LOSING FAITH

LOSING FAITH

Denise Jaden

Simon Pulse
New York London Toronto Sydney

SIMON PULSE

An imprint of Simon & Schuster Children's Publishing Division

1230 Avenue of the Americas, New York, NY 10020

First Simon Pulse paperback edition September 2010

Copyright © 2010 by Denise Jaden

All rights reserved, including the right of reproduction in whole or in part in any form.

SIMON PULSE and colophon are registered trademarks of Simon & Schuster, Inc.

For information about special discounts for bulk purchases, please contact Simon & Schuster Special Sales at 1-866-506-1949 or business@simonandschuster.com.

The Simon & Schuster Speakers Bureau can bring authors to your live event. For more information or to book an event contact the Simon & Schuster Speakers Bureau at 1-866-248-3049 or visit our website at www.simonspeakers.com.

Designed by Mike Rosamilia

The text of this book was set in Berling LT Std.

Manufactured in the United States of America

2 4 6 8 10 9 7 5 3 1

Jaden, Denise.

Losing Faith / by Denise Jaden. — 1st Simon Pulse paperback ed.

p. cm.

Summary: Brie tries to cope with her grief over her older sister Faith's sudden death by trying to learn more about the religious "home group" Faith secretly joined and never talked about with Brie or her parents.

ISBN 978-1-4169-9609-5 (pbk)

[1. Death—Fiction. 2. Grief—Fiction. 3. Sisters—Fiction. 4. High schools—Fiction. 5. Schools—Fiction. 6. Christian life—Fiction. 7. Cults—Fiction.] I. Title.

PZ7.J153184Los 2010   [Fic]—dc22   2010007296

ISBN 978-1-4169-9670-5 (eBook)

To Shana,
my ever-present sounding board and friend.
In case no one has told you this yet today,
Shana, you are brilliant.

LOSING FAITH

chapter ONE

*t*he statue has got to go.

That's my first thought as I prep the living room for Dustin's visit later tonight. I know I'm the only one who would notice the discriminating eyes of Mom's four-inch Jesus staring down from the mantel. Dustin probably wouldn't look away from my breasts if the room were two feet deep in holy water. Still, I reach for it.

When my hand fumbles and the statue topples sideways, I pick the thing up and scan the hearth for any other too-holy housewares.

"What are you doing?" My older sister rushes in from the kitchen, scuffles across the carpet, and ignites a spark when she snatches the statue out of my hand. She settles it back into its ring of dust, adjusting it to its all-seeing viewpoint, and then eases her hand away like she's afraid the thing might fly right up to heaven. Turning, she glares at me.

Great. Caught in the act of abducting a religious icon. Not exactly the act I feared being caught in tonight.

"Actually, Faith"—I stare into her eyes so she won't miss this—"I was wondering if you could give me a lift to the church."

As expected, her whole face lights up, and I'm tempted to let her believe she's finally fished her heathen sister out of the sea of despair. It's better than telling her the truth.

"Amy's going to meet me at a coffee shop near there," I add. Not complete honesty, but close enough.

"Oh." Her face falls. "I'm not sure, Brie. I mean, I wasn't going to—" She flicks her fingernail against her thumb a few times and looks away.

She wasn't going to what? Wasn't going to youth group like she has every single Friday night since she was born? I glance at the clock above her head. Good thing Dustin's not waiting down the street somewhere, which was my initial idea. But me staying home alone on a Friday night would be far from ordinary and I don't want to raise anyone's suspicions. I stare back at Faith until she goes on.

"Celeste doesn't want to go, my car's out of gas, and I

can't find my Bible." She starts for the kitchen. "Sorry, Brie, I'm not going tonight."

Usually, I strategize about as well as a fly caught in a screen door. But tonight I had taken the initiative to plan something nice—really nice—for Dustin, and tonight, of all nights, Faith's turning into someone I don't even know. What happened to her Big Salvation Plan, the one that wraps around her life in giant, multicolored jawbreaker layers of certainty?

I can't do anything about Celeste cutting out on her. They argued on the phone earlier and I learned a long time ago that I don't understand their friendship well enough to get involved. But I can fix other problems. I reach for my purse. "I have gas money."

She stops in the kitchen doorway.

I dig out the only bill I can find, walk toward her, and push it at her chest. She looks down at my hand like it's covered in warts.

"I know it's only five bucks, but that'll at least get your car to the church and back, right?" Heading to the bookshelves in the living room, I scrunch my nose because the dog, curled up on the couch, must have farted. I pull off a Bible with *Brie Jenkins* inscribed in the bottom corner of its black leather cover. "Here," I say, coughing from the flutters of dust. "Take mine."

"That's a King James Version," Faith says. "I really need my N.I.V."

Faith and her New International Version. Like it matters. And here I thought getting my parents out of the house would be the hard part, but they left before six, barely taking time to say good-bye. When I don't move my outstretched hand, Faith lets out a sigh and takes my Bible from me.

She opens it, apparently figuring this is the perfect time for her daily devotional, and I call the dog to get him and his raunchy smell out of here. "Nuisance, here, boy."

Our overweight golden retriever has selective hearing. It's probably too late anyway; Dustin will certainly end up with blond dog hair all over his pants, but I want to at least try to give the cushions a once-over with the lint roller.

I pry my fingers under the dog's mass, using all my weight to lug him off. He takes my gesture as an attempt to play and jumps up, frothing all over my freshly made-up face. I fall on my butt and let out a giggly yelp. When I look up, expecting to see Faith laughing, she just stares into the open Bible, and nibbles on her lip.

She shakes her head, and at first I think it's at me and my stupid predicament, but then she flips the page and scowls hard down at the words. I'm baffled, since I can't imagine her disagreeing with anything in The Good Book.

The loops of her blond hair mimic the paisley wallpaper behind her. It's hard to remember when my hair used to be even curlier, before Amy permanently lent me her straightening iron. It takes me a second to notice Faith's whole body trembling.

"Faith, what's—"

"Nothing." She snaps the book shut, and heads for the foyer. Her renewed determination makes me wonder if it had been my eyes that were trembling. "You wanted a ride, right? Let's go."

I follow her, but she picks up the hall phone and dials while she slips on her shoes.

"Oh, good, you're still there," she says into the handset. "I'm driving my sister to the church, so I think I am going to go. That's my sign." Her forehead creases as she stares at the floor listening.

At least she doesn't sound angry with Celeste anymore. Though she doesn't exactly sound cheery either.

"Nothing dangerous, but I need you, Celeste," Faith prods.

I wonder what kind of crazy, shake-in-your-shoes idea the church has planned for them tonight. Perhaps they'll play tag in the parking lot in bare feet.

When she glances up from her call and notices I'm still there, she whispers, "Hold on," into the receiver and moves down the hall with the phone pressed to her chest.

Fine. Not like I wanted to listen in on *that* conversation anyway. I open the door, calling, "Don't worry about me. I'll just be in the car," loud enough so they can both hear me.

Whatever. So what if they don't want me in their stupid inner circle. My own circle's coming together and it'll be much better than their little saintly one.

I collapse into the front seat of her Toyota and decide once again that I'll have to try harder to get Dad to take me driving so I can finally get my license. Then I won't have to ask Faith for anything, won't have to concern myself with what she and her friends are up to. Swiping the chip bags from around my feet, I shove them into her already full garbage bag. As I reach for one more wrapper on the dash, a new sticker above the stereo catches my eye. Or at least it wasn't here the last time I was in this traveling garbage dump. The round yellow sticker has an artsy cross on it. Almost scribbled-looking, but preprinted on there.

Faith slides into the driver's seat and I'm about to reprimand her for defacing her vehicle—I mean, at least she has one—but I stop myself when I see the tense look on her face.

"All worked out?" I ask, even though I know Faith almost always gets her way with Celeste.

"You need a ride home, too?" she asks, backing out and then driving down the street with her eyes straight ahead.

6

Her fingers grip the steering wheel at ten and two like it's a life preserver.

"No. Amy'll drop me." I haven't thought of a reason why *Amy* couldn't pick me up, and I hope Faith won't think to ask.

Her hands loosen and drop to the lower half of the wheel. She nods, apparently relieved that I'm not going to be any more of a burden. For a second I wonder why things had to change between us. Why aren't we still friends, or at least siblings who can have a normal conversation? But the thought is gone as soon as it enters my head.

After stopping at the corner gas station, she reaches to turn on the radio, confirming there'll be no sisterly chatter on the car ride over. Once she starts singing along, I decide I much prefer listening to her singing voice over arguing with her anyway. I nudge the radio volume down. Faith is used to this move of mine, and keeps singing without any reaction. And this is the way I like her voice—not tied to her church worship group or up on stage with everyone staring in amazement. Just her singing and me listening.

We pull into the large church parking lot, and Faith backs into a spot near the perimeter. She turns off the engine and we sit there, both staring ahead at the looming steeple.

"You okay, then?" Faith asks after several seconds.

I take that as my cue to reach for the door handle. "Sure." Something in me wonders if I should ask her the same question. "Are you—"

But a dark-haired girl with a ponytail scurries over to the driver's side and interrupts us. "Faith, oh my gosh, it's so good to see you!"

Faith and I get out on either side, and I raise my eyebrows. Only at church can people get so excited to see each other after only a day or two apart.

"Oh, you brought your sister." The girl nods approvingly.

I pull my arms across my chest and feel the scratchy condom wrapper I'd stashed in my bra. More teens move in toward Faith, toward us, and I get a mental picture of them grabbing my hands and singing "Kumbaya."

And just then, Faith's dark-haired friend makes her way around the car with a hand outstretched. I stare down at it.

"I'm not staying," I say, tucking my hands behind my back. "I mean, I'm meeting someone . . . over there." I point over my shoulder. "Thanks for the ride," I call out, but Faith waves me off, since she's now surrounded by several of her elated youth-group buddies.

I dash across the street and make a show of ducking into the Rio Café. After waiting a few minutes to make sure it's safe, I slip out into the dark alley alongside the coffee shop and race through to the next street over. The street is deserted and I hug my purse to my chest. I wish Dustin could pick me up in front of the coffee shop, but I can't chance Faith catching sight of me heading back to the house with my boyfriend.

I slink into the shadow of the art supplies store so I won't be obvious to any stray, lonely men driving past, and pull out my cell phone. After checking the street sign, I text Dustin with the coordinates.

I snap my phone shut and blow on my sweaty palms. *What if I'm not ready?* Dustin's been patient—too patient, Amy says. And now that I've given him so many hints, how could I say no?

I won't, I decide only a second later. Even though I'm not completely at ease with this, who is, their first time?

I look up just in time to see a familiar red Toyota sail by. The smiley antenna ball catches my attention, and I squint at the back of a blond curly head in the driver's seat. It's Faith.

Worse, she's headed back in the direction of our house. There goes my special night with Dustin. Though the thought does make my racing heart slow a little.

When Dustin's lights gleam around the corner and onto the deserted street where I wait, I put Faith out of my mind. I paste on a smile, smooth down my straightened hair with both hands, and step out of the shadows into the bright lights.

chapter TWO

i slip into the passenger seat of Dustin's yellow Mustang, lean over, and kiss him on the cheek. He smiles, and slides a sandy-colored lock of hair behind his ear. The dimple on his cheek makes my heart flutter.

"Where to?" he asks, sliding one hand onto my knee. I place my hand on his, stopping him before he reaches the hem of my skirt.

My mind works fast and I remember a barn bash one of Dustin's friends mentioned. "Evan's party?" I say.

"I thought we were going to your place." He inches his hand up my thigh.

I hadn't actually told him that but I guess I'd been

obvious enough. "We can't. My sister's home." I add a pouty huff to pretend I'm just as upset about it as he is.

He looks over at me with a suggestive smile, and then past me to the backseat. "We could . . . park somewhere."

I follow his eyes. Oh, how romantic. Sticky vinyl clinging to my bare ass. Perfect.

"I heard it's supposed to be a big deal at Evan's." I make my voice sound light.

"Oh." He meets my eyes.

I flinch away, not wanting to give his gaze time to convince me.

"Right." He turns and studies the mirror on his visor.

I can't tell if I've offended him. "It's just . . ." I tug my skirt back down. "I was hoping to get to know some of your friends."

He stays quiet for a few seconds, letting the car idle on the edge of the curb. Then, without a word, he puts it in gear.

I spend the first few minutes of the car ride thinking about how to make things better with him. I take about a hundred deep breaths and make a mental promise to myself to set up another night for us soon. Now that I've had a practice run, I'll be much more comfortable with it next time.

"Did you finish your poem?" Dustin interrupts my thoughts

and with that one question, not a hint of abrasion in his voice, all is right with my world again.

"Um, almost." My face heats up. I'm flattered that he remembered what I'd been working on earlier when he called. That he cares enough to ask. But I just hope he doesn't want to hear some of it. My poetry's not good, not like Faith and her music or anything. Still, it gives me hope that one day I will share all my inner workings and passions with him. When I figure out what those are.

He shoots me a grin and one solid nod, but doesn't say anything else. It's like he knows my exact thoughts and he won't ask for more until I'm ready. I can't hold back a little internal squee. We're so perfect for each other.

It takes longer than I expect to get to the farmhouse out in the middle of nowhere, but I don't mind. Dustin talks about some of his classes this week and asks me what I think about every little thing. We're in different classes, different grades even, but I appreciate the fact that he wants to talk to me about the stuff in his life so much when we're alone, so I try to offer intelligent replies.

When we pull up the dirt drive of the party house, a crowd assembles by Dustin's door. I let myself out and stand on the passenger side while Dustin slaps a few hands and says his hellos. A couple of I-don't-need-to-shower-more-than-

once-a-week guys partying in the back of a pickup truck call
for me to come over. Not by my name, but by a more endear-
ing alias, "Hey, baby." I ignore them.

The thing about guys in Sharon, Oregon, is that the
majority of them wear this tougher-than-granite act, cracking bottles open with their teeth, their jean buckles, their
forearms. I figure it's to make up for living in a town with a
girl's name.

Dustin and I walk across the yard and look for our friends.
Well, Dustin's friends, if one wants to get technical, but I'm
sure it won't take long before they'll be my friends too. I
reach over and intertwine my fingers with his, pulling my
shoulders back and standing a little taller. The number of
people who watch our trek feels a bit unsettling, but exciting
at the same time. This is my third big party with Dustin and
I think I could get used to this.

A bonfire blazes in front of an abandoned farmhouse on
our left. The barn, missing a side wall and lit up by a half-
dozen hanging lanterns, sits straight ahead with the guts of
the place in plain view.

Dustin and I don't acknowledge anyone else in the yard.
Mostly guys. Mostly drunk. We're heading to where the rest
of the party rages, on the upper floor of the barn. Juniors
and seniors, less drunk and less biceps-flaunting than the lawn

crowd, chat and joke in small groups. A large table displays a full spread of alcohol.

"Cool," Dustin says. "Let's go."

He pulls my hand, but I don't move. My feet are wrapped in lead weights. The open-air platform—with no railings, fences, or even chicken wire—combined with all levels of inebriation, terrifies me. I swallow at the lump lodged in my throat.

"Why don't we just stay down here for a bit," I say.

"Yeah, right." He looks at me like I've just suggested we play hopscotch on the mounds of manure. "Let's get a drink."

I scan the yard around me looking for an excuse, but there's nothing. Nothing enticing about ditching the fun crowd above for the guys who are vomiting by the swing set, or the ones lying flat on their backs with draining beer bottles propped in their mouths like frothing baby bottles.

I try a different, more honest, approach. "Um, do you really think it's safe up there?"

Dustin belts out a laugh like I've just said the funniest thing he's ever heard, then gives my arm a good yank toward the barn entrance.

My mouth feels like I've sucked on a lint ball. *The loft is probably safer than it looks*, I tell myself over and over and over again on the thirty feet it takes to get to the barn. *Dustin wouldn't take me there if it wasn't. And so far tonight, no one's fallen.* I scan the ground around me to make sure.

Inside the barn, a stereo above cranks out some old Fergie tune. Halfway along the wall, there's a staircase. It's a curlicue access that looks like the fries they make in the school cafeteria. Dustin drags me toward it while I try to keep my mind on cafeteria food. Fries, ketchup, that disgusting, overcooked pasta.

I take deep breaths and concentrate on the rickety railing and cross-mesh metal of each stair. When the light from the top floor comes into view, I back up a step. Dustin almost trips, and gets his bearings before tugging on my hand once again.

When I force myself to step onto the platform at the top, vertigo hits me and I drop Dustin's hand to grasp the wall. The dim lanterns streak across the ceiling like a crazed disco ball. People, laughing and talking, come in and out of focus.

"Let's just hang out here for a bit." I focus on the dusty wood-plank floor and force some steadiness to my voice. By the time my breathing evens and I look up, Dustin stands across the platform, filling a shot glass at the booze table. Did he even hear me?

He chats with a group of guys, knocks back the drink, and makes a face that for a second I can't recognize as someone I would ever be attracted to. Someone comes up the stairs behind me and I'm forced to slide over so they can get through.

My BFF Amy stands a few feet away from Dustin, talking to a group of girls near the ledge. Actually, Amy's not *really* my BFF. Not like Faith and Celeste, who've been attached at the hip since kindergarten. Amy and I are more like BFFN—Best Friends For Now. Or BFWIW—Best Friends While It Works.

Amy has Big Plans, just like everyone else in my life. Hers include makeup artistry and working at MAC Cosmetics. I've learned to apply perfect eyeliner and toenail polish, but try as I might, I can't drum up the kind of excitement it would take to organize my life around flawless foundation.

I wave. She holds up a drink toward me, her eyebrows raised.

I smile back, because Amy doesn't really drink. She had too much at the first pep rally last year and ended up passed out half-naked in the school parking lot. Since then, she discreetly nurses one drink throughout a whole party.

She gestures for me to come over, even though she knows about my fear of heights. I can hardly remind her from here. I shake my head, and then motion for her to come over to where I'm glued against the wall.

She nods and holds up a *one second* sign to me before turning back to finish her conversation.

Perfect. At least I won't look so completely alone. Dustin now holds a beer in one hand and a shot in the other, though he still doesn't seem to be making a move back in my direction. Maybe I should have just parked with him somewhere. I let go of the wall with one hand and try to wave him down, but he's caught up telling one of his jokes and doesn't notice.

I'm startled by a vibration in my pocket, and at first I slap at it, thinking a bug crawled on me. Then it dawns on me, and I dig for my cell to look at the display.

My parents. *Crap.*

The deal is, I can go out late on weekends because my parents are actually pretty cool despite their heavy church involvement, but I always have to tell someone in the family where I'm going and I have to answer my phone when they call. One time I forgot to charge the stupid thing and got grounded for two weeks because I didn't pick up. And that was on a Sunday afternoon.

Of course they might alter the rules a little if they knew about the booze table, the lack of parental supervision, and the guy who picked me up. I press my cell to my ear, cupping my hand over my mouth to help deaden the music and voices.

"Hello!" I yell. My parents' meeting shouldn't be over for at least another hour. I can't believe one of them ducked out to check up on me.

A muffled voice sounds on the other end. I plug my other ear to hear better.

"Hello?" I say again.

"Brie . . . can you . . . are you . . ."

"Dad, there's a band here at Café Rio. I can barely hear you." I step into the stairwell and crouch down, pulling my arms over my head to deaden the sound. Things are slightly quieter, in the way a football game might be quieter than a rock concert. "Dad, you there?"

"I need—" He sounds like he's choking or sick or something. I've never heard him like this. He's always so . . . composed.

"Dad, are you okay?"

". . . the hospital . . . I can't . . ."

The hospital? "Are you hurt?" I bring my fist to my mouth. *Or maybe it's Mom.* "Dad?"

"Just come . . . the hospital . . ."

Silence follows and I look at the display on my phone. It reads CALL ENDED.

I click on my phone book and dial Dad back. It goes straight to his voice mail. Following the tone, I ramble on in a panic. "I don't know what's going on, but I'm coming to the hospital as soon as I can. I hope everything . . . everybody's okay. Is Mom with you? Okay, I guess I'll see you soon."

Next, I scroll to my sister's number and hit send. Hers also goes right to voice mail. Faith always has her phone on, even when she's at home. She's the super-responsible one. Never been grounded for anything.

Turning cell phones off must be a hospital rule. Which means she's already there and I, of course, will be the last of the family to arrive.

One minuscule step at a time, I move along the wall toward Dustin, who's now near the open edge of the platform.

I can do this, I tell myself. I focus on the floor and attempt to slow my breathing.

At least I'll be there for only a second. Long enough to drag Dustin out so he can drive me. I slide my hand along the wall until I reach him. He doesn't notice me right away and laughs too loudly at another guy's joke.

Keeping one hand on the wall, I reach over and tug at his plaid overshirt. He finds my hand, laces his fingers through mine, and with a sudden tug, I'm at his side. By the edge. My heart beats like a thunderstorm in my chest.

He looks over. "Hey, babe. You gotta hear this." He turns back to his friend. "Evan, tell Brie about this guy."

"Dustin, I gotta go." My sweaty hand nearly slips from his. I wrap my other hand around his wrist for some sense of security.

"It's the funniest thing," he says, as though he doesn't hear me. "Tell her what his mom made him do."

I pull him toward the staircase. "I mean it, Dustin. There's some kind of emergency with my family. I need a ride."

Dustin takes a big swig of his drink, and then passes it to Evan. "The girlfriend wants to get out of here. You know what that means." He raises his eyebrows at Evan. His words slur, but I don't care. Nor do I care about the show he's putting on for his buddy. I force my mouth into a smile and hold my lips tight to keep my teeth still.

When Dustin reaches in his pocket for his keys, the motion knocks him off balance. The edge is so close. Suddenly, he jerks me down by the hand. The whole barn spins and I scream, squeezing my eyes shut. A roar fills my ears, Dustin's hand slips from mine, and black spots blur my vision. The next thing I know, someone else's arms grip my waist and I'm pulled, lifted . . . saved. I pry open my eyes and am amazed to see I didn't go over.

Dustin rummages on the floor of the loft, still near the edge. "Where the hell are my keys?"

The group around him laughs, but he doesn't notice. Evan, my apparent savior, leans over me, asking if I'm okay. I still hear my scream echoing into the night.

I nod. "I just . . . I gotta go."

I crawl away from the edge, over to Amy, and grab her leg.

"Yeah, he's so cute. I swear—" She stops and stares down at me like I'm some kind of psycho poodle.

"Amy, I need a ride. It's an emergency. I have to get to the hospital."

After a second, recognition crosses her face. She glances at the girl she was talking to, then back to me with more concern. "Oh. Okay. I'll drop you off."

She doesn't say anything until we get into her brother's beater Hyundai, and I'm glad. I just need to concentrate on my breathing for a few minutes.

"So, are you and Dustin on the outs, or what?"

"Huh?" I rattle the door to make sure it's shut. "No, he's just drunk."

"I don't know." She shakes her head. "I wouldn't leave him there like that. You better be careful. He could have anyone—"

"I've kind of got more important things to worry about at the moment, Amy." She hasn't even asked about the hospital. I could be dying of internal bleeding for all she knows.

As if she can read my mind, she asks, "So someone's hurt, or what?"

"I don't know. I mean, my dad sounded awful, and what if—" I stop myself. Faith's big on speaking things into existence. Not that I believe in that stuff, but still. We sit in silence through the next traffic light. Small beads of rain land on the windshield, and when she turns on her wipers they sound much too loud in the quiet car.

"Wow, I sure hope everyone's okay," Amy says.

But something's really wrong and she isn't driving fast enough. When we round the corner and the hospital comes into view, I fling the door open. "You know what? It's fine. Just drop me here."

She screeches the brakes. "Are you nuts? I'll drive you, Brie. I'm driving you, aren't I?" She shakes her head. "Shut the door and stop being such a bitch about everything."

Amy calling me a bitch is like Faith calling me religious. But Amy's the least of my problems. I yank the door closed. The quicker I can get there and find out what's going on, the better.

She turns into the parking lot. "Look! Your dad's van!" She uses her "making amends" voice.

"Great." I jump from the car and force out my reply. "Thanks a lot for the ride, Amy. I really appreciate it." I wave as I run past her car. She doesn't offer to park. To come in. To find out if my family is okay. Instead, she nearly hits a light post when she zooms backward to spin in the direction we came from.

Amy's always been pretty self-absorbed and I don't have

time to be offended about it now. I race through the automatic doors and straight for the elevator, accosted by the antiseptic smell. Pushing the up button, it hits me that I have no idea what floor they're on. I scan the wallboard and see EMERGENCY CARE—4TH FLOOR just as the elevator doors open.

When I step off the elevator onto the fourth floor, the first thing that strikes me is the seriousness of it. Nurses and doctors bury their heads in clipboards. A man inches along with a walker as though it's stuck in sludge. I'm almost positive people don't have cute, healthy babies on this floor.

At the nurse's station, I spot my sister's blond hair, and the frumpy gray sweatshirt I saw her in earlier tonight. She leans over the counter toward the receptionist. I let out my breath and march over. At least she'll be able to tell me what's going on.

As I'm about to grab her by the shoulder, the red stitching on the seam of her top makes me stop. It's not the same shirt.

She turns to face me, the striking blonde who's not my sister, and moves aside so I can speak to the nurses.

"It's awful," one heavyset nurse is saying to another, completely ignoring me. "They must be having a horrible time."

"Excuse me?"

They both stop and turn to me.

"Jenkins?" I say as a question, since I'm not really sure who

I'm looking for. My mouth tastes like metal when I speak.

The gossiping nurse frowns. She glances at the other nurse, and then points down the hall. "Uh, yes. The last door on the left."

By the time I'm halfway down the wide hallway, the word "Chapel" posted above the last set of doors comes into view. Of course. Where else would Dad be? Must be on his knees in there with the hospital chaplain. My parents' Big Plan is called predestination, and this is what they do in times of crises. Or anytime, really. They meet with other churchies.

My heart still beats hard against my ribs, especially when I notice the police officer pacing in front of the chapel door. I shimmy past him and nudge the door open. My parents are both inside, alone on either side of the small room, and I let out a small breath at the sight of them. The wood walls and ceiling seem jarring after the sterile hospital hallway. Mom perches on a chair to my left, bent forward, and in shadow. The solitary light from the far side of the room shines down on Dad, hunched over the pulpit.

"I got here as fast as I could. What's—"

Dad looks up with tears streaming down his face. I glance from him to Mom, then to the rest of the sparse room. The four empty benches. The plants in pots along the side of the room that look too similar and too perfect to be real. Dad holds a gray sweatshirt, one without red stitching, and crumples it in his tight grip.

"Where's Faith?" I ask.

There's a pause and time stops. Suddenly, Mom and Dad come at me so fast and so panicked that I feel like a baby choking on a penny. Having no idea what's going on or how to react, I ball my fists and pull them to my face. My parents throw their smothering arms around me and I feel explosive heaves from their chests, as though the only air in the room is coming from them.

At least *they're* breathing. My lungs are stuck together with Krazy Glue. "Where's Faith?" I ask again, but it comes out in little more than a squeak.

Mom lets out a howl of a cry.

My parents squeeze me tighter and pet my head as though I'm a dog or a farm animal, and suddenly, I understand.

Faith isn't here. Isn't coming here.

I gasp, and my Krazy-Glued lungs tear apart.

I'm no longer the black sheep of the family.

I'm the only one.

chapter THREE

S everal hours later, the police follow us up our
driveway without a word. I eye Faith's Toyota
and try to work out in my head, for the hun-
dredth time, how she could be gone. Just the sight of her car
makes my brain default to thinking she must be inside the
house waiting for us. I blink hard to try to reset my internal
algorithms.

*Focus, Brie, focus. You need to get through the rest of this
night without falling apart.* I don't know why I think this. To
be strong for my parents? No, that wouldn't make sense.
They're much stronger than I am.

I take a deep breath and try to distance myself enough to

set a plan for at least getting through the police statements. Setting some logical parameters has always helped me to keep a cool head and not fall apart in emotional situations. Like when Dad and I had that huge fight about me not going to church. I was just about in tears because he was forcing me to go, then suddenly I stopped speaking in the middle of our argument and went to my room. I calmly made a list of my reasons and passed it over at dinnertime. And okay, this is totally not the same thing, but it did work.

If I speak as little as possible, I can keep my delusional thoughts to myself until I've had time to process. That's my plan, my guide to getting through this.

She's really gone, I tell myself again as Dad opens the front door.

Nuisance lets out a loud bark when the two male police officers walk through into our house, but no one bothers to quiet him. Nuisance would sooner lick them to death than actively assault them.

Mom sits on the edge of our sofa, and turns her eyes to the floor a foot in front of her. Her hair is falling out of its clip at the back and her wrinkled white blouse hangs loose out of her skirt. Dad unbuttons his suit jacket when he sits beside her.

No one's mentioned whether I should be here or not, so

I lean against the French door joining the living room to the foyer, not committing to staying or leaving. Since the only other open seats are on the love seat across from Mom and Dad, the police officers spend a couple of uncomfortable moments adjusting themselves into it. If one of the cops wasn't severely underweight, it could be a real problem. Nuisance likes this skinny guy though, and by the way he nudges his head under the cop's hand, I suspect it'll only be a matter of time before he attempts to find his own place on that love seat.

The other officer clears his throat and the large pockmarks on his cheeks vibrate. "I know this has been an unimaginable night," he says softly, looking between my parents. "These are just routine questions we have to ask. Please feel free to take all the time you need."

The phrase seems so weird since it's not like they're giving us time for anything. Sleep. A shower. All the time we need for what? To grieve? To let strange men into our house to ask questions? I take a few steps backward and hover by the coat rack. *Fell off a cliff. Dead. Gone.* I try to remind myself again of what is real, so I don't laugh or something.

"Can you tell me the last time you saw Faith?" the pock-faced cop says.

Dad doesn't hesitate. "Around six tonight." He checks his watch. "Er, last night."

Skinny Cop marks it down in his small notebook. "And did she leave by car?"

"We weren't here," Dad says. "But yes, she would have taken her car."

I guess no one noticed when we parked right behind her Corolla five minutes ago. "Actually, I think she got a ride with Celeste," I say. Just after it leaves my mouth, I berate myself for so quickly neglecting my oath of silence.

"Celeste?" Skinny Cop runs a finger over his notes.

"Schwartz." Dad fills in the blank. "Celeste Schwartz. Her best friend." Skinny Cop makes a note in his book.

Pock-faced Cop distracts me from wondering whether or not they've talked to Celeste yet with another question. "When was the last time you saw your sister, honey?" The way he says "honey" makes it clear that it's just as uncomfortable for him as for me. This guy should be in traffic or something.

"She dropped me off at quarter after seven at the church. But her car's outside, so she must have come back."

Skinny Cop marks this down too. "And do you remember what she was wearing?"

Now this seems ridiculous. It's not like she would have changed clothes at the top of the mountain. "Um, jeans and a sweatshirt." I point to the one beside Dad, and wonder where they found it. At the top of the mountain? Or the bottom.

I'm strangely numb at the thought. It doesn't seem like it could be real.

"And how was her mood when she left?" Both officers look at me.

"Um, okay." I gnaw on my thumbnail, wondering why they keep talking to me.

Skinny Cop, thankfully, directs the next question to Dad. "Did you know she'd be up on Blackham Mountain last night? Does she regularly go up there?"

"Well, no." Dad runs a hand over his face and stretches out the skin on his jaw. "She was going to youth group. They must have had a special event of some kind up the mountain. She has a close-knit group of friends and they always look out for . . ."

The room falls silent. We all know we can't blame Celeste, or any of Faith's other friends. Accidents happen. I'm glad I've heard something that makes sense for the first time tonight though. The youth group went to the mountain. Faith had to drop off her car because my five bucks wasn't enough to get her up there.

"We spoke with someone at the scene—er, on the mountain," Pock-face says. "From what we've heard so far, Faith went for a walk alone. No one was close by when she fell, but her scream was heard in the nearest subdivision."

Trying not to visualize this, I grip the coat rack.

"So the youth pastor wasn't there?" Dad asks.

The cop shakes his head. "Only minors present."

"Have you ever known Faith to use alcohol or drugs?" Skinny Cop asks.

"No. Never." Dad shakes his head with a scowl, but in a way the question is a relief. It makes obvious just how routine these questions are. In fact, even the idea of Faith drinking or doing drugs makes the whole situation seem completely ridiculous. Like it isn't even happening.

Mom's stooped position hasn't changed since she sat down. Her shoulders appear rigid, like if she tries to straighten up they might break.

Skinny Cop's voice sounds abrupt in the stillness. "Is there anything that might lead you to believe that Faith would take her own life?"

Mom lets out a gasp, and the shock of her sound hinders my ability to process the question for a second.

"Suicide?" Dad shakes his head roughly. "No way. Not Faith."

I can tell by Dad's tone, he isn't feeling the same relief at these over-the-top questions as I am. "You're kidding, right?" I add.

"These are all standard questions." Pock-face runs a hand

down the arm of the love seat. "As soon as we get through them, we'll be able to get out of your way."

"Faith didn't believe in . . . she would never have . . ." Dad is processing aloud.

Skinny Cop clears his throat, standing. "No, no. Again, Mr. Jenkins, we're not trying to imply anything. We'd like to see her room if you don't mind, and—"

"No!" Dad shouts. "We will not listen to this . . . garbage. Why don't you two *officers* come back when you get your facts straight, and stop putting my family through this cruel charade." While he speaks, he marches toward the door, obviously expecting them to follow.

They do. "Mr. Jenkins," Pock-face starts, but Dad doesn't let him finish.

"I said we've had enough for today, gentlemen."

The two cops look at each other, and a subtle agreement passes between them. "We're very sorry again for your loss, Mr. Jenkins . . . Mrs. Jenkins," the skinny one says as they back out the door.

After the cops leave, we spend a few minutes staring after where their squad car disappeared around the corner. Dad squeezes my shoulder and even though I notice his hand there, I barely feel it. Barely feel anything. Everything is surreal, including my parents, who blend into the wall behind them like a mural. But then I notice Mom's intense shivering and she comes to life again in my vision. Dad moves beside her and slides an arm around her shoulder.

"How was she . . . when you left her?" Dad asks me, not meeting my eye. Mom's shivering turns into quiet crying spasms.

I swallow. "Fine. Good," I say, holding my face straight so they won't see through me. Faith might have been a little stressed, but not suicidal stressed. And my parents don't need to work themselves up any more right now.

Dad's eyes flitter between the walls and he looks like he's trying to find the words to make this better. Words to bring me and Mom comfort. But there are none and I want to let him off the hook, at least as much as I can.

"I'm okay," I tell him. "We should probably all try to get some sleep."

With Dad's arm cradling Mom, they trudge to their bedroom without another word. I stare around our empty house and have flashes of Faith in the living room, by the front door, on the stairs. The visions exhaust me. I know I can't let my mind go with them, but I can't seem to stop them either. Instead, I head for the stairs and force myself to think about things I shouldn't. Things that are selfish and shallow, but that's all I can deal with right now. I think about Dustin. Is he still at the party? If only I could be back there where my reeling mind could just have a break.

Nuisance nudges his nose at my leg and I'm glad. I could use the company. At Faith's door I grab the knob, ready to pull it shut, but stop, unable to help myself. Instead, I push it open a few inches.

I've always felt like an intruder when I step over the threshold into my sister's room but tonight the feeling is amplified. I turn back to Nuisance and whisper for him to stay.

I take in the clean floor and bed—not made, but for once not covered in books and clothes either. I wonder if Mom slipped in to clean it up. But no, she couldn't have. Feeling dizzy at the sight of all Faith's things, I grasp for her bedpost. All the tangible items in her room make it seem all the more unbelievable. She can't really be gone.

Beside Faith's bed, I find not one, not two, but three Bibles. I run my hand over the covers, trying to feel the texture, trying to feel anything beyond this disorientation. The top Bible says "Amplified Version." The next one doesn't even look like a Bible until I open it up. The third is titled "New American Standard" at the bottom. When I place them on her bed, my eye catches sight of my red sweater underneath the bed skirt. I remember the way Faith looked at me when she borrowed it over a month ago.

I was wearing it out one night, and she told me how good it looked on me at least three times. Finally, I took it off and passed it to her, but she shook her head, saying she didn't think she could wear red. For the first time ever, I swear I saw something close to jealousy on her face. I forced the sweater at her, begging her to just try it. Even though I had no idea why, the thought of Faith being jealous kicked me in the gut. Maybe it was because I knew she had it so wrong.

She took the sweater but I never saw her wear it. Not once. And now I wonder how much that might have bothered her. If it made her feel somehow inadequate because she didn't feel comfortable in the bright, attention-grabbing clothes that I wore.

I scoop the sweater up, but hidden underneath it is one more Bible stuffed almost to the back of her bed. This one's title reads "New International Version."

My hands fumble to open it. This is the Bible she was so desperate to find. After flipping only a few pages, I can tell it's well used. Lines upon lines of yellow highlighter catch my eye as I fan through. The lines blur in my vision and I wipe my eyes, surprised that there are no tears. Shouldn't I be crying? I squint my eyes shut and try to force some moisture. But my face is a desert.

I stand, holding the book closed against my chest. It

surprises me that I want to keep it to remember her by. If anything, I hated her for her religion. For finding her place and being so much better than me at all of it. But I stop that thought before it can fully form. I can't hate her. Not now. I head back for the door, trying to swallow down my overwhelming guilt.

When I'd come in, I hadn't noticed the three boxes stacked up just inside her doorway. I run my hand over the long piece of packing tape on the top one, confused. Why are these here? Why near the door, like they're all ready to go somewhere? Then I stare back over her unusually tidy room. My heart stops.

Did she . . . pack up? The sick feeling in my gut intensifies and I press my palm against the wall to still the swaying room. I couldn't imagine it of any other person on earth, but I could believe this of my sister. That she wouldn't want to be a burden to anyone, even in death.

The words of the police officers ring in my ears. *Is there anything that might lead you to believe that Faith would take her own life?* I jerk my hand away from the box.

No. I can't handle that thought. I can't. Searching for shallow thoughts, safe thoughts, I concentrate on the coloring of the carpet and follow it through the doorway and into the hall. I've always thought of it as beige but now that I'm driven, I can see the flecks of gray and brown and follow it like a trail of bread crumbs leading toward my sanity.

I ease Faith's door shut and race into my own room, not lifting my head. Finally, my chest loosens, and I can breathe again. I call Nuisance in a whisper and drop onto my bed. Folding forward, I rake my hands through my hair. It's all too much. All I can picture are Faith's eyes on my red sweater, and I wonder if she really could have been so messed up.

chapter FOUR

t he next morning, I'm unsure whether I'm waking up or just living in the midst of a horrible dream. I'm sure I must have slept some, but all I can remember is staring at my digital clock, watching the minutes tick by, tossing and gripping my sheets every time my mind returned to Faith and what happened.

The edges of my room blur in my vision and even when I stare into the bathroom mirror, it seems like I'm looking into a murky pond. At least I can't see how bad I look.

One thing I know is that I need a new plan. A plan for how to face today. Since last night's plan didn't work out so well, I'm calling this one **Plan B: talk to Mom and Dad about everything and we'll get through it together.**

Hearing Dad's voice on the phone downstairs, I creep halfway down the steps to listen.

"Yes, I know," he says, "but I'd really like Scott to handle the service. He was her leader." His slippered footsteps brush across the tile floor. Dad's not normally a pacer, but I swear he's wearing a trench in our kitchen. "I trust his decisions on those things. He can e-mail me the details. Gina isn't ready to talk about it."

I'm glad Dad's taking the reins, though I wouldn't expect any less from him.

"You can put Brie down for one. Why don't you start with her."

Whatever he's volunteering me for, I already know I don't like it. I tromp the rest of the way down the stairs and into the kitchen. Dad keeps pacing, not noticing me.

"Sure, okay. Whatever you think," he says. "Tell Scott I appreciate him doing this. I know this is what"—his voice cracks and he clears his throat—"she would have wanted."

After Dad hangs up, a big lump lodges its way into the back of my throat. Even though I don't drink coffee, I head for the coffeepot and pour myself a cup. Dad stares at the phone receiver on the counter. I take a big gulp, then wince at my scalded tongue and throat.

I don't know if it's from my burning mouth or the sunlight in the kitchen, but my world morphs from hazy to real. The miniature dents in the edge of our teal countertop magnify in my focus. Dad, with his wrinkles like the Grand Canyon, turns and aims every gold and brown fleck of his irises at me.

"What is it I can do?" I ask.

His brow furrows.

"You told someone on the phone, 'Brie will start.'"

He takes a moment to shake off his own daze. "I thought maybe you could say something at Faith's service. But you don't have to, honey."

Dad sounds so sad, I don't know what to say. I'd be completely heartless not to agree to whatever he wants right now. "Oh. Okay."

His eyes are dry, but red. They dart to the newspaper as though he doesn't want to look at me. It's so strange seeing this fragile side of him. It scares me.

I zip over and snatch the paper from the table, before he makes a move for it. For sure they'll have something in there about Faith, and I feel the need to save him from seeing it, like maybe it would be one more thing than he could handle and then he'd fall apart too.

I head out of the kitchen and up to my room. The write-up about Faith is easy to find on the second page. I snip it out, crumple up the rest of the clipped page, and throw it in my trash can. The write-up doesn't say much—seventeen years old, survived by her family—but something about seeing it there in black and white makes it seem truer. I stare at the junior year picture of her with her hair tied back, her honest smile, and think for the first time of how pretty she was. Why had I never noticed that?

A few minutes later, I pick up the journal and pen from beside my bed and head back downstairs. Dad is mumbling the funeral details into the phone again.

I pick up my cell phone and consider calling Amy. Or Dustin. But they're both probably still sleeping after the party last night, and I'm not sure I can say the words just yet anyway. Instead, I text them.

Faith fell off a cliff.

This can't be happening.

Funeral Wednesday. 2 PM.

I hit send.

Mom still hasn't come out of her room and I wonder if she'll stay there all morning. When the doorbell rings, Dad doesn't make a move from the kitchen, so I open the door to chubby Mrs. Ramirez, a lady who's been going to my parents' church for a million years. She taught Faith and me at Sunday School.

She pushes a large white casserole dish in my direction. "I'm so sorry." When she says the words, I have a déjà vu feeling. But not the "post" kind. More like the "pre" kind. Where you know this is going to be repeated over and over and over again, exactly the same.

I take the dish and thank her. After stuffing the casserole into the fridge, I burrow into my journal on the couch again.

I'm not really a journaler, or a girl with things to say all the time about everything. But for as long as I can remember I've made up little poems. When I'm confused, their rhythm helps me sort things out.

Plan C: Write something meaningful for Faith's funeral service.

When I put my mind to it, all I seem to remember about my sister is that she fell off a cliff.

I shake my head, still unable to wrap my head around it. I run my pen around the outside of the page. What does anyone say at a funeral? I miss my sister? First of all: duh. Everyone knows that much. But secondly, is it even true?

We haven't hung out since I was in middle school. The last time I can think of was when we went to Disneyland three years ago.

"Come on," Faith had yelled, grabbing my hand, and pulling me from ride to ride. We laughed so hard on Space Mountain, I thought we might pee our pants.

But so much had changed since then.

Disneyland, I write near the top of my page, right underneath *Cliff*.

But I can't really talk about Disneyland. Not at a funeral.

I lay my head back on the armrest and stare at the ceiling. The dark paint splotch above the window catches my eye and suddenly I remember more.

"We're just supposed to do the trim," Faith had teased me, paintbrush in hand.

I didn't laugh. Not at the time, not now. At the time, I was convinced Mom would throw a fit. She'd just redecorated the living room, had the walls painted by a group from the church, and Faith and I were supposed to worry only about the trim around the windows.

But the worst part wasn't the dark brown paintbrush splotch in the middle of the wall. Faith leaned over to try to make my error less noticeable and caught the gallon paint can with her foot.

The memory is so fresh, I feel like I have to see the stain. I push myself off the couch and crawl beside the piano. When I heave the large storage ottoman out of the way, there it is—

the basketball-size splotch on Mom's white rug. Of course it's still there. Where else would it be?

"Get some paint thinner from the garage," Faith had said. By the time I raced back into the living room, she was rubbing at a corner of the stain with a bottle of bleach and a tea towel.

But nothing worked.

Finally, after we edged the heavy ottoman into place, I convinced her not to say anything to Mom and Dad. I wanted to go to a party that night and I told her we'd find a better time to tell them.

That was three months ago.

When I hear Dad hang up the phone, I put all my weight into pushing the ottoman back over the splotch, and launch myself onto the couch. I write *PAINT* in large letters on my page, just to look like I'm doing something when Dad lumbers past the French doors and up the stairs.

But I won't be telling that story either.

Lying my head back, I close my eyes. I picture her face, see her bending down, scrubbing at the carpet. Her hair was pulled into a red bandana that day, but as I see her in my mind's eye, the bandana falls off and her curls flounce around her face. She stands and puts her arms out, and I notice the gray sweatshirt, though I know she wasn't wearing it that day.

There's fear in her eyes, and I try to force her face into a smile in my mind. But it won't budge. The longer I focus on her image, the more petrified she appears. I whisper not to worry, that I'll take the blame for the carpet, but her face doesn't change. If anything, it becomes more panicked.

She looks down at her feet and so do I, but it's not the living room carpet I see. Instead, her feet stand on bits of rock and gravel. And there's an edge, so close, and one foot starts to slip. A look of horror crosses her face when she looks up at me, and then she's gone. My eyes dart down and she's falling, past jagged rocks into what appears to be a bottomless pit.

"No!" When the word bursts from my mouth, everything goes black, and suddenly I feel the rush of wind past my eyes, my face. And it's not Faith who's falling, it's me. I can't see the ground, I can't see anything, and my cheeks suck upward. I scream, but barely hear my voice.

"Brie!" someone calls out to me, but I can't tell if it's from above or below.

"Help!" I try to gasp, but nothing comes out. My ears echo with the loud rumble of rushing wind.

"Brie!" I feel a jerk to my shoulder. "Brie, wake up." A shake to my arms. "It's just a dream. Wake up!"

I stare up into Dad's face, but I don't know where I am or how I got here.

"Are you okay, sweetie?"

Glancing around, I see the couch under me, the love seat across the room, the paint splotch above the window. I nod, but I can't find my voice.

"It was just a bad dream," Dad repeats.

And I want to tell him it wasn't. It seemed so real. But he pats my knee with a shaky hand, gives it a squeeze, and suggests I go find something to eat. It'll make me feel better.

After he leaves the room, I take a deep breath and sit up. I'm still tired, but the last thing I want to do is accidentally fall asleep here again. And the second-to-last thing I want to do is eat.

I tiptoe to the front door and ease it open just enough to slide through. Fresh air will help me get my bearings. But the first thing I see is Faith's Toyota.

I'm drawn to it. The driver's door is unlocked, which isn't surprising, since Faith trusted everyone. But I've never sat on the driver's side, so it takes me a few seconds to work myself up to get in.

When I click the door shut beside me, the space feels much smaller than it ever did before, like there's barely enough room for me. Maybe it's because I'm huddled in by the steering wheel. I reach my hands up and run them over it. Then over her gearshift and her dash. My hand circles the yellow sticker with the scribbly-looking cross. I slide my finger up the cross and then sideways, wondering why God would take someone so good. Someone who loved him so much. Then I trace the tiny black dots arching along the top and bottom. Looking closer, they appear to be letters and not just dots. I lean forward and try to make out the words.

Live 4 Him.

Sounds like something Faith would have pasted in her car. I peer even closer to read the minuscule bottom text.

Die 4 Him.

I suck in a breath and my thumb quickly covers the words, as if I could take back reading them.

chapter FIVE

Plan D: Greet some mourners. Read a poem. Go home.

Five days after the barn party, I hunch on a pew in the front row of the church, hiding behind my notebook while I wait for the dreaded service. My parents' church doesn't feel the same way I remember it. The decor seems so outdated. So orange. It smells different too, like the old people my grandma lives with. I don't remember the congregation having more than five or six people with white hair, but those few must be leaving their scent.

I used to call it *our* church, back when all four of us attended weekly services come sickness, tiredness, or even major catastrophe. But then I started spending more time with Amy, who wouldn't get out of bed before noon on a Sunday if her eternal soul depended on it—which, according to my family, it did—and eventually I reasoned my own way out of Sunday mornings.

Mom and Dad huddle in a corner. Mom's been crying since we got here, but not the normal kind of crying. More like a constant huffing that builds to a wail every five minutes or so.

Faith's coffin sits less than ten feet away from me, but thankfully it's closed. Whatever she looks like now, I don't want to know. Even the thought of having her body so close gives me this creepy feeling, like having a dead animal carcass in the room. I've heard that funerals often have open caskets to give the family some measure of peace, but how could it?

As the church fills up, I recognize some faces from the parking lot the other night. The dark-haired girl who tried to include me mingles with a few distraught-looking youth group types. Some others from Sharon High, Faith's school friends, avert their eyes, which is fine with me. If one of them died, I wouldn't know what to say to their siblings either. I haven't been in school all week and the appearance of all these people out of their natural habitat only adds to the hallucinatory feeling of this whole day.

My eyes stop dead on my silent-yet-intimidating locker neighbor, Tessa Lockbaum, leaning against the back wall.

What is she doing here? She wears her usual death garb: black turtleneck, dark baggy jeans, silver belt buckle in the shape of a skull. Rumors permeate the hallways at school about how many kids she's beaten up over the years. Students give her a wide berth whenever she makes her way to classes.

Being my age and the antithesis of holy, Tessa definitely wouldn't have been one of Faith's friends. With stray empty seats all around, I wonder why she just stands there, her arms crossed as though she's judging the world.

All of a sudden, she glares right back at me and I realize how long I've been staring. I turn away, but feel holes burning into my back. Not only am I confused about her presence, but what's with that look, as if she blames me for something?

A stab of guilt hits me, and my mind rebounds to that night. All I could think of was Dustin. The last time I saw my sister, I lied to her, used her, barely said thanks for the ride.

"Hey, babe. You okay?"

Dustin's voice jolts me back to the moment. I slap my journal shut, swallow hard, and take my time looking up. He had texted me back to tell me he was sorry and that he'd be here, but that was the last I'd heard from him. In a way I'm glad. I wasn't ready to talk to anyone earlier. Still may not be. Amy sidles up beside him. Dustin wraps an arm around my shoulder and gives me a squeeze and Amy mimics him on the other side.

"I'm so sorry," they both say at the same time. Even though they don't laugh, I feel like I've missed out on some private joke.

Amy called me right after she got my text, asking if I wanted her to come over, but I let it ring and then e-mailed her back using the excuse that I didn't think my parents were ready for outsiders. The truth is, I was waiting for the whole idea of what had happened to hit me. I didn't really want anyone around when that happened. Of course I'm still waiting.

"What's she doing here?" I ask, changing the subject and trying not to focus directly on Tessa. But when I speak, I realize how long it's been since I've really talked to anyone. My voice feels strange. Echoey.

"Holy shit!" Amy says. "Did you invite Tessa Lockbaum?"

I stare at Amy, eyebrows raised, until she realizes the idiocy of her question.

"Maybe she's paying her respects or something," Dustin says.

That doesn't make sense, but I'm not about to argue, especially with Dustin. I motion to the pew behind me. "I saved this row if you guys want to sit here."

He shifts uneasily. "Actually, I left my jacket at the back."

Sure enough, his brown leather jacket hangs over the pew of the very back row. I'm disappointed, but turn to Amy.

"I'll be right back," she says, before I can speak. "You know, the bathroom."

With the church nearly full, the pastor ambles up onto the stage and rustles his papers at the podium. The way he spreads the papers out, stares at them, then shuffles them back together, I wonder if he's at all prepared for this. Then again, am *I* prepared for this? I haven't faced people all week and now I have to give a speech about my dead sister. How *could* I be prepared?

When the pastor taps on the microphone, Mom and Dad slip into their seats beside me.

This disorganized Pastor dude looks like he's barely out of high school. He wears a sweater that I saw on a manne-quin at American Eagle last month, which probably adds to his pubescent appearance. He must have started pastoring in kindergarten, because he's been Faith's youth leader for, like, ever. For all Faith used to prattle on about him, "Pastor Scott says this and Pastor Scott says that"—she never mentioned he was hot. No wonder Faith spent so much time at youth group.

"I'm Scott MacDonald," the guy says in a much deeper voice than I expect. "For those of you who don't know me . . ."

He scans the crowd for several seconds and the earring in his left ear gleams across the room like a neon sign reading *I miss the nineties.* "I'm the Youth Pastor here at Crestview Church. Or, as some of my crew like to call me, Captain Scotty." He clears his throat and crinkles his brow, apparently just now remembering he's leading a funeral. "We are gathered here today to celebrate the life of Faith Jenkins."

Mom lets out a whimper at my sister's name. I slide my hand over hers on the bench and leave it there, even though I'm tempted to pull away from her cold clamminess. I wish Dustin and Amy would have stuck close by. Someone to hold me up while I hold up Mom.

The pastor launches into the Bible, and since Mom's breathing seems almost normal, I open my notebook low on the bench beside me. I finally wrote a poem this morning, but looking over it now, it's way too embarrassing. When my turn comes, I'm going to give my head a little shake, and hope that Junior up there gets the picture. Surely somebody with a little more distance can start off the tributes.

The pastor goes into his philosophical take on the accident. He keeps repeating, "She wasn't alone," which gets redundant real fast, since Faith was never really alone. She hung out constantly with her friends from youth or, at the very least, Celeste.

I crane my neck to look for Celeste in the crowd, but can't see her anywhere.

I'm thinking about how whacked it is that Tessa Lock-baum lurks in the back while Celeste isn't even here, when Pastor Scott motions to the sound-tech guy and a song starts playing through the speakers at the back. A picture of Faith at her full-immersion baptism comes up on the screen at the front. Age twelve, her hair hangs straight and straggly from the water. Her glasses are covered in so many droplets I doubt she could see a thing.

Of course Celeste must be upset, but she, more than any-one, should be here.

I bite my tongue when Faith's clear voice bursts through the speakers behind me. I didn't know they'd be playing her music today. I ball a fist at my side to keep my strength, my balance. *It's not really her,* I tell myself. *She's gone.*

The picture fades into another, now with Faith propped on a girl's shoulders at youth camp. Her smile seems to take up the whole screen.

"Hallelujah, praise to my Lord," my sister's voice resounds through the back speakers. Not an actual song, but one of the improvised tangents the worship team used to attempt on Sunday mornings. They did that regularly back when Faith sang with them, because she could sing to anything.

I glance back to find Dustin and Amy, figuring they'll help me get some equilibrium. But all I see is the top of Dustin's head. The way his hair jitters every few seconds, he must be playing games on his cell phone.

I'm not mad. Jealous, if anything. I wish that could be me, that I could find a distraction that takes me anywhere but here. Amy, nowhere in sight, is likely giving herself a make-over in the bathroom.

I almost scream when Mom grasps my leg. But the picture of Faith in church shocks me, too. She stands up on that same stage in front of us now, with arms outstretched in abandon-ment. She'd been part of the worship team for years, so it isn't an unusual sight, but because she'll never stand there again, it makes me catch my breath. Makes everyone in the whole room catch their breath.

Pastor Scott rests a hand on the podium, but doesn't say anything when the picture fades. The silence is eerie. I fight the image of Faith in my dream with the same outstretched arms.

Even with the music stopped, Faith's voice echoes in my head. Not any particular words, just a humming melody. Finally, the pastor flips through papers, clears his throat, and uses his forced professional voice to read an excerpt from the Bible. It ends in, "These three remain: faith, hope, and love."

My stomach lurches at the words. No, they don't remain. They don't! Gripping the pew on either side of me, I suck in through my nose. I can hold it together if only her voice in my head would shut up.

Pastor Scott rustles through his stack of notes again, the congregation silently watching. Waiting. At last he pushes the papers aside, and without any notes, leans toward the microphone ready to ad-lib. "I don't mean any disrespect," he says, using a different tone now, like he's ready to cheer us all up, "but there is a great side to all of this."

A murmur covers the congregation. Mom's choked cries intensify and Dad moves closer to comfort her.

"Of course we'll miss Faith, but let's think of the glory she's enjoying now. She gets to be with her Lord! This is what she wanted!"

There's a bustle around me. I want to check on Mom, see how she's taking this, but I can't seem to turn my head. *Deep breaths, Brie.*

"I hadn't spoken to Faith much lately," he goes on. "Last year, when she was more active in my group, she was a real welcoming force for the new kids. Everyone really loved her."

Last year? More active? How could she possibly have been more active? Faith was a youth group junkie since the day she turned twelve.

Mom's breathing becomes quick, like she's hyperventilating, so I place my hand back over hers. I glance at Dad, but he's busy stroking Mom's hair.

"So we thank you, God," the youth pastor bellows, "for the time we did have with Faith."

I feel a jerk to my hand as Mom pulls away and stands in one quick motion.

"The time we had with her?" Mom laughs a loud, cynical laugh, almost choking on her tears. "*We* didn't spend any time with her!" She drops back to her seat, as though she can't hold herself up any longer.

I get Mom's point, though. Even the years we did have with Faith, she was either in school, or at some youth event. The youth group at Crestview surged in the last couple of years, and they have their own church services at the old fire hall, so Mom and Dad stopped seeing her Sundays, too. Still, I don't think it's really fair for her to blame Pastor Scott for that.

Dad stares straight ahead, like Mom's outburst didn't happen. And no one else steps in. When I glance around, people look away as if they aren't really watching us. Mom folds over, almost in half, sobbing so loud I want to cover my ears.

Dad puts his arm over her, but keeps his eyes straight ahead. Apparently, the wall in front gives him strength. With his face scrunched tight, Pastor Scott stands behind the podium. He blinks, clears his throat, and attempts to recover.

"I'm, um, terribly sorry." He runs a hand through his shaggy hair. "Perhaps now would be a good time to open it up for those who would like to help us remember Faith." His words are so quiet, he sounds like a different person. He backs away from the microphone. Now is the time when he's supposed to give me the nod (so I can give him the corresponding *no way* shake) but he doesn't angle even slightly in my direction. He probably doesn't want to look at Mom.

I scan the room for an aunt or uncle, for someone who I can give my most pleading puppy-dog look to, but everyone avoids my eyes. Gripping my notebook with both hands, I totter up on shaky legs. Dad wants me to say something? Well, here goes, I guess. The people in the pews around me are still like a photograph while I inch my way up to the podium.

Everyone's eyes fix on me at the microphone. Hopeful eyes. Like I'm going to say something that will make it all better.

"I can't," I blurt.

Pastor Scott immediately steps beside me and places his hand on my shoulder. He thinks I can't bring myself to say anything. I scan the crowd again. That's what they all think.

Flipping open my journal, I decide to just read the stupid

poem. People will be grateful for whatever I say at this point.

"I wrote this poem," I say into the mic. The pastor's hand falls off me and he backs away. "I've never read my poetry for anyone, not even Faith. But somehow I think she would want me to read this today." I glance around the upper part of the room to catch my breath, but then realize how stupid I look.

I drop my head and race through the first lines.

"I wish I could talk about things from our lives
Faith would have retained it all, had she survived."

I look up and smile a little to make it clear that I know it's pretty lame, but then with all the somber faces staring back at me, I clue in to how inappropriate I look. I stare down at my journal.

I scan over the next lines and they're all about me and my struggle to get through this. That suddenly seems inappropriate too. Shouldn't this be about Faith? I run my finger halfway down my page looking for something about my sister. I swallow down my nerves and start again.

"That time with the tuba and breaking her arm
Will no longer conjure our whimsical charm."

I can't stop the flashes of memories in my head. The tuba that was bigger than she was. The coat hanger she used to shove down her cast to scratch with. It's hard to clear the images. Part of me wants to keep concentrating on her face. But everyone is waiting for my next words and I can barely feel my tongue now from nerves.

> *"Disneyland seems like forever in the past.*
> *That vacation, apparently, would be our last."*

My voice cracks and I stop for a second to catch my breath.

> *"The paint on the carpet will always remain."*

Just for a moment I visualize moving the ottoman permanently, so we could see the splotch all the time. Remember it.

> *"Why take the good things and leave us the stains?"*
> *Even with these memories, I'm keeping calm*
> *And wondering why I don't lose it like Mom."*

I snap my mouth shut. When I wrote it, all I thought about was the fact that I haven't cried all week. Now it looks

like I'm just bringing even more attention to Mom's outburst.
I know I need to push on. And fast.

"Whatever I say doesn't help with the grief
If only I didn't feel so much relief."

As the words leave my mouth, they shock me. I know
what I meant when I wrote them: the relief of having the
cops out of our house, of Dad and his strength, of every
moment I seem able to put one foot in front of the other.
But saying it out loud, it sounds all wrong. My face heats
up and I start to close my book in embarrassment. But the
words ring out in the air, and I can't just leave them there.
With only two lines left, I reconsider and decide to just
finish.

"All I can hope is she's somewhere above
My sister, Faith, who I hated and loved."

When I finish no one moves, and the buzz of the
sound system takes over the silence. The moment is way
too uncomfortable and when I peek up, stares come at me
from all around the room. The relief line still rings in my
head and I swallow hard, wondering just how wrong people

could have taken it. Or was it wrong to admit that sometimes I hated Faith, even if it is the truth?

I try to come up with some words, but suddenly Mom leaps out of her chair again, taking everyone's attention, and before I can open my mouth, she runs for the back of the church.

The echo of her sobbing resonates, even after the doors close behind her.

Oh no.

"Excuse me," I whisper, and don't wait for a response. Rushing through the pews, I fly out the back doors into the lobby.

She's not there, or in the bathroom, so I open the outside doors and scan the parking lot. Nothing. I race up the stairs to check the balcony. With no sign of her, I start to panic.

As I'm about to find a side door leading into the sanctuary and grab Dad, people start filing out of the main exit into the lobby. Somehow, Pastor Scott must have wrapped things up.

When people make their way through the main doors, they all give me concerned looks, like they wonder how I could possibly have said what I did. And now I wonder the same thing myself.

Okay, I'm sorry! I feel like shouting. *But give me a break.*

Someone had to say something and it's not like anybody else was taking over!

But I guess we all have to deal with grief in our own way. I just deal with mine by, oh, I don't know, writing bad poetry.

Tessa Lockbaum comes into view. I've already assumed my defensive stance, due to the stares coming at me from every direction, so I'm ready to confront her. But when she lifts her head, my scowl stops at the tear on her cheek.

A tear. From Tessa Lockbaum.

How could she have even known Faith? Them hanging out would've been like Hitler consorting with Mother Teresa. In fact, I'm almost positive I've seen Faith move aside in the hallways right along with everyone else when Tessa tromped by.

Just as she spins away and hides her face, Dad grabs me by the shoulder. "Where's your mother?"

"I don't know," I reply, my words drenched in apology. All I can think of is how I can ever get her to forgive me.

chapter SIX

*d*ad makes a beeline for the van while I tag along behind, rattling off all of the places I've searched for Mom.

"Maybe she walked?" Craning my neck in both directions, I see no sign of her in the parking lot. "She must be headed home, right? Where else would she go?" I'm not a babbler, so my incessant muttering makes me want to pinch my lips shut with my fingers. But I don't. "Do you think she's angry?"

Dad finally looks at me, but not in the way I expect. He studies me, eyes circling my face, as though I'm a mathematical equation, something he has to figure out. "Angry," he murmurs. "Angry." He turns away again and I can't tell if he's thinking of how horrible I am or if his mind is somewhere else. We ride the rest of the way in silence.

Inside our front door, Mom's coat lies across a chair. I let out a breath, but snatch up the coat and hang it in the closet. Mom's the one who always nags at the rest of us to do this, and I try not to think about the oddity of cleaning up after her.

After seeing the coat, Dad heads back out the front door. "I'll put the van in the garage."

The house is quiet, which means Mom's already gone up to their room. Good. I don't have a clue what to say to her yet.

As I unzip my boots, a shadow appears behind me from the living room and I almost come out of my skin.

"What? Oh, Mom. It's you." Still with my other boot on, I stand there, lopsided. "You're home. I mean, I'm glad you're home. I didn't mean what I . . . I'm so sorry about what I . . . said. Mom, are you . . . okay?"

She stands as still as the empty room behind her with her head down, listening, or not, to my rambling. If we were normal right now, she'd be pondering my apology, wondering whether or not she should let me off the hook. But if we were normal, I guess I'd have nothing to apologize for.

"Mom?"

Her clammy hand reaches to the back of my neck and

pulls me in. She kisses me on the forehead, something she never does, backs away, and turns for the stairs. In her right hand, she grips the Jesus statue from the mantel.

The way her hand wraps over his face makes me think she's not taking it upstairs to pray.

During the burial the next day, the three of us are zombies. Thankfully, none of us have to speak or actually do anything. We're all just there for show. I keep my eyes on the ground as the pallbearers lower the casket, as Pastor Scott reads from his Bible, as the small group of extended family and my parents' friends say good-bye. Still no Celeste. Faith's humming in my head is the constant that's keeping me distant from it all. Keeping me in an alternate reality.

I try to focus on the least emotional people of the crowd. Men are the safest bet and I count how many are wearing dark suits. Back by the trees there's a guy in jeans, which is a bit out of place, but if Dustin had come I'm sure he would have worn jeans too. This guy's so far away from everyone else that he doesn't even look like part of the service, but I can tell by the way he stares toward the closed casket that he must be here for this. For Faith.

I inch back from my parents and they don't seem to notice. I'm lost in my thoughts and in Faith's humming, when

I notice the guy in jeans glancing around. His features are chiseled, even from a distance. I've always loved longer hair on guys, and when he pushes his dark bangs away from his face, my heart skips a beat.

I know this is not the time to think about cute guys, but still, I take another step toward him. How did he know Faith? How come I don't recognize him? He doesn't look like the clean-cut guys from church youth group. I take another step, edging out of the circle of mourners this time. They're all so captured by Pastor Scott's speech, none of them seem to notice.

Mystery guy wears a red and black checkered jacket and now that I'm closer I can see the crease down the front of his blue jeans. He holds a bundle of carnations down at his side. I try to ignore the clothes and concentrate on his etched expression, intent and contemplative. Something about him seems different and I'm drawn toward him.

Maybe he senses this, because he turns in my direction. I'm not sure what I'm doing exactly. I have a boyfriend. I guess I just want to say hi, maybe ask where he knows Faith from. But suddenly he jolts like he's been woken up from a dead sleep, drops the flowers, which scatter around him, and backs quickly behind an adjacent tree.

I dazedly look behind me, wondering what spooked

him. Nothing. No one in the service seems to have moved a muscle.

Staring in the direction of the tree where he disappeared, I drop my bag, check over my shoulder to make sure my parents are still occupied, and inch into the woods. But he's not there, behind that tree. In fact, I don't see him anywhere. Did he just vanish into thin air? I focus on a path through the trees, and when I'm out of sight of the burial group, I take off in a run.

Soon the path fades into bushes and stumps, and I'm not sure which direction to head in. When I look around, I think I catch movement straight ahead. I pick up my pace again. I don't even know what I'll say if I find him, but now I need to. It feels like my sanity depends on it.

Well into the forest, I take in my surroundings. Everything looks like it's moving now. The rustling of leaves envelops me like surround sound. I make a false start, but then realize it's only another gust of wind.

"Hello," I call out. "I just want to talk to you."

But there's no response. It takes me several minutes to admit he's gone, whoever he is. And if I don't return soon, I'll have no idea how to find my way back to the cemetery.

My lungs ache after the jog back to Faith's grave and I've questioned my muddled brain the whole way. Did I really see him? Maybe my mind was so desperate for distraction that I created a mirage of a hot guy. That makes more sense than anything.

When I near the clearing, I slow down and peer around a tree until I'm sure no one will notice my reappearance. People are consoling my parents and the service must be finished.

The sky has clouded over and I wish I'd brought a heavier sweater, but when my parents glance over and give me the look that it's time to go, suddenly I'm not ready. I wasn't here for the service and didn't get a chance to think about what just happened. They're burying my sister.

People clear quickly, either from the cold or from the realization that my parents want this to be over. I get Dad alone and ask if he minds if I hang around a few minutes and catch a bus home. "I'll be home before dark," I add.

I half expect him to say no, but he must be too emotionally exhausted. He nods, then leads Mom back toward their car.

When the last car pulls away and I walk over to collect my backpack, I spot the carnations. They're blowing around the perimeter of the cemetery. The boy *was* here. But he couldn't have known Faith well if he brought full-bloom carnations. Flower buds were her favorite—didn't matter what kind, as long as they were young flowers. The promise of new blossoms, she always said.

I pick up each carnation and bring them over to Faith's plot. Even in full bloom, Faith would want them. It's tempting to keep thinking about the boy, keep wondering about him, but I don't let myself.

Faith's gravestone isn't up yet, but there's a plaque propped up that emblazons the dates of her birth and death. They look like the expiration dates on a can of soup. Seventeen years doesn't appear like nearly enough time for the life of a person. The rest of the flowers surrounding the plaque and atop the casket are barely buds. I keep my eyes from the lowered casket and distract myself by wondering if people will come down here to change the buds so they don't bloom.

Under the date and her name reads a simple Bible verse and I have to ask myself, *Can't anyone be a little bit original and come up with something other than Scripture to say something about her?*

I shake my head, suddenly realizing maybe this is what she would have wanted. Still, a part of me knows there was more to her than youth groups and Bible verses.

Gnawing my lower lip, I read the verse. "He said to her, 'Daughter, your faith has healed you. Go in peace and be freed from your suffering.'"—Mark 5:34.

I know this is meant to bring some kind of comfort, but when I read the word *healed*, all I can picture is Faith's mangled body at the bottom of Blackham Mountain.

I try again to focus on anything but the casket and I'm done looking at her plaque, but my knees feel glued to the ground. I can't leave yet. I fiddle with the handle on my backpack.

"There's this thing," I say quietly. As if she can hear me anyway. "I guess I should read you this thing."

Digging through the front pocket of my pack I find the folded piece of paper. "I've been kind of confused these last few days. And angry." My eyes drift over the first couple lines. "Yeah, it's not Shakespeare or anything." After the complete mess I made at the funeral yesterday, I can't believe I'm even thinking of this. But I glance around and the cemetery's empty. Just her and me.

Even though I know this is stupid, I can't stop staring at the words. "Well, I'm going to read it to you. Because you're the only one I can read it to. But take it with a grain of salt, okay?"

I smooth out the paper and clear my throat. "It's a poem just for you."

> *"Everyone knew you much better than me.*
> *Our empty house mutters instead of sings*
> *Your voice annoys me wherever I go."*

I choke a little on this line, but don't let myself stop.

"You went before me, taught me to grow."

I glance at her grave. "Way too sappy, huh?" I brush a tear from my cheek and press on.

"They wanted me to be more like you
I hate that this is probably true.
But most of all, I'm mad that you left
I hate you for that. Your greatest theft."

The last words are barely recognizable because I sob through them. I fold up the paper and her humming trickles back into my head, softly at first, like the flutter of butterfly wings, then louder so I can almost make out her words. Even though I don't know when her humming stopped, now, hearing it, I feel like I can breathe again.

"You always wanted to hear my poetry. I told you it was bad. And this is one of the better ones." I choke out a laugh. "You know, the one thing I should scratch out is the part about your voice. I can't say anything bad about it. I just can't."

I rub at my throat, as if I suspect her voice might erupt

out of me. But no such luck. I push myself up from my knees and lean down to pick up my backpack. "It sucks, you know?"

When I turn to leave, my legs don't let me. Looking back at her grave, the buds of newness, I wipe away my tears one more time.

"I miss you, Faith," I whisper.

And then I'm done. I know I am.

chapter SEVEN

*t*he next day is Friday and I spend the whole day and most of the weekend in bed like I haven't slept in weeks. The truth is, I feel as though I've been sleeping more than ever, since my whole life is like one big hazy dream. But my body is exhausted and each time I wake up, it seems just as easy to shut my eyes again and let Faith's hum lull me right back to sleep.

Sunday afternoon I get around to checking my cell phone and e-mail and find several "How R U?" messages from Amy and a couple from our friend Steph. I double-check to make sure I didn't miss anything from Dustin, but there's nothing.

It's not personal, I know that. Just discomfort. It's better if I see him at school, where we have our history of how we act together.

I hit reply and tell both Amy and Steph that I'll be back in class tomorrow. Even though I haven't discussed this with my parents, it seems obvious to me. Get on with things so I can find some part of my life that feels normal again.

When I head downstairs for something to eat, Dad sits on the living room couch staring at the wall.

"Hey," I say, trying to make my voice as even as possible.

He blinks and looks both directions before dropping his eyes to a pile of papers on the coffee table in front of him. "Oh, hi, sweetie."

"Hungry?" I ask, heading for the kitchen. I'm not even sure *I'm* hungry, but I've barely eaten lately and I've been getting more and more dizzy since the burial. At first I assumed it was an emotional reaction, or a consequence of too much sleep, but now I'm wondering if it could just be lack of sustenance.

"I'm busy," he says, which doesn't answer my question.

I look in the fridge and the most obvious thing is a pizza box on the middle shelf. It's not until I open it up and see the pineapple piled up on half of the remaining pieces that I realize how old it is. Faith was the only one in the family who liked pineapple. The thought of eating it, even if it isn't filled with salmonella, makes me want to hurl. I dump the whole thing in the garbage and cut up some cheese to go with a box of crackers from the cupboard. After making a plate up for Dad and one for myself, I push through the door into the living room.

This time Dad's not zoned out, but rather looks like he's had too much caffeine. He picks up papers, places them down again. Grabs the phone and starts dialing, only to shut it off and drop it back onto the table. I watch from just inside the room as his behavior becomes more and more frantic.

"Where's Mom?" I finally walk over and place the plate of cheese and crackers beside his papers. Just as I do, he decides he needs that space to spread out his work and holds the plate up, darting his eyes around in frustration. Doesn't seem like a hard problem, but it shocks me that Dad, of all people, can't find the simple solution. "Here." I take it and put it on a side table instead.

Since he doesn't seem able to answer my question about Mom—it's pretty obvious she's up in their room again anyway and besides, I was only trying to make conversation—I head back for the stairs.

Being alone is just so much easier.

Plan E: Somehow we all need to get back to normal.

Monday the Jenkins Family of Three returns to real life. Dad looks like he's been doing hard labor through the night when he drags himself to the coffeemaker first thing in the morning. He spent the last five days taking care of all the remaining incidentals surrounding Faith's death. It would probably have taken me a year to get around to contacting everyone affected, but Dad's already called her optometrist, dentist, and schoolteachers, old and new. Taking care of all the details is obviously helping him get through it.

His real job, Concord Financial Services, could do without him for another week I'm sure, but he's pushing himself, getting back on that horse. And I understand how it would be easier to just think about numbers right now.

I've tried all weekend to come up with a way to tell the church ladies to stop bringing us food. Mom needs to cook again. Cooking is numbers for her.

And for me, numbers, I've decided, is school. I'd never admit it to anyone else, but I actually don't mind school. Of course that wouldn't be apparent from the amount of homework I've done this week. Each time I open my schoolbooks, all I can think of is how Faith will never spend another day in classes. She'll never graduate, even though she was a good student. I want to keep up on my schoolwork, I do, but at the same time it almost doesn't feel fair.

Instead, I've spent most of my mind-numbing hours thinking about how I'll act with Dustin when I go back.

Amy and everyone else will be easy, business as usual, but I don't want my boyfriend to think I'm a basket case and not know how to talk to me anymore. I practice phrases like "Hey, how's it goin'?" and "Yeah, actually, I'm doing okay" in front of my mirror until I can pass them off without a flinch.

But it's far from business as usual at Sharon High Monday morning. It appears that way when I first step through the school doors, but then two kids near the entrance stop mid-conversation and stare. They go back to talking, but in nearly a whisper.

Give me a break! I drop my eyes away from every silent stare and angle for my locker. I was positive the hum of Faith's voice wouldn't survive the busy hallways at school, but the odd tranquility makes the humming seem even louder. Amy stands only a few doors down from my locker, chatting with another girl, and hasn't noticed me yet. Which is amazing, since the rest of the school seems to be on Brie Alert.

Tessa Lockbaum's locker, right next to mine, is marked with a dull black lock that looks like something out of a junkyard. A sticker covering the number of her locker reads F*** YOU, the asterisks added overtop in her own handwriting in order to not officially break school rules. At least she's nowhere in sight.

I call out, "Hey, Amy. How's it goin'?" a little too loudly, so all the students in the vicinity can take in my even-keeledness.

She peeks past the open door of her friend's locker and smiles. "Hey."

We walk toward our first classes together, and I know it's my obligation to break the silence. I mean, what's she going to ask about?

"So what'd you do this weekend?" I say, pulling from my repertoire of pre-practiced phrases.

She nibbles at her lip like this question is just way too difficult.

Come on, Amy. You can do this. I'm fine, really, I try to say with my eyes.

"A few people got together at Tabitha's."

"Tabitha's?" I say quickly. "Cool. Who was there?"

She glances both directions as we cross another hallway. "Oh, you know. The usual."

Silence. She's certainly not making this easy. I wonder if she feels guilty about that night. About not coming into the hospital with me. But I know Amy well enough not to bring it up. She doesn't deal with guilt well, and would definitely get defensive.

"So was Steph there? Or Dustin? I haven't talked to him since the funeral." My mind races to keep my part of this discussion going as long as possible. "I probably should've called him this weekend, but then I thought . . . I mean, I could've . . ."

Crap. Somehow I meandered back to home life.

"I haven't seen either of them," she says, looking straight ahead. "But I'm sure Dustin will understand that you didn't call."

I study her profile to make myself believe what she's just said. During my last three months with Dustin, all she's ever told me was that I wasn't doing or being enough and I better pick it up. The thought of her suddenly being so supportive and caring right now makes tears well up behind my eyes. I blink a couple times to diffuse them.

"They had an assembly last week. About Faith," she adds.

I cringe. I don't want to picture the whole school sitting in the auditorium trying to process what I can't even seem to process. I scratch at my jeans, unsure of how to change the subject.

"I've got Chem." Amy stops in front of an open classroom.

I give her a quick hug, which feels strange. Neither of us are really huggers. But I have to tell her, without actually saying it, how much I appreciate her company. "I'll see you at lunch?" I ask, another weird question. We always eat lunch together.

She offers a quick nod before ducking into her class.

• • •

My first class, English, I make it just through the door when my teacher catches sight of me.

"Oh, Brie. You're back," Mrs. Edwards says from her desk. "How are you doing, dear?"

Just the mention, the out-loud recognition, seems to make the surrounding students uncomfortable and they move away from me like I'm a drop of oil in their otherwise placid water.

I don't want *this* kind of attention. I give Mrs. Edwards a slight nod, but keep my head down all the way to my desk. This seems like enough to give her the hint and she leaves me alone through the rest of the hour.

At Dustin's locker between classes, I study myself in the window across the hall while I wait for him. Even in a reflection, the wrinkles in my shirt are obvious. I pull at the bottom of it in a vain attempt to flatten them out and wonder if I should be wearing something more somber than my bright orange retro tee.

My hair is no better. I guess I forgot to straighten it this morning. Or brush it. I run my fingers through until I hear Dustin's loud voice and turn to look for him.

"Oh. Brie." He sounds surprised to see me.

"Hi." I smile, glad that my voice comes out steady. But I don't touch him. Let him make the first move.

He pulls me in and slides his arm around me. At first, I'm

relieved and let out a long-held breath, but then he kisses my neck and nuzzles into it and I feel smothered, like I can't get any air. "You want to go somewhere?" he whispers.

I pull back, but his grip on my back holds strong. Turning my head, I take a big, calming breath. I guess I wasn't expecting just to fall back onto the *losing my virginity* train so quickly. "Um, no," I say. But in a flash, I wonder if I'm overreacting. He's being nice to me and I should appreciate it. He hasn't taken offense because I didn't call all week and I don't want to say or do anything I'll regret.

But I can't go off alone with him and make out. I just can't imagine his mouth on mine right now. The thought of not being able to breathe brings me to a cold sweat. And after the way I almost cried with Amy earlier, I might totally fall apart on him. I just need some time to get my footing. "I mean, I've got Geometry next. I was gone all last week so I really can't miss it."

He stares at me but doesn't let go, and I'm really starting to feel panicked, trapped.

When Evan walks up behind him and grabs his shoulder, Dustin jumps and pulls away in one motion.

"You coming, or what?" he asks Dustin, giving me a half nod.

"Oh, yeah, right." Dustin looks back at me, then raises his eyebrows. "I'll see *you* later."

Later is okay. It's better than now. I force a smile and suck in another lungful of oxygen.

When Dustin and Evan turn the corner and move out of sight, I realize how few people are left in the hallway. In fact, only one person remains.

Tessa Lockbaum.

She leans beside the water fountain, and when I look at her, she doesn't avert her eyes the way most people would. I wonder how long she's been there. Was she watching Dustin and me?

The next bell sounds, which means I'm officially late. Perfect. But at least my classroom is in the opposite direction of where Tessa stands. I scurry down the hall away from her, trying to ignore Faith's humming.

When lunch rolls around, I can't find Amy anywhere in the cafeteria. Either I missed her or she's starving herself again. Since Dustin's a senior, he has a different lunch period. Steph and the other girls Amy and I usually sit with are laughing and chatting across the cafeteria. I'm tired and don't feel like putting in the effort of a strong front right now. Instead, I plop down at a lonely table and ignore the eyes and whispers of those at the tables around me.

What can I expect on my first day back? I knew it was

going to be weird. I guess this is just a different weird than I anticipated.

"Give it time," I tell myself.

The rest of the afternoon, I keep to myself, which my class-mates make extremely easy for me. I walk home alone and when I round the corner onto our street, a big, rectangular truck with the Family Thrift Store logo sits in our driveway. I catch my breath. It's way too soon for this. Dad must have seen the packed-up boxes and decided to just get them out of the house. But I wonder, in his super-efficiency, if he's packed up the rest of her stuff as well. I gave Faith's room only a cursory glance. What if I want to keep something else?

When I get closer, I see Mom at the front door. She's still in her robe and slippers, shaking her head violently at the pudgy man in gray coveralls. Sections of her hair stick out like legs on a spider. She holds her hand up like a stop sign, and even though I can't picture this man busting into our house to steal all Faith's possessions, I don't blame Mom for the added caution. Before I reach our driveway, the man heads for his truck and hops back into the driver's seat. Mom still stands with her hand outstretched.

"Hi," I say when I get to the door.

This seems to break her from her trance. She lowers her hand and nods, but looks like she won't even be able to say hello without breaking into tears.

"Let's go back inside," I tell her, and don't have to give directions beyond that. Silently, she lumbers up to her bedroom. I think about following her upstairs to peek into Faith's bedroom, but I'm not sure I'm ready to see it in case it's empty and bare.

The doorbell rings a few minutes later. For a second I'm worried it's the thrift store guy being pushy, but I answer it to another outstretched casserole.

"That's so nice of you," I say, "but my mom . . . Well, I'm really hoping she can get back in the kitchen soon. To take her mind off of things."

"Put it in your freezer, dear," Mrs. Ramirez says. "It's there if you need it."

I thank her and Nuisance nuzzles his nose into the opening when I attempt to close the door.

"All right, I'll take you for a walk."

Normally when I walk Nuisance, it's not really a walk, more of a sprint, with me being dragged behind. But today he meanders, like he's waiting for me to take charge. At least choosing a direction gives me something to think about. Something to distract me from my other thoughts, like whether or not I should call Dustin. Or if it's still too early to invite Amy to the house. Or maybe I should make plans to go out with her. I need to get a foot back into my social life, but I'm just not sure how to do it right now. Even the thought of spending a whole evening hanging out seems exhausting.

For half a second I consider talking to Amy about what I'm going through. But the thought doesn't take root. She's my path back to normalcy. Besides, she's not the type to get into heavy emotional conversations.

When Nuisance and I get back to our street, there's another van in our driveway. I jog to the house, hoping they haven't rung the bell yet so I can intercept them before Mom has to deal with whatever it is. Nuisance keeps pace, but I'm sure it's using all his resources.

"Hello," I call to the sandy-haired guy walking to the doorway.

When he turns, I see the vase of flowers in his hands. "Is this the Jenkins house?" he asks, reading from a swatch of paper stuck in the arrangement.

I nod. "Thanks." After taking the flowers, I open the door and put them on the hall table. They're buds, of course. I turn to offer one more thank-you, but the delivery guy is already back in his van. After closing the door, I scan the buds until I find a small card nudged in the top.

Dear Mr. and Mrs. Jenkins, and Brie,

So sorry I couldn't be with you at the memorial service
for Faith. My grandmother is having health problems
and we had to leave town suddenly to be with her.
I don't know when we'll be back, but my heart is with
you all during this difficult time.

Love,
Celeste and the Schwartz family

I prop the card beside the flowers. Poor Celeste. As if losing your best friend isn't enough. I consider e-mailing her,
but what would I say? It's not like we were really close, and
I don't seem to even have any comforting words for my own
parents.

I head to the living room where the cushions and blankets
sit balled up in a pile at the end of the couch. I pick one up
and start folding. Toast scraps decorate a plate on the hutch
beside haphazard papers. They must be Mom's since Dad has
been at work all day. I'm glad she's at least eating something.

Everything looks different. Of course the only real changes
to the room are the mess and the little empty spot on the
mantel. A ring of dust sits where JC used to be. Maybe Mom

threw Jesus in the garbage. I don't know why, but the thought makes my gut clench like I've swallowed a coat hanger. Whatever she did with the thing, I don't want to know.

Dad marches through the door just after six. I take it upon myself to heat a pot of church-donated stew. Maybe I shouldn't have said anything to Mrs. Ramirez. She's probably already passed on the message to the rest of the church ladies.

"When's Mom going to cook again?" I ask Dad. "Don't you think it would help distract her or whatever?"

Dad shrugs and then turns to the window. "Did you hear that?"

I concentrate, and Faith's hum resonates loud and clear in my head. I'm starting to like the sound, even need it. And now I wonder if Dad can hear it too, since he moves across the kitchen in perfect rhythm. He looks out the window, and then shakes his head, as if it was nothing.

Going to the fridge, he grabs the milk and pours himself a glass. When he's done, he slides the milk into the cupboard where the glasses go.

"Dad? You okay?"

"Oh, yeah, yeah, honey. Just had kind of a rushed day." His voice, gravelly like he just got out of bed, makes me wonder if he spoke to anyone at the office, or just locked himself away until five-thirty.

He sits and stares across at the refrigerator. I follow his eyes, expecting them to be on the church meeting schedule he keeps there, but instead he focuses on our wipe-off family calendar, at an entry in the right bottom corner, written in red: *Faith—Contact lenses. 3:00.*

Most girls are eager to get contacts, but not Faith. Mom had to talk her into making the appointment. "They're nice to have for special occasions," she'd told her again and again. Finally, almost eighteen years old, Faith was getting them. More for Mom than for herself.

I never involved myself in the conversation. I was the prettier sister, at least with my hair and makeup done, and I kind of liked it that way. She had confidence and innocence, solid friends and beliefs, not to mention an amazing voice. But now my mind wanders back to my red sweater and I wonder if it was no coincidence that she'd finally decided on contacts. I wonder if she really was jealous. Of *me*.

"Did you walk the dog?" Dad asks, breaking me from my thoughts.

I nod. So strange hearing Dad call Nuisance "the dog." Dad named Nuisance when I was in kindergarten, making a big show of his brilliant sense of humor. Mom laughed and laughed, so the name stuck. Faith and me, even to this day— well okay, until last week—we rolled our eyes every time he called Nuisance in that tone that made it obvious he still thought it was hysterical.

And that's not the only household item he christened. The fridge is "Ms. Frostbite," his van is "Ol' Granny," and the TV remote is "The Maestro." But I guess Faith and I will never roll our eyes at any of those things again. In fact, the thought of the nicknames suddenly seems sad.

While Dad's head is down, I take the milk out of the cupboard and slide it into Ms. Frostbite. I place a bowl of stew in front of him.

He blinks at it, then murmurs, "Thanks."

I perch on the chair across from him with my own bowl. "Mom's been upstairs all afternoon."

He clinks his spoon around his bowl a few times. "Give it time, honey."

"I know." I take a bite. "I'm just sayin'."

After a few minutes of slurping, Dad asks, "How was school?"

"Weird, actually." I chomp a big bite of bread, thinking of how to explain this. "No one really wants to talk to me."

He nods and I wait while he processes so he can give me an insightful "Dad" answer.

"Give it time," he finally says again.

I get my practical side from Dad. I've said the same phrase

about fifty times to myself already and I know he's right. The more I can get on with life, the more normal it will become.

"Did work go okay?" I ask, just to say something. It's not like we ever have deep conversations, but this one feels so forced.

He stares into his stew, and I'm not sure if he heard me.

I look down and blurt out in one big breath. "Hey, that Pastor, uh, Scott, the youth guy, he said something at the service about Faith not being in youth group much lately." I spin my spoon. "Do you know what he meant by that?"

"Hmm?" Dad clears his throat. "I don't think he said that, honey. You know Faith's been, or was . . ." His tone is annoyed, probably because I asked a question that forced him to answer. He clears his throat again. "She was always involved with youth. You know that, Brie."

He's trying to shut down the topic, I can tell, but I'm not ready yet. Just saying her name, I realize how much I need to talk about this. About her. "Yeah, but Pastor Scott said—"

"I'm sure you misunderstood, sweetie."

His jaw tightens, he picks up his bowl and spoon, and heads for the sink. He clanks his bowl on the counter and walks out of the room.

I wish I'd never asked.

Halfway through cleaning the stew pot, the phone rings.

I hope it might be Dustin or Amy, even though they've never called on the home line. But I wonder if my cell's turned on. I dry my hands and head for the handset on the kitchen wall. On the fourth ring, I pick up and say hello, but I guess I'm too late because a click sounds on the other end. Then silence. Out of habit, I scroll through the caller ID.

Missed Call. 6:37 PM

E. & T. Lockbaum

Tessa. I drop the phone on the kitchen counter and hug my arms across my chest.

What does she want from me?

chapter EIGHT

Plan F: Find my long-lost social life.

The next day at school, I catch Amy in the hallway. The first
bell rings, and I can tell she's in a hurry, but I grab her by the
shoulder anyway.

"Hey."

"Oh, hey." She glances around like she's trying to find an
escape route.

Maybe the whole dealing-with-tragedy thing is too much
for her. Maybe that's why I couldn't find her at lunch yesterday.

"I'm okay, Amy. You don't have to avoid—"

"I'm not avoiding you," she says, way too fast. "The bell . . .
Henderson hates it when I'm late."

I run alongside her. "No, not just today. We haven't hung out since before Evan's party." I know that's mostly my fault, but at school it should be easy enough to get back to normal. I'm trying to make it easy.

"Oh, that. Yeah, I guess I've just been busy." Her eyes don't leave the hallway in front of her, but even from her profile I'm sure I see the guilt. "Have you talked to Dustin?"

She's changing the subject. "No, not really." It's hard to talk with saliva in my ear. But I don't say that. Amy would be way disgusted. She fiddles with her books, itching to get away, but instead I offer a solution. A way to make up for leaving me at the hospital. "You could be there for me now," I say in just a murmur, like it's a subliminal message.

She stops suddenly and faces me. "All you can think of is yourself." She points a finger at my chest. "Did you ever consider maybe this has nothing to do with you, or your sister who you didn't even give a shit about until she died?" She turns her head so I can't see her eyes.

Stunned into silence, I back up a couple of steps. I know I pushed her too far, pushed her into defensive mode, but did she really just say that?

She takes my retreat as an ending to the conversation, spins, and stalks off to her class.

•   •   •

History class: always a great opportunity for thinking, doodling, and writing bad poetry. Mr. Clancy, Clairvoyant Clancy, knows I need a break, a chance to process. He told me so yesterday, but today when he says it again, I can't stop thinking about Amy's words.

Once I've calmed down I'm not all that surprised that she went from zero to bitchy in 2.7 seconds. What I am surprised about is how her words hit home. Maybe I didn't give a shit about Faith until she died. Maybe I do think about my own needs too much.

The other students work feverishly on this week's test that I don't have to take.

Not today, I decide in a flash. I don't want special treatment. I'm fine. It's everyone else who thinks that I'm not. Marching to the front of the class, I'm about to snatch up the sheet of test questions and head back to my seat, when I notice Clancy already holds a copy outstretched toward me. He looks at me but doesn't say a word.

I scan the quiz twice and quickly realize this was not my best decision. Without much choice, I fill in the only historical figures I can drum up in my mind. Napoleon, Christopher Columbus, Thomas Jefferson. It's been weeks since I've opened my textbook.

By the time I finish scribbling in answers that don't make any sense, I've decided I'll back off for a while with Amy and everything will be fine.

After the lunch bell sounds, I stand at my locker feeling very alone. If I go to the cafeteria, who will I sit with? I won't want to approach Amy's table—my table—and the rest of the student population can barely look at me. While I rearrange my books, then rearrange them again, trying to appear busy for the hall monitors, I mull over the possibility of finding somewhere outside to eat.

A bang on the locker next to mine startles me. But I don't look over. That's Tessa Lockbaum's side.

The binder I'm fiddling with falls to the ground and I scramble to pick it up.

"Hey," she says, talking to someone she knows behind me. Even though I can't remember her ever talking to anyone so casually, I don't bother to check who it is. Keeping my eyes straight ahead, I shove my binder into a space that suddenly seems too small for it.

"Hey, Jenkins," she says.

My heart stops. During middle school it was obvious why she never spoke to me. My churchy reputation didn't exactly fit with her death metal, extra-black-eyeliner image. "Rockin'

Lockbaum" was the nickname she had for herself. Terrifying Tessa, Troublesome Tessa, Tormenting Tessa—those are what we actually called her.

"Hey, Jenkins," she says again.

"Me?" I ask, which is over-the-top stupid, since I'm now the only one in the school with that last name. I turn toward her, but keep my eyes on her black leather boots.

"Pretty screwed up what happened to your sister, huh?"

What's even more screwed up is that you're talking to me about it. "Yeah," I whisper. And when the word comes out of my mouth, something changes. It feels good to have someone talk to me. To talk about *it*. Even if it is Tessa Lockbaum.

"Meet me in the bathroom on the second floor after last class," she says. "We've got something to discuss."

Her tone makes my throat go dry. What would she have to discuss with me? And why can't we just discuss it right here and now? But I'm not sure how to challenge Tessa Lockbaum and by the time I look up to respond, she's gone.

I feel sick all through lunch, and even though I head out to a stoop at the back of the school with my brown bag, I don't bother to open it.

Plan G: Talk to Tessa.

After last class, I'm on my way to face her when I practically barrel into Dustin, still sweaty from P.E. A strand of his sandy hair sticks to the side of his face.

"Hey, babe." He tries to hug me, but I put a hand to his chest as a knee-jerk reaction. When I realize what I'm doing, I pull my hand away and move in close to him.

"Hi." I feel a bit better with the proximity today and take quick, shallow breaths.

He ignores my jilt and whispers in my ear. "We should do something tonight, just us." He plants a sloppy kiss at the base of my neck.

It seems like all he wants to do lately is grope me, and I try to remember if he's always been like this. After all that preparation of how to answer him, he hasn't even asked how I am.

I realize a second later that I'm probably overreacting. Any girl at Sharon High would give up her first car to date a guy like Dustin. And here I am thinking of throwing it all away. But I need to find an excuse to take things a bit slower. Just for a while until I'm a little more balanced.

"I can't tonight," I tell him. "My parents have this thing planned." I don't mention that "this thing" is the fact that they'll probably never let me leave the house again at night after what happened to Faith.

He scowls at the word "parents," but I don't care. I push him harder with my hand. And for a second he looks offended.

"You going for a shower?" I try to pass it off and scrunch my nose for effect.

The offense fades as he remembers the sweat dripping down his chest. He leans in for one more quick, slobbery kiss to my cheek before heading off in the direction of the changing rooms.

I walk to the second-floor bathroom, resetting my thoughts on Tessa and taking deep breaths the whole way. I know I need to face this or I won't sleep tonight. But only two girls are in the bathroom applying makeup at the mirror, and neither of them is Tessa. I head to get my things, relieved. She probably just wanted to scare me.

When I turn the corner, Tessa stands in front of her locker. I consider heading home without my backpack, but then remember that I need to face this eventually.

"Hey," I say, forcing a calm, cheerful tone. I don't look at her when I sidle up beside her.

She doesn't respond. Did I imagine our whole conversation earlier? I dial my combination and push my binders into the bottom of my locker in a big pile.

Tessa's door slams beside me. I jolt, but keep my eyes

focused into my cavern. My heart beats so loud, I swear it's echoing through the hallway.

"So are we meeting, or what?" she demands.

"Um, I have to get home." Pure nervousness makes the excuse fall out of my mouth.

I feel her studying me, like she's not sure if she can believe this.

"I guess I can stay a few minutes," I force out, knowing I need to get this over with.

"Good. Let's go."

Following Tessa down the hall and up to the second floor, I ignore the stares of the few stray students still left in the building. *So what if she wants to meet me in a bathroom,* I tell myself. *We're still in the school, and surely someone will hear if she bangs me up against a stall door or something.*

But when I step off the top stair, the upper floor is deserted. When Tessa pushes open the bathroom door, the same two girls are still in there with makeup strewn across the counter.

Tessa kicks the bathroom door to the wall, which instantly brings their conversation to a halt. The girls grab their purses, shove the strewn makeup into them, and rush out the door.

"Come on," Tessa says.

I swallow, moving inside, but glue my backside to the wall

nearest the door. "You wanted to discuss something."

Tessa faces me and leans up against the counter. "Does everyone act idiotic about Faith's death, or just the freaks near our lockers?"

I'm so surprised by the question, I don't know what to say.

"You'd think people would grow up a little by the time they reach high school," she adds.

I have a difficult time grasping where she's going with this. Could Tessa be the most levelheaded person I've spoken with in ages? "I guess people just don't know what to say." My words are quiet, but in the small space they're enough.

"My sister died when I was . . . six." She mutters it like she's figuring out which class she has first thing tomorrow. "I get it. Kinda."

I feel her eyes on me, but I'm still a little scared to look up from the counter.

"What's even more messed-up than funerals," she says, "is the way people treat you after the funeral. Like you're diseased or something. I mean, come on."

"Yeah. You're right about that." I can't believe we're having this conversation. Or I guess she's having the conversation. Mostly I'm just agreeing.

I look up at her for the first time. Her eyeliner doesn't seem nearly as scary close up. It's as if the black marks are there to hide her eyes, not to make them spine-chilling. I remember her glaring at me from the back of the church. Or was she just watching?

"Corey was hit by a truck."

I blink, not knowing what she's talking about, but also not about to ask.

"My sister, Corey. I was supposed to be watching her while my mom went inside to get us a snack," she adds, without emotion, like she's said it a hundred times.

"Oh." I don't know what else to say. Does she want to talk about it? I mean, obviously she does if she's brought it up. "Were you and Corey close?" As soon as it leaves my mouth, I bite my lip. It's so not what she wants to hear. I, of all people, know that. "I mean, does it get easier? Like, after a few years."

Even though she doesn't answer right away, the question feels much better. And the look on her face tells me she's thinking about it.

"Yes and no," she says, finally. "Sometimes you have to force things to get easier."

I think about that. About her wardrobe and attitude. I try to think of ways I could force my life to get back to normal, force my parents to talk to me, but I can't imagine myself taking such drastic steps. Things must have been pretty bad for her.

"Is that why you were at Faith's funeral?" I ask, picking at the stitching on the side of my jeans.

She shrugs. "I guess. I just thought, you know, we should talk."

I offer a smile, thinking we're having a bonding moment. But suddenly she walks straight for the door beside me, and whips it open so hard it bangs against the wall again.

"I gotta bail," she says, and tromps down the hallway without even saying good-bye.

chapter NINE

y the time I get back to my locker, it's after four and I've almost regained my proper breathing pattern. Who knew Tessa and I could relate on any subject, especially this one? I grab my backpack, stuff it with books, and head for the door. My cell phone beeps through the canvas, and I bend down to dig it out.

Three missed calls. Two from Dad's office, and one from home. Dad doesn't like wasting minutes on my cell phone, so whatever it is, it's important. My hands tremble while I scroll to the last call and hit send.

All I can see in my mind is Mom's depressed face.

"Are you okay?" Dad asks when he answers the phone on the first ring.

"Uh, yeah, of course," I say. "Is everyone . . . is Mom okay?"

"Yes, yes. Where are you?"

I start to clue in that he's worried about *me* because I'm late getting home from school. "I'm on my way, Dad. I had to stay after class to catch up." He doesn't need the whole background on Tessa Lockbaum. He's got enough to worry about and I don't know how I'd even start to explain.

"When will you be home?"

He suggests picking me up, but I talk him out of it and promise to be home within minutes. I hang up and break into a run.

Plan H: Apologize profusely until Dad calms down.

After catching my breath, I push through the doorway and wait for Dad to start his lecture so I can reply with my apologies. Then, while we're at it, I can tell him how confused and alone I feel. Get it all out before I start dying my hair black and covering my body with piercings. I've spent the last few years avoiding talking to my parents, but maybe now's the time to start. Maybe this one good thing could come of Faith's death.

"I have to get back to the office," Dad says, reaching

past me for the door, not saying another word about it.

My mouth drops open as I watch his back all the way to the van.

The rest of the week, I focus on avoiding Amy in the hallways. Tessa doesn't come by our lockers while I'm there and I wonder if it's coincidence or if she's avoiding me now. I've been coming up with fresh excuses of why I can't be alone with Dustin. Thankfully I haven't had to use the "my sister just died" excuse yet, but I can feel it coming, especially Friday afternoon when he tells me he has the whole weekend free for me.

"My dad, he's not letting me go out at night right now," I say.

He cocks his head like he doesn't understand, and I feel like a child, an elementary school student who has to ask permission to go to the neighbor's and play.

"Maybe we could go to a matinee or something?" I offer.

He purses his lips, not like he's considering it, but like he doesn't quite have the words to reply. Like he's caught on to my sidestepping and is about to call me on it.

"Or maybe I can sneak out," I add quickly, not meaning to, hardly comprehending that I could do that to my parents right now, but feeling him slipping away.

He smiles and kisses my cheek. "That's my girl. I'll call you," he says before backing into the school for wrestling practice and leaving me to walk home with my horrible self.

Saturdays are not a usual workday for Dad, but he's gone by the time I get up the next morning. Mom ignores me, which is nothing new. Since the funeral she pretty much ignores life, but today I take it personally. I think it's my fault for scaring her yesterday when I didn't come home right after school. Obviously Dad wouldn't have had a clue if she hadn't called him to come home from the office.

Mom pads around the kitchen in silence, and I know it won't be long before she ducks back up to her bedroom.

"I'm sorry," I say when we bump into each other at the kitchen sink. And I am. Sorry they got stuck with me. I'm sure they've wondered about it too: Why couldn't we have kept the good one?

Mom doesn't respond, just fills her coffee cup and walks out of the room.

I drop my head to the counter. Why won't my parents talk to me?

When I lift my head several minutes later, I stare around at our drab kitchen. My loneliness personified. Mom used to breathe creativity and life into our house. Used to bring home flower arrangements from the shop almost daily. Then she'd change up tablecloths, artwork, whatever, to give the place a fresh feel. That's what she called it. Fresh.

Not that I ever showed any appreciation for it.

The dust on the blinds, scum around the usually shiny stainless steel sink, and crumbs accumulating on the edges of the floor make the place feel old and used-up.

Stale.

It wouldn't kill me to do something about it.

For the rest of the morning, I don't leave the kitchen. I wipe down the blinds and the counter; I pull out the scrub brush and go to town on sink scum. Scrubbing. Polishing with a vengeance. The harder I scrub, the harder I need to scrub. Hating myself. Hating Faith for leaving me to be the sole hope for my parents. Even hating Tessa for making me feel for only one second like I wasn't alone.

When Dad walks through the door after lunch, he looks different. His suit jacket is folded neatly over his arm. He places his car keys down deliberately and walks across the room with measured steps.

"We have to talk," he says, and pulls out a kitchen chair.

At first I can't believe my ears. He finally wants to talk to me! I sit across from him but don't pull my chair up to the table, since something still doesn't feel right.

"I spoke with the school," he says. "I've requested that any teachers who plan to keep you after class phone me first."

Is he serious? I used to always come home way later. And okay, things are different now, but still. "I'm sorry, Dad. I should've called. I guess I didn't think you'd worry as long as I was home by—"

"I'd appreciate that," he says, and the way his voice sounds, he's not angry. Not at all. Just scared. "But that's not what I wanted to talk to you about."

I lean forward, putting my hands flat on the table between us to show him I'm ready for this.

"It's not healthy to go through this"—he clears his throat—"time alone. There's a pastor at the church I want you to talk to about . . . uh . . . well . . . about how you're feeling. I know you haven't been attending youth group, but it's important to lean on God and the church in times like these."

He's passing me off to the church? "Dad, if we could just . . ." I want to say more, but I know that look on his face. "Fine. When?" I ask.

His eyes stay fixed on the table between us. He can't even look at me to see how much I need him. "I made an appointment for you at three today."

I flick the edge of the table where the varnish is peeling off. Then again, going to the church would give me a chance to get my mind off Dustin. And if my parents won't talk to me, maybe the youth pastor, someone else who knew Faith, will.

"Sure." I nod. "Three o'clock."

Dad doesn't say anything else. Just slides back from the table, spins, and marches out the door.

Great. Thanks, Dad. Glad we could have this enriching conversation.

Plan I: Track down Captain Scotty.

At five to three, I get out of Dad's van and walk across the carpeted foyer of Crestview Church. The last time I was in the building was for Faith's funeral. The time before that, the Easter service nearly six months ago. Faith's voice booms in my head, and I notice it for the first time all day. Her ever-present hum has become so commonplace that it doesn't even interrupt my thoughts anymore. It comforts me now as I grasp for my inner strength. I'll need an extra dose of it to brush off whatever they're going to preach at me here.

At the front office, I give the secretary my name, and wait while she looks up my appointment.

"I see you're scheduled with Pastor Overly at three," she says.

Pastor Overly. My parents have had him over for dinner

before. They should call him "Pastor Olderly" though, since he's practically a fossil. "Shouldn't I be seeing a youth pastor?"

She scrunches her wrinkly face at me. "Oh, yes, of course." She scrolls down her computer screen. "Pastor Scott keeps his own calendar, but if you want to check at his office, it's right that way." She points down the hall. "If he's busy, feel free to come back to see Pastor Overly. He's wide open." Her face is slightly smug and I have the feeling I'll be back within minutes.

When I reach Pastor Scott's office, I take a breath and knock. I shouldn't be nervous, I tell myself. I'd much rather talk to someone who really knew Faith.

I wait several minutes before deciding he's not in there. Maybe I could leave a note. Pushing the door open tentatively, I see books. Tons of books, all over the desk and the floor, but not neat, like in Dad's office at home. Some left open, others stacked in precarious-looking piles. I scan the desk to see if there's a day planner there somewhere, but it's impossible to tell among all this crap.

The room is windowless, which makes me feel claustrophobic. I step inside anyway.

"Hello?" The booming voice of Pastor Scott sounds behind me and I knock the door open into a tower of books, toppling them over.

"Oh, I'm—I'm sorry!" I scramble to the strewn books, not even turning to acknowledge the guy. I do my best to scoop them into something resembling a pile.

He lets out a deep laugh. "Oh, leave them, please. Those things fall over all the time."

No doubt. I start to pull away, but it feels way too awkward leaving this haphazard pile. "I don't mind," I say. Lifting a big textbook from the stack, I start a new pile, quickly taking stock of the biggest books and arranging them in a structurally sound way.

He walks past me and drops into the chair on the far side of the desk, placing his freshly filled coffee cup down.

When I finish assembling the stack, I stand and would offer my hand, but Pastor Scott is busy sorting through his mess of papers with his head down. He is wearing that American Eagle sweater again and, even though I think it would look better on Dustin, it does do something to endear him to me.

"I'll just be a second," he says.

I wait in uncomfortable silence until he finally clears his throat and looks up.

"How can I help you?"

"I'm Faith Jenkins's sister. Brie," I say.

"Of course. I remember you from the funeral." He checks

his watch. "Have a seat." He motions to the one across from him. "How are you doing?"

His voice sounds kind and I want to give an honest answer, but I proceed carefully. "Um, okay. My dad thought I should come in and talk to someone here at the church."

He nods, encouraging me to go on.

"I have some questions about my sister."

"Obviously, I don't know how you feel," he says, "but I loved Faith. I love all the kids in youth, of course, but Faith was special. She had such a soft heart."

I take a deep, slightly guarded, breath. It feels good to have someone talk about Faith so openly, like she really was real. "My dad wanted me to see someone because he can't really talk about everything yet."

"Has he told you that?"

I stare at him for a second. I'm not used to people being quite this forthright. "Look, my parents don't want to talk about anything right now." I stand up, feeling like it might make me come across as stronger so he won't think he can manipulate the things I know are true. "I know you're just doing your job. Talking things out is the best thing, and all that, but my parents just need some time right now, and to not worry about other stuff."

Pastor Scott stands too. "You're not other stuff, Brie. Whether you like it or not, you're their daughter." The force of his voice makes me look at him. "I know it's been hard, but maybe if they focus on you right now, it'll help them through this. I know you're trying to think of them, but maybe what you're actually doing . . ."

He goes on, but I tune out. So I'm the cog that's holding them back, huh? Whatever. These aren't the kind of answers I came here for, and they make an anger burn within me. *I've tried!* I want to yell at him.

"You and Faith are so different, but it still makes me feel like a piece of her is around when you're here."

His comment takes me back and makes me think about Faith's voice. How I can hear it and he probably can't. And it is nice to have a piece of her. "How exactly do I remind you of her?"

A small smile tugs at the side of his mouth. "I don't know. It's something. Maybe your eyes. Or maybe it's your smile. No, wait. I haven't seen yours yet to compare."

I let my mouth form into a smirk. Faith and I did look alike. Before she got her glasses and I discovered the world of straightening irons, people used to mix us up all the time.

"It is." He nods. "It's the smile."

Suddenly, I miss Faith. Like, really miss her. And a tear escapes from my right eye.

"I know," he says, like he can read my mind. "I miss her

too." He doesn't look away and let me save face, but keeps his warm eyes right on me.

I sit down and wipe my cheeks with a tissue from his desk. "Can I ask you something?"

"Of course."

"You said something at the funeral. Or maybe I heard something wrong. I don't know."

"Go on."

"You said Faith hadn't been in youth group for a while."

"Yeah, it's been pretty crazy, I guess. I was supposed to meet with her—" He pulls a day planner from the bottom of his stack of papers and opens it. At first, he thumbs through, but then he picks up the book and fans it. Stops in the middle and fans it again. Finally, he puts it down. "Well, I can't find it right now, but we were supposed to meet, and then she had to cancel. I thought maybe the group was getting too big for her, maybe the music was getting too loud, and I thought we should talk about it."

"But she went to youth events all the time. Like six nights a week. Why didn't you just talk to her there?"

Pastor Scott crinkles his forehead. "Well, she hadn't been coming to my Friday night meetings. Maybe she was going somewhere else. I know Grass Roots has a pretty big youth group, and they meet at least a couple times a week."

I think about this, but it seems so strange that she wouldn't mention it if she'd changed youth groups.

"I don't know about six nights per week," he goes on. "The home groups only meet once a week. And Faith's was held at your house, right?"

I shake my head. "I've never met her home group." In fact, she never mentioned one.

He looks up to the corner of the room, his face contorting. "I'm sorry, Brie. I have no excuse, I should know what was going on with their small group." He pauses for a minute, squinting. Suddenly, he snaps his fingers, remembering something. "Celeste was in it."

Well, duh. But with the mention of her name, I wonder if she's back in town yet. Maybe I should e-mail her, since I haven't seen her at school.

Pastor Scott's eyes droop a little. "I'm afraid when the youth group expanded so quickly, I just lost track."

"Oh. That makes sense." I can't blame him. I'd completely lost track of my sister too, and we lived in the same house.

Pastor Scott stares down at his desk.

"Do you think," I say, "I mean, when you did know her better. Do you think her death could have been . . ." I can't say the word *suicide*, it gets stuck in my throat. ". . . um, intentional?"

Pastor Scott stares at me for a few seconds, tilts his head

as though he doesn't understand the question. Finally, he shakes his head. "No, Brie. Faith didn't kill herself. That's one thing I'm sure of."

His words make me feel so relieved I want to jump out of my chair and hug him. I didn't know how badly I needed to hear this. "How do you know?" I venture.

"I don't have all the answers," he says, "but she loved the Lord. She trusted Him." He stops and takes in a big breath through his nose. "What I do know is He has a plan and a grace for all of us and what we're going through."

He who? What plan? I scan Pastor Scott's face and quickly catch on. Right. The Big Plan. The Big God Plan. "Yeah, I know," I say, standing to leave.

"If you ever want to talk again, Brie . . . Just wait, I want to give you my phone number." He just stares at me though, and after a second I realize that finding a scrap piece of paper would likely upset his whole world. So finally I pull out my cell phone and punch in his number as he rattles it off. "You don't have to do this alone. . . ."

He goes on, but I tune him out, force a smile and nod. Here it comes, his Christianese spiel. I've heard it, and I just don't want to hear it again.

"Don't lose that smile," he says, as I back through the door and shut it behind me.

chapter TEN

*a*ll evening I watch movies with one eye on my cell phone, but Dustin doesn't call. This relieves me and freaks me out at the same time. Does he see through me and know I didn't really want to meet up with him?

But as worried as I am, I can't bring myself to pick up my phone and dial. After Dad's fit about me coming home late from school, I can't even imagine what would happen if he found my room empty at midnight. I have woken up a few times to my door cracking open and one of them checking on me in the middle of the night. And part of me likes that.

I dial Amy, ready to apologize, say whatever I have to in order to set things straight. But when her voice mail clicks on, I chicken out and decide it's much better to talk to her in person.

Sunday morning, I don't know how Dad does it, but he prods Mom out the door and they look just as fixed up as they always did for church. I spend the whole day feeling like a stranger in my own home. Feeling like our house has been taken over by ghosts.

Plan J: Back to school. Talk to whoever still wants to talk to me.

Tessa eyes me as I open my locker beside her on Monday. "You look like shit."

"Thanks." I reach up and smooth my hair, but several of the wisps won't stay. "It's been a long weekend."

She pulls wrinkled papers from behind her books, straightens them out, and reads them one at a time, like she's looking for a specific one. "Your parents acting weird?"

Amazing how much she knows, without me having to say a word. I nod. "They freaked out when I didn't come home right after school last week. Then they sent me to talk to this guy at my dad's church."

Tessa muffles a laugh. "My parents sent me to some preacher a few years ago too. I told him a thing or five." She shoves the crumpled papers back into her locker. They almost fall out but she shuts the door on them.

I smile. So this is how it is. The most normal conversation I can have is with Terrifying Tessa. She's the closest thing I have to a friend.

"See you later?" I ask as I shut my locker door.

"Yeah." She nods. "Later."

Just as I leave my locker, I spot Amy at the other end of the hallway, but when she sees me she ducks into the girls' bathroom. I can tell she's avoiding me, but I don't care. I pick up my pace and push through the door.

The bell rings and the five or six girls inside disperse out the two end doors, but none of them are Amy. Two stall doors remain shut and I lean against the counter waiting, not caring that I'll be late for class. The first girl to emerge is my friend Steph.

"Hi!" I try to sound chipper.

She doesn't respond and looks away as soon as she sees me, which makes the few seconds while she washes her hands incredibly uncomfortable. I guess if I'd known there were sides to choose, it would have been obvious she would take Amy's. They were friends first, and Steph truly belongs in the makeup-and-fashion-fanatics club. Or maybe she's just playing it cool because Amy can hear us.

Obviously I'll need to put things back together with Amy first.

While I'm thinking this, the other stall opens, but it's not her. Steph and the other girl skirt out the far door and I can visualize Amy having made a beeline through the bathroom just to escape me.

Right. So maybe she needs another week to get over her PMS.

I track down Dustin outside the gym before I leave for the day.

"You didn't call." The moment it leaves my mouth, I know it sounds like an accusation. "I mean, it's probably a good thing because I ended up having to do this . . . stuff." *Like meet with the church pastor, watch old movies I couldn't even concentrate on, phone ex-best-friends and hang up on their voice mail.* Obviously I can't elaborate.

He glances into the gym like he's in a hurry. "Well, no worries, then, right?" He looks back at me and flashes one of his sweet smiles. My anxiety from last week almost totally subsides, and I hope he'll pull me close again. Give me another chance to prove I can be a good girlfriend. But I can tell he needs to go.

"Well, next weekend for sure," I tell him. His sexy face is pulling me in and I can't seem to help making promises.

Besides, it's a whole week away. My parents can't expect me to stay home forever.

He offers a nod, a peck on my cheek, and then disappears through the door.

At home I'm glad to hear Mom puttering in the kitchen again. When I walk over to see what she's making, she meets me on the opposite side of the swinging door.

"I just need a little time to myself," she says.

I'm so happy she's back to cooking, I decide not to push it. Instead, I head toward my room to start on homework— something I haven't been able to concentrate on for a while. Maybe life *is* getting back to normal. Or at least as normal as it can be. The thought makes me stop in place on the stairs and wonder. What will life be like for us in a year? Will we be over this and used to living without her? Or will our house always feel empty? Will we have to move somewhere else to get away from the holes?

An hour later, I haven't solved any of life's questions or a single math problem. I tidy up the living room, but when I dust the bookshelves, I notice half of them are empty. My first assumption is that Mom started to clean out some of Faith's things. But when I read the spines, all I see are Faith's Christian novels. It's the rest of our books that are missing.

I squint to try and figure out the logic in that.

When Ol' Granny rattles into the driveway, I peer out the window and watch Dad get out. His shoulders are straight; his jaw isn't in that tense, forced smile he usually wears.

Plan K: Talk to Dad.

"Can I talk to you for a sec?" He hasn't even hung up his coat yet. *Down, Brie, down.*

"Sure, honey. I just have to make one call. . . ." He trails off when he sees my face.

Do I look too serious? I blink hard to reset my expression.

He walks over and puts his hands on both my shoulders. "What's up, sweetie?"

"Oh, no big deal," I say too loudly. "I was just, well . . ." I have no words. I can't say her name. Not to him. "It's about youth group," I say finally.

Dad looks confused, but only for a second. "Did you talk to Pastor Overly about it?"

Right. He thinks I want to join the youth group. And that may not seem like the safest place in the world right now. "Well, mostly I wanted to clear something up."

Dad tugs me over to the couch and sits down with me. "Oh, okay. You have some questions?"

Great, now he thinks I want him to lead me in some

special salvation prayer. He must not remember I said that whole spiel when I was eight.

"It's about Faith," I say.

Dad's face immediately adopts the tense, rigid look. I go on anyway.

"I don't know what I'm asking, Dad. I guess I just don't get her, and maybe I never got her, but now that she's gone, I need to and I don't know if I can figure this out on my own." When I finally shut my mouth, the seconds ticking on the wall clock sound amplified.

His voice is quiet. Controlled. "I think you're looking for something that isn't there because you're having trouble letting go, Brie." He loosens his tie. "We have to try to move on."

"I'm moving on, Dad, believe me, I'm trying."

"There are things we'll never know, honey. But God knows everything. That needs to be enough."

Mom opens the kitchen door. "Dinner's ready," she says.

Both of us stop and turn in her direction. It's like we've gone back in time. We stare at her, stunned for a moment.

It must be the uncomfortable silence that makes me speak. "We were just talking about Faith."

Mom drops her eyes to the carpet in front of her and then backs through the door into the kitchen without another word.

Dad lets out a loud breath through his nostrils, then pushes himself up with both hands and marches for the kitchen.

Several minutes later when my conscience gets the best of me, I walk for the kitchen too. Mom and Dad both sit at the table with their heads down. Normally, I'd think they were praying, but for the tense feeling. Nuisance is splayed under Mom's chair, his head drooping across his paws like he has no plans to move anytime this year.

I lift the lid from the pot on the table before I sit. Franks and beans. I scan the counters and see two cans, lying empty on their sides. What had Mom been doing in the kitchen the whole afternoon? And how could she, of all people, stoop to canned mush? But from there, my eyes go to Ms. Frostbite and take in the preschool drawings now plastered across the front, Faith's name at the top of every one.

Silently, I scoop some of the sweet muck onto my plate and sit down. I assume the same position my parents are in and listen to the kitchen clock tick.

Well, as long as all the weirdness is gone . . .

chapter ELEVEN

Plan L: Youth group, here I come.

Since Mom and Dad won't talk about Faith, I decide to try
another route to reconnect with my sister. After dinner, I flip
through the Yellow Pages and scan the plethora of church
listings. At first I don't know where to start, but when I see
Grass Roots, I remember Pastor Scott mentioning that one. I
look up their website, and the fancy flash screen tells me their
youth group meets on Tuesday and Friday nights.

After school Tuesday, I call and let my parents know I'm
sticking around school to work on a project and will be home
by ten. My cell phone will be on. Since Dad's still at work and
Mom won't pick up the phone for anybody, I just leave the

excuse on the answering machine. It is pretty crazy though, that I'm lying to my parents because I don't want to tell them I'm going to youth group.

I head to the school library to find the online city bus schedule. It doesn't take me long to figure out my way to Grass Roots Community Church, and once I arrive I sit outside on the bench to attack some of my homework while I wait. The church looms high into the sky behind me, much bigger and newer than Crestview.

Just after six, I call home to make sure my school project plan is kosher. Dad answers on the second ring.

"Hey, Dad. You're home. You must have gotten my message, then, right?"

"Yes, I did. Are you done? Should I come and get you?" He sounds anxious.

"Um, if you don't mind me missing dinner, I have a ton to catch up on. The school will be open until ten." At least I hope it will. I did overhear something about an evening volleyball game.

Dad assures me he'll be waiting out front for me at five to ten. His voice wavers and I want to try again to talk to him, for both of us. But as if he senses this, he clears his throat, tells me not to be late, and hangs up.

An hour later, when I've almost fallen asleep over my

Macbeth essay, a dilapidated pickup truck pulls into the parking lot and an older guy with scraggly gray hair hops out of the driver's door. Two teen guys and a girl step out of the other side. If it wasn't a *church* group I was waiting for, I'd swear it was a party mobile.

I wait a couple minutes before following them inside. A few other teens trail behind me and I hang back to see which direction they go. I'm nervous, not being comfortable in church groups to begin with, let alone one my sister might have attended. A girl with braids smiles my way. I flash her my own quick grin, but quickly break eye contact. Seconds later, she walks on ahead.

I follow the braids girl at a distance through a double set of doors, and into a cozy room with benches around the perimeter. The group from the truck sits cross-legged in the middle of the room. The girl I followed waves and says hello to everyone. I feel invisible until the old guy spots me.

"Oh, hi!" he says, standing. "Come on in and join us." He motions to the kids on the floor to shove over.

I hesitate, and he heads across the room toward me. This guy looks way old to be a youth leader.

"Are you here for Senior Frenzy?" he asks.

I nod.

"Well, we're happy to have you. Come meet some of the others."

He starts to back up, but I don't follow. The rest of the crew in the circle eye me curiously.

"Listen," I say, "I'm actually just trying to find out if my sister ever came to your group."

"Well, we keep an attendance board in the lobby, but what's her name?"

"Faith Jenkins," I say, trying to keep my voice even.

He shows immediate recognition. My heart beats faster.

"Oh, dear, I'm sorry," he says, his face making it obvious he really is. "I didn't know her, but we all heard." He pauses to let out a pained sigh. "She hasn't been here to Senior Frenzy, I'm afraid, but I know how difficult it is to lose somebody. You're more than welcome to stay." He steps closer. "Fellowship can be of great comfort at a time—"

"Right," I say, backing up. "I appreciate the offer, but I have to go, actually." I cringe inwardly at my curt reply and back a few more paces away. "Maybe another time."

He doesn't come after me, but reaches his hand out like he's still willing to usher me into the group if I change my mind. I pull my arms across my chest and back the rest of the way out the door.

Almost across the lobby and out the main doors, I

remember what he said about an attendance list. It's not that I don't believe the guy, but somehow I just need to see it in black-and-white, to know for sure that this avenue is exhausted. I walk to the large bulletin board. Two more teens amble for the double doors and I duck my head down before they can say hi.

Once they move around the corner, I scan the board. The list is easy to find. Large, bright-orange poster board with a zillion names down one side, dates along the top, and "I ♥ Jesus" stickers marking which days different kids have been present. The words "Senior Frenzy" are scrawled across the top in thick black marker.

My eyes go first to today's date. I scan down the empty row. They must fill out the attendance board at the end of group. The list of names on the left takes only a minute to go through. At first I just look for *F*s at the beginning, but when my eyes get to the bottom, one messy last edition catches my attention. I'd recognize that handwriting anywhere.

Celeste Schwartz. I never did e-mail her to see if her grandma's okay.

It seems impossible to me that Celeste would have gone anywhere—especially to a youth group—without Faith, so I check the names again. But Faith's name is definitely not on the list.

Running my finger back to Celeste's name, I scroll sideways. How long could she have possibly been coming here
without my sister? There's only one sticker on Celeste's line.
I slide my finger up to the date. My hand flies to my mouth.

September twenty-fifth.

The night Faith died.

I check my watch. Nearly eight PM. Absorbed by the
sight of the peppy sticker on that date, I stumble backward
toward the exit, completely ignoring the girl who holds open
the door for me.

My head spins all the way to the bus stop. If they don't
mark attendance until the end, what would that be, like ten
o'clock? I was at the hospital way before ten the night Faith
died. And Celeste was . . . at Grass Roots Community Church.

I suddenly feel like I don't really understand anyone. I
know there must be some logical explanation, but everything
feels surreal again. Like it did after the night of the accident.

On the bus, I root through my bag for my cell but when
I open it, it lets out the *ding* that tells me the battery is dying.
Since I definitely can't risk missing a call from Dad, I jump
off the bus on Garibaldi and head for the closest pay phone.
I dial information and get the three listings for Schwartz. No
one answers on the first two and at the third an answering
machine picks up with a digitized recording.

I leave a message after the beep. "Hi, I'm looking for Celeste, if she's home yet. This is Brie Jenkins, and I really need to talk to her as soon as possible." I leave my cell number and hang up.

The street I've gotten off on is near the local college and full of restaurants and pubs. Even though I haven't eaten, I can't stomach food right now. At least it's a safe area and if I walk, maybe my head will clear.

As I'm about to round the corner by Applebee's, a familiar head of dark hair in the window catches my attention. Amy's hairstyle is unique, with tight loops and straightened sections alternating, so I know it's her without having to see her face, and Applebee's is her favorite restaurant. I wonder if she's with Steph and the rest of the girls who don't even say hi to me anymore. When a hand reaches out and brushes over Amy's hair, I clue in. She's on a date. The plant in the window obstructs my view of the guy, though. I'm glad, at least, that this may be the reason she hasn't been in contact. A secret boyfriend is one of the better reasons to forget a friend.

Since we're on Garibaldi, I suspect it's a college guy. I check my watch—still an hour before I have to meet Dad—and then back up to pull open the heavy front doors of the restaurant. I scoot between tables in the direction I saw Amy.

A waitress station stands right in my path, and several

servers try to get into it at once for supplies. I have to wait, but stand on my tiptoes to see if I can find Amy. I catch a glimpse of her curls, and the top of the head of the blond guy she's with.

I smile. Even if we haven't talked in over a week, I know that once I catch her with this new guy, she'll want to seem like the sweetest thing in front of him. Much easier to solve things with her that way. When the last waitress clears out of my way, I barrel around the station toward the table.

But then I stop.

Their hands are clasped on the table and Amy looks at me first. Then Dustin.

No one speaks, but my mouth drops open.

"I, um . . . Brie," Dustin says.

"Holy crap," I say, backing away. My heart triples its speed and feels like it's going to explode all over the floor around me. I really *don't* know anybody. Not my parents, not Faith, not Dustin. And definitely not Amy.

Dustin stands, dropping Amy's hand. "It's just—"

"No way." I shake my head. "Not tonight. No flippin' way."

chapter TWELVE

*a*fter Dad picks me up, I bury myself under my covers in bed and cry all night long. I hear the door creak open and quiet my tears to see that it's Mom looking in on me sometime after midnight. Part of me wants to let out a sob so she'll come in and put her arms around me. But the other part of me won't allow it. My insides are vibrating with anger and I don't want to spew it on anyone except the two people who deserve it. Besides, Mom's not ready to handle anything else.

The next morning I've had no sleep but I'm ready to take on life—at least the school part of it. Amy and Dustin hooked up. Whatever, they deserve each other. Tessa is my new best friend. Great, can't wait to get my first skull-and-crossbones tattoo. I'm taking exams that I don't know any of the answers for. How could life get any better?

When I trek through the school entryway, I immediately spot Dustin standing at the far end of the hall near the gym. When he sees me, he drops his head and ducks through the doors. I walk in his direction, but then stop.

As angry as I am, I'm also emotionally exhausted. Between my sister dying and Amy de-socializing me . . . no one wants to talk to me as it is. Do I really want to make it worse by telling off a popular senior like Dustin?

Besides, I have more important things to worry about.

Plan M: Take a short cut through the Senior Wing to see if Celeste is back.

I'm not sure exactly which locker belongs to Celeste, but I know it was near Faith's, so I head there.

When I find number 893, I stand in front of it for several minutes, staring. It's stupid, I know. It doesn't look any different than the rows and rows of shiny yellow lockers on either side. But it *is* different. I run my hand along the sleek yellow door, searching for some school memories of Faith. But I avoided her in school, so the only ones I can think of are of me walking the other direction. I stare down at the floor.

A group of senior girls walks past and takes my attention. I recognize the rail-thin Asian girl. She has smooth hair, like opaque glass, and I wonder if she straightens it between classes. I'm not sure if I recognize her from the hallways, or if I've seen her with Faith before.

Celeste doesn't seem to be showing, so after looking back at Faith's locker for a second, I trail them by a few feet, trying to fake some interest in the binder I'm holding.

"So she killed herself?" the tallest one asks.

"No, I heard it was an accident," one of the other girls replies.

"Uh-uh. I know it for a fact," the glass-haired girl announces. "I overheard a phone call. . . ." I'm too far back to catch the rest of her sentence.

"Are you sure he's talking about her?"

"That's all I know. They didn't say a name, but I know it must be the Jenkins girl."

The moment she says my last name, I gasp and it sounds like a trumpet in my head. I feel like I'm on display. Like the entire student body is pointing at me. And suddenly, the tallest girl stops and turns back toward me. I drop my binder and the rings clack open. I scurry to the floor to shove the papers back inside.

Right, I guess acting natural is out of the question, then.

Several seconds later when I glance up to see if they're all staring at me, the hallway is empty and the second bell rings.

After lunch, I have History. If I go, Clancy will be as nice as ever, probably give me a C for the test I bombed, and I'll feel like a failure all over again for not being on top of my life. Instead, I head for the guidance counselor's office. I need to talk to somebody because I'm seriously starting to think I've lost it.

Ms. Lamberton is available when I get there. I sit in a chair and stare at her for a long time, trying to decide how to start up this conversation.

"Nice family," I say, pointing to the picture of two preschool kids on her desk.

She smiles. "Oh, these aren't mine. They're my nieces." She turns another picture to face me. "This one's mine."

It's hard not to smile at the picture of Ms. Lamberton holding a cute, brown Chihuahua on her lap.

"I call her Appy," she says, and rambles on about the history of the dog. Where she got her, how she named her, why that's her only real family. I'm surprised she doesn't have kids of her own. She's older, in her forties maybe, but pretty.

"My sister died," I blurt.

"Yes," she says softly, switching gears instantaneously. "How are you?"

Ms. Lamberton reaches a hand out toward mine. I don't reach to meet hers, but I feel like she cares.

"I'm trying to get things back to normal here at school, but it's not easy. No one acts the same." I wait for her to interrupt me. To step in. But she just lets me talk. "Anyway, I thought I was ready to go to all my classes and concentrate on schoolwork, but I guess I'm not." I want her to send me home so I don't have to see Dustin or Amy or listen to people spread horrible rumors about Faith. I plead with my eyes.

She nods. "Why don't we work on getting you caught up first," she says, scribbling out a permission slip, "and then we'll worry about the classroom. Many kids, or people, really, don't know how to deal with death."

I'm so surprised at her understanding that I sit there for a moment without a reply. She takes that as a hint to go on.

"I'm going to give you a pass for today, Brie. Go get some work done in the library. And if you need a pass tomorrow, too, come back and see me." She smiles warmly. "Okay?"

The library. That's at least a good second choice. I thought I would have had to beg to get out of class. Go into the whole story about Faith and all about my feelings. Maybe even start crying.

I leave feeling strangely comforted. Ms. Lamberton is not what I would've expected.

chapter THIRTEEN

Plan N: Update Facebook page.

When I get home, I head straight for the computer. Seeing some graffiti on one of the library tables at school reminded me of all the cutesy love notes about Dustin I have on my Facebook page. I need to get them off there. Now.

When I go to log in, Faith's username comes up. Has it really been that long since I've been on here? Well, I guess I haven't had too many people to keep up with. Nor do I want to display any new pictures of myself at the moment.

I've really let myself go over the last couple of weeks and now that I think about my Facebook page, it hits me how much. I run a hand through my stringy hair. When was the last time I washed it? It gnaws at me that maybe this is the reason that Dustin and Amy got together. Not only was I avoiding being alone with him, but I'm not exactly enticing at the moment. The thought hits me with a wave of nausea. My looks had always been my one thing to hang on to.

I gnaw on my lip, willing my mind not to go there. Not to doubt myself.

Still, Dustin or Amy should have had the decency to tell me.

My mouse hovers on the login screen. I click on Faith's username. I'm sure her page is still up and untouched. Even if Mom was in a place where she could get rid of some of Faith's stuff, she wouldn't have a clue how to deal with her web presence.

In the password box I type "G-O-D-I-S-G-O-O-D." It was Faith's password for everything.

Her news feed comes up and since I don't really care about the church activities her friends are going on about, I click to her profile page instead. Her photo makes my heart stop. She looks so alive, her eyes glinting back at me. I reach out to touch her face, running my forefinger over her smile, then when it becomes too much, I pull my eyes away to scan the rest of the screen. A handful of friends' pictures run along the side. She'd sent me a friend request about six months ago. When I click to see them all, I don't see my photo, so I likely never responded. "Bitch," I say to myself.

No new messages or condolences decorate her wall, which surprises me. The last post is from September twentieth—the week before she died—and shows more photos that include Faith. The post is from a girl named Reena M. Black, who has dirty blond, shoulder-length hair with a slight kink at the ends. Her close-up photo stares through the screen with these huge blue eyes, the kind you have trouble looking away from. But they're kind and compassionate, and her teeth are super-white. She looks a little older than Faith, though still the type of caring person Faith would have been drawn to.

But I've never seen her before. I'm sure I'd remember those eyes. I click on her link, and seconds later the screen fills with her profile. More pictures of her and Faith display and I click through them. Celeste's in some, and her smile hasn't changed since kindergarten. Really, except for the boobs, she looks like the exact same girl who came over and played Barbies when I still wore diapers. I make a note beside the computer to e-mail Celeste when I'm done to see if she's back yet, since I can't imagine how she'd handle it if a message from Faith's Facebook turned up in her inbox.

The longer I browse around the pages, the less I feel like an intruder. Four or five other girls fill out the rest of the pictures. Just one boy with spiky white-blond hair and a couple of those stupid advertising buttons from the supermarket pinned to his shirt. This must be her home group, whoever they are and wherever they meet.

Another rod of guilt stabs at me. I should at least know who these people are.

I run my mouse over the photos, considering checking out Celeste's page, but none of the people are tagged. Under each one is a comment from Reena M. Black with a reference for a verse from the Bible. It looks so odd to have Bible verses splattered among pictures on a Facebook page. I jot down a couple of them out of curiosity. I'd always brushed off my sister's allegiance to her Bibles and everything in them but now that she's gone, I do want to know. What verses did she like best? And why?

Nothing much else to look at in Reena's pictures. A group of kids laughing and having fun. A few of them are so tightly crammed together, I wonder if they were taken in one of those photo booths at the mall. There's something charismatic about Reena though, her electric blue eyes pulling my attention in every single photo.

But since I don't know the girl, I click back to Faith's page. Her "alive" picture comes up again, and I know I can't mess with this part of her. Not yet. Instead, I send another friend request from her page to my sorry ass.

This time I'll answer it.

Plan 0: Track down Celeste.

The next day, I haven't heard back from my e-mail to Celeste and she still hasn't returned my call, so I leave for school early and detour over to her house. I've decided I don't even care about the Grass Roots youth group. I just want to talk to her about Faith. Let her jabber on about the things she knew so well until I stumble across the things I knew too.

Their van is in the driveway and Mrs. Schwartz answers the door only seconds after I ring the bell.

"Brie, honey, how are you?" She tilts her head the same way everyone does when they ask that. Her two-year-old boy squirms against her ample hip. I couldn't imagine having a sibling so much younger, but then I wonder how long it'll be before I can't imagine having a sibling. "We were so sorry we didn't make it to the service. We didn't hear—"

"Oh, that's okay." I wave a casual hand in front of my face. "Is everything okay with . . ." I'm not sure if it's her mom or her husband's mom who was sick. ". . . um, the rest of the family?"

"Oh, yes." She stares at me, studying my face as though she's not quite sure why I would ask. "Celeste's been having a hard time, of course."

I figure maybe Mrs. Schwartz doesn't want to talk about it if it's one of her parents, and I, of all people, can understand that.

"Is Celeste here?" I ask.

She pulls her hair out of her toddler's hand. "I'm sorry, she isn't. She left for school a few minutes ago."

After thanking Mrs. Schwartz, I rush toward the bus stop, so excited that Celeste is finally back at school. I'm determined to catch her before first class.

I get into the school five minutes early and wait it out in the Senior Wing.

The first bell sounds, and I catch a glimpse of Celeste down the hall. I'm not sure if she sees me, but suddenly she turns the opposite direction heading toward the school offices. Maybe she has to check in after her long absence.

I race through the crowded hallway, getting bumped and prodded, but when I get to the foyer I don't see her anywhere.

"To class, please," a hall monitor says.

"Um, I'm just going to the office." I skirt around him toward Ms. Lamberton's room. But when I turn the corner to the main bank of offices, I stop.

Celeste slips out a door and away from me toward the main exit, her arms loaded with books. This time, I'm pretty sure she didn't see me. Ducking past the office windows, I bolt after her, keeping silent to avoid the hall monitor's attention. I make a point of stopping to make sure the double doors close gently behind me. Halfway across the parking lot, Celeste climbs into her SUV.

"Celeste!" I wave to catch her attention. I'm so glad I caught up with her. The outside air suddenly seems so much easier to take into my lungs.

Her eyes dart to me. I expect at least a slight smile, even if she is pretty sad. Nothing, though. She just stares across the empty cars.

I wonder if her grandma did die. When I take a step toward her, something jolts her back to the moment and she starts her ignition.

I pick up my pace. She must have seen me, unless she's in that same dazed state I've been in. When she backs out of her space, I break into a run. She stops to switch gears and I land right in front of her red SUV, bending forward to catch my breath.

I look up and meet her eyes. Not only is she not happy to see me, her eyebrows tilt inward and she looks downright scared. I walk toward her driver's door, but as soon as I leave the front of her vehicle, she hits the gas, sailing past me and out of the parking lot.

Watching her taillights, I'm stunned. I grip the car beside me for balance and try to swallow a breath of thick air. What's wrong with her? It's not like I blame her for not being at the funeral. I just wanted to talk.

Plan P: Get some answers from someone.

After last class, I march to the Senior Wing again. No sign of Celeste, of course, but I scan the halls for the gossipy glass-haired girl I followed the other day. As I stand leaning against a locker, I notice whispering down the hall, and by the stray glances, I know it's directed at me.

There's something almost giddy about their whispers though, and it's not until I see Dustin round the corner at the other end of the hall with his buddies that I realize what they're murmuring about. Right. Now that I'd caught them, Amy was probably spreading around her happy boyfriend news.

I blow a breath through my nose. Dustin catches sight of me, but then obviously diverts his eyes. When one of the guys he's with says something to him, he laughs too loud. A fake laugh. He's uncomfortable. I'm at least glad for that.

Dustin doesn't stop at his locker, but keeps moving until he turns another corner away from me. The whispers intensify and now I feel like everyone in the hallway is talking about me. As much as I want to run out the doors, I stand my ground. Faith used to get teased about her glasses in elementary school, and I remember Dad telling her, "Don't show them that it gets to you, and they'll get bored and stop." I concentrate on breathing in and out and recite those words inwardly as my mantra.

Several minutes later, I notice the glass-haired girl chatting outside a classroom with a couple of others. They don't seem to have noticed me, so I doubt they're part of the Ridicule-the-Dumped-Girl Brigade. I stand across the hall, trying not to stare, but probably not succeeding. When I catch the girl's eyes a couple of times, she moves toward me.

"You waiting for me?" she says.

I nod. Swallow. "Are you, um . . ."

"Sammy," she says.

Not what I meant, but as I see her close up, I wonder if she was in one of the pictures from Faith's Facebook page. "Did you know Faith Jenkins?" I ask, skipping my own introduction. If she recognizes me as Faith's sister, now will be the time she'll show it. I'm not sure if the nerves I feel are from being watched or from hoping she won't recognize me. Or maybe hoping she will. I study her eyes. They close for a second, and then open with the same composed look.

"I didn't know her very well," Sammy says. "She was in my history class."

This saddens me. I don't want to talk to another person who barely knew Faith. I live in the head of one of those already. But I remember their gossiping the other day, and I want to hear what the rumors are.

"Did you hear how she died?" I ask, forcing a casual tone.

"Yeah." Sammy's eyes light with a flicker of interest. "Suicide. Off a cliff," she says slowly, like she's sad about it. "She was really a nice girl."

When she says that it was suicide, outright, in my face, I suddenly feel like I have to defend Faith. Stand up for her name. I bite my lip to rein myself in.

"Somebody in her family told my parents the details. I don't remember much else, sorry."

Somebody in *my* family? If my parents aren't talking to me, they sure aren't talking to strangers about it. Why is she spreading this around? Just for a little excitement?

"No," I blurt. "She didn't kill herself. She couldn't have."

Sammy nods. Her straight hair looks like it's ice misted in place and each piece moves like a spear with her nodding. "It's sad, but true."

"It's not true! You didn't even know her. You said it yourself!" I try to calm down, remembering I'm not sure of anything. Backing away, I say, "Maybe you shouldn't talk about stuff you don't know."

Tears well up in my eyes, so I turn and jog out the doors before she says anything else. I've been doing a good job at holding myself together, but something about Sammy's words, her confident tone, just broke me. Even if it could be true, how would she know? I can't fathom my parents telling her or anyone else that it was suicide, especially if they can't even tell me.

At home, I race to my room and pull out Faith's Bible. I scrounge for the list of Bible verses I'd found on Facebook, feeling an urgency to know something, anything, true about my sister. Flipping to the table of contents, I scan for the Book of Acts. It doesn't take me long to locate the proper verse. It's one of the ones emblazoned in yellow highlighter.

> And when the blood of your martyr Stephen was shed, I stood there giving my approval and guarding the clothes of those who were killing him.

I've never understood this gibberish. I thumb back to the table of contents to find the Book of Romans. Maybe the next one will be in English.

> Therefore, I urge you, brothers, in view of God's mercy, to offer your bodies as living sacrifices, holy and pleasing to God—this is your spiritual act of worship.

Bodies as sacrifices? I know what that means. People in the Bible were constantly killing animals and offering them as sacrifices, I'd heard about it in Sunday School. But I'm sure this is talking about people. I have to read it again, because I can't believe it actually says that.

Then again, I guess Jesus was sacrificed. Still, I don't know much, but I'm pretty sure the Bible doesn't tell people to go out and kill themselves. After all, it does say "living" sacrifices. This verse has got to be out of context here. I scan the other verses to make some sense of it all but it's like reading another language.

I try to reassure myself that these verses were posted on Reena's Facebook page, not Faith's. But a glob sticks in my throat.

The verses are highlighted in Faith's Bible too.

I drop the Bible wide open on the floor like it's burning my hands.

Faith never would have committed suicide, but would she have become a sacrifice?

I wish I could tell myself flat-out *no*. But I can't.

chapter FOURTEEN

*m*y parents don't want to talk. Amy and Dustin are out of the question. Celeste doesn't want to speak to me either, but I don't care. She's the one person who can clear some of this up for me. She's going to talk to me whether she likes it or not.

By the phone there's a list of frequently called numbers. It's a dry erase board, so I promptly remove Amy's number. Then I pick up the handset and dial the Schwartz house, which I don't recognize as any of the ones information listed off the other night. Celeste's mom answers.

"Hi, Mrs. Schwartz. Is Celeste home?"

"Can I ask who's calling."

"It's Brie Jenkins."

"Oh, hi, honey. Celeste isn't here. Everything okay?"

"Yeah, yeah, fine. It's just . . . do you know where she is?"

"She's at work until ten, I think." The toddler must be on her hip again, because he wails into the phone.

I didn't even know Celeste had a job. "Oh, right," I say. "Um, where does she work again?"

A pause, and she babbles a few sentences of baby talk. The little guy finally quiets down. "Over at Starbucks."

I'm about to ask which one, since there are at least five Starbucks locations in Sharon, when the kid starts whimpering again.

"Okay, thanks," I say over the noise, and hang up.

Plan Q: Go for coffee.

Only three of the Starbucks are on our side of town. One I need to take a bus to, the other two are within walking distance. I glance up at my parents' closed bedroom door and consider whether or not I should disturb Mom. I leave a note on the hutch instead, and decide to start with the two closest Starbucks.

I find Celeste at the second one, the one nearest our high school. When I walk through the door, the chimes jingle. The dim lighting in the place makes it feel calm, peaceful. She glances up from where she takes orders at the counter and her easy countenance becomes rock hard. I've never seen her so rigid and I can't believe that I have to swallow down a lump of nervousness over talking to Celeste, who I've known since I was a little kid.

"Uh, hi," I say when it's my turn.

"What can I get you?" She won't meet my eyes.

"I really need to talk to you," I whisper.

"I'm sorry, Brie. I'm working here. Either order something or get out of line."

"Okay, um, tea."

"What kind?" She points to a huge list at the edge of the chalkboard.

"I don't know, pick one for me. When's your break?"

"What size?"

"Um, small. When, Celeste? When can I talk to you?"

She takes the five-dollar bill from my hand and works out my change. "Tall chai," she calls over her shoulder. Then she looks behind me and says, "Can I help you?" to the man next in line.

I don't move until she looks back at me. "You can pick it up over there," she says, motioning to the far end of the counter.

Fine. I pick up my tea and look for a seat where I can keep an eye on her. Over half an hour passes while my cup empties and she completely ignores my presence. The questions running through my mind overwhelm me and to put myself at ease, I try to concentrate on the memories of when everything made sense.

I remember Celeste and Faith on the trampoline we used to have out behind our house, when they hooked up the sprinkler and squealed like hyenas each time the water hit them. I'd watch out the kitchen window and wonder what it would be like to jump so high, completely forget my fear of heights, and be so carefree.

Looking over at Celeste's crease of a mouth, I can barely wrap my head around her being the same person.

I get back in line.

When it's my turn again, I've come prepared with an order. "Tall skinny vanilla latte. So when exactly is your break?"

"Three eighty-five." She stares at me and her right eye turns in ever so slightly. Over the years I've known her lazy eye to mean either she doesn't have her contact lenses in—which I highly doubt today, since she's counting out change pretty efficiently—or she hasn't been sleeping well. "Are you going to stay here all night?"

"Is there a problem with that?" I cross my arms to try and have the upper hand.

She shrugs. "Suit yourself." Then looks behind me. "Next."

I slowly sip my latte, but another half hour passes and she still doesn't take her break or even glance in my direction. Every time there's a lull in customers, she ducks behind the counter or through a swinging door. I just hope she isn't escaping through a back exit.

I arrive at the counter again, this time with no one behind me. "Listen, Celeste, I'll wait as long as I have to. I don't know why you're trying to hide from me, but—"

"I'm not hiding from anything." Her eyes dart back and forth. "What makes you think I'm hiding?"

Oh, I don't know, your freaked out response just now? Not to mention nearly driving over me in the school parking lot. "Well, something's definitely wrong."

"It's not . . . Are you going to order something?"

"Low-fat brownie." I know I can't sit here without purchasing something. And it *is* low-fat.

A man in a white button-down shirt moves up beside Celeste on her side of the counter. Obviously her boss, he looks at her register, glances at her for a few seconds, and heads to the baking display unit a couple feet away.

I give her a hard stare so she knows I won't let up, even if it means getting her in trouble with her boss.

"I'll . . . we'll talk, okay. On my break in ten minutes," she whispers.

Smiling my thanks, I head back to my table.

"Hi," she says when she sits across from me with a dark coffee.

"Hi." I'm not nervous anymore. After being here so long processing memories, I feel strong and ready for whatever she tells me about Faith. I've got a thousand questions, but I don't want her to run away again, so I start easy. "I get it if you're having trouble talking about it. I can't say I'm having the easiest time either, but my parents, well, they don't talk about her at all, and nobody at school does . . . and it's making it all really weird."

"So you just want to talk about her, then? About Faith?" Celeste's voice wavers a little on the name.

"Well, yeah." I nibble on my lip. It looks like this relaxes her a bit, but she doesn't respond and I'm not sure exactly where to start. "There's something I wanted to ask you about too," I say, finally.

Her eyes rest on the table between us. She takes methodic sips of her drink. "Okay. What's up?" She sounds casual, but her tensed forehead and non-smile make me think it's an act.

"I was just wondering where you and Faith had been going to youth group. Pastor Scott said—"

"Yeah, we haven't gone there in ages." She waves her hand in front of her, another casual motion that doesn't quite match the rest of her. "We didn't, uh, we didn't have a church youth group, really. I mean, not in a church."

Okay, that makes sense. So maybe their home group was it. "Yeah, because I checked around, and it seems like Faith wasn't going, but you—"

Celeste glances to the counter and then to the outside window. "I should probably get back."

"No! Celeste, please just talk to me. Were you at Grass Roots the night of the accident? Because I thought you were with Faith, but then I saw your name listed on the roster there." I don't even know why I'm asking this. I want to know about Faith's life, not her death, but because Celeste is acting so strange, I just need for it all to make sense.

Her forehead wrinkles and she looks down at the table between us for so long, I don't think she's going to answer. But the longer she stays quiet, the more I need to hear something. I sit patiently, rubbing a dent in my thumb under the table.

"I . . . you're right. I was at Grass Roots that night." Her voice sounds like a songbird with a vice around its neck. She's trying so hard to sound like this is normal. I just wish I could figure out why it isn't.

"When I heard Faith on the phone with you that night, I just assumed she'd be going out with you," I say, more to myself than to her. "And when the police said she'd been with friends—"

"I—I don't . . . I wasn't." She stands and backs away from the table so I start to follow.

"Rumors are circulating at school that Faith killed herself," I say, "and I thought at first no way, but I don't know, maybe she did, and—"

"No! No, she didn't. Brie, you should know better than anyone." She backs up so fast, she bumps into another table, the two coffee cups on top splattering. The women seated there stop chatting and stare up at her. Celeste doesn't say anything, doesn't even apologize, just turns back to me and says, "I gotta go."

"Wait, Celeste!"

She moves away from me but I feel like my feet are stuck to the floor. I reach out, pleading with her to stay.

"I'll call you later," she says, scooting behind the counter. Before I know it, her boss stands between us, glaring at me.

My hands shake and I don't have it in me for any more confrontation. I grab my purse and place hand over hand on tables and chairs to get myself to the door. Maybe Celeste just needs some time to calm down too. Maybe she hasn't talked about any of this either and so it all came out wrong.

When I make my way across the parking lot, I notice Celeste's red SUV parked a few feet away. I walk over and peer through the back windows. I don't know what I'm looking for. A worship CD case on the back seat? A sweatshirt I'd seen on her a thousand times? Something that makes me feel like my memories aren't all lies.

Her back windows are tinted, and it's hard to see anything, so I move to the front ones. Clean and empty. Just before I turn away, my eye catches a familiar sight on her dash. In the exact same spot as in Faith's Toyota, there's a small round sticker.

It's yellow, just like the one in Faith's car, but this one looks like someone's tried to scrape it off.

My heart pounds inside my chest. I'm sure it doesn't mean anything, just some "Sisters in Christ" type of bonding thing. But still, somehow it feels like this is important. That I have a new piece of Faith that matters.

chapter FIFTEEN

the next day after last class, I call Dad and stay an extra half hour in the locker room eavesdropping on all the after-school teams. I hear about a couple of parties, a bit of celebrity gossip, but nothing about Faith or even about Dustin and Amy. My dead sister and my dead relationship are already old news.

I trek toward my locker to pick up my backpack, but remember along the way that I wanted to get a reading list from Mr. Clancy so I can catch up with the rest of the class. Just as I turn the corner, a guy emerges out of Mr. Clancy's classroom. Red and black Mack jacket, dark, shoulder-length hair. I have instant recognition. He's the same guy I saw at Faith's grave site.

It hadn't occurred to me to look for him at school, but here he is, right in front of me.

Once I get past the fact that he isn't a mirage, I call, "Hey!"

He looks my way and his dark bangs fall over half his face. My heart beats faster and I step toward him. He flicks his hair back and our eyes meet. His gaze pulls me in further, questioning me. I bet he's wondering who I am or why we haven't seen each other at school before. The same things I wonder about him. But then, abruptly, he spins and jogs the other direction.

"Wait!" I pick up speed. When I turn into the hallway that leads to the back of the school, there's no sign of the guy, but the double doors at the end clack shut. I burst through after him.

Still no sign of him, but since there's a fence in the other direction, he must have gone for the parking lot. Taking one deep breath after another, I keep my sprint until I stand in the middle of the twenty or so cars that are left.

Did he drive away already? I scan all directions and don't see any movement. Well, except for the couple sucking each other's tongues off at the car beside the fire hydrant.

One more search around the area and I give up. He's gone.

But who is he? I need to know.

Finally I sigh and head back into the school, straight for Clancy's classroom. The door's ajar and he sits solemnly at his desk with his eyes closed. It doesn't surprise me. I pegged him as a meditator.

I stand there for several seconds letting my heart slow before scuffing my foot to make a noise.

No reaction. I clear my throat. "Mr. Clancy," I say, just above a whisper.

Slowly, his eyelids open. He stares ahead for several seconds before turning to me.

"Ah, Miss Jenkins." He says it like he expected it to be only a matter of time before I appeared here before him.

"I'm sorry to disturb you," I say, "but I was just wondering about a boy who came out of your classroom."

His eyes scan the desks, as though he might find someone still sitting there.

"I mean a few minutes ago. He was wearing a red and black jacket?"

"Oh, yes, yes. The homeschool class."

"The what?"

"There were a few homeschool students who came in to take a test."

"Oh." That explains why I'd never seen him in the hallways. It also gives me hope. If he doesn't attend Sharon High, maybe he doesn't know about all the stuff that makes me a leper around here. "Can you tell me his name?"

Clancy looks up at the ceiling. Is that where he keeps his class list? I follow his eyes, but the plain, white expanse reveals nothing. I wipe a sweaty palm on my jeans with anticipation.

"Hmm . . . I'm afraid I don't remember which of them wore a jacket like that. Mr. Monakey maybe." He turns back to me. "Ms. Lamberton just picked up their tests a few minutes ago."

Clancy eyes my purple top, which is riding an inch or so above my jeans. Not quite school regulation.

I tug it down before he comments and slink toward the door. "Thanks, Mr. Clancy. I'll be sure to ask Ms. Lamberton."

By the time I get to the school office, I realize I forgot to ask about the history homework. And Ms. Lamberton's already gone for the day.

It's four thirty when I walk through the door to our empty house. It appears exactly the same as I left it this morning. The blender from my protein shake still overflows with water in the kitchen sink, the newspaper is spread open on the table.

I wonder if Mom went back to work. The thought makes me smile. I know it will take her much longer to get over Faith, but if she's working with flowers, doing something she used to enjoy, at least there's hope she'll be able to function normally again, at least one day.

I pull the curtains back, let in some light, and begin my regular dusting routine. It's not looking any fresher in here, but at least I'm keeping it at a consistent stale. Even though it's into October, I crack a few windows.

Mom walks through the front door just before six with Dad trailing behind her. I've made scrambled eggs—my one culinary ability—and set the table. Sure enough, Mom wears a skirt and blouse. Her hair is tied back, and a sprig of baby's breath pokes out from the ponytail. She's been working at the flower shop again.

But she hasn't brought any home, in fact she appears quite worn-out from the day. Maybe she's not ready to go back full-time yet.

"I made scrambled eggs," I say.

Mom gives me a look that says I'm her saving grace. The best daughter in the world.

Of course it's not much of a competition anymore. The thought drains my smile.

Dad's jaw is tense and I wonder if they've been arguing.

When we sit down to dinner, Dad eats fast, like he's in a contest.

"What's up, Dad? Somewhere to be?"

He takes a drink; his chin is a mess of ketchup. "I'm at the church tonight." He says it the way he's always said it. And in that moment, I realize it's Friday night. Praying Parents night. Is he really going back to lead it? So soon?

"Oh," I say and turn to Mom. They always led it together. "Are you going?"

Mom flattens her napkin several times on her lap until it looks like it's been ironed. "No. I don't think that would be the best thing for anybody." Her words are quiet, and she takes her flattened napkin and carefully folds it exactly in half. Then in half again. She places it on her still-full plate and pushes herself back from the table. I watch her back as she lumbers out of the kitchen.

Dad doesn't seem to notice the whole conversation. Or he ignores it. He slurps the last of his eggs a mile a minute, barely taking a breath. The fact that my parents barely talk to me is one thing, but barely talking to each other? It makes my stomach twist in knots.

By the time I clean up the dinner dishes, Mom is zoned out in front of the TV, and Dad has left to teach his class. I head upstairs for the computer. Even though I do have homework, I can't concentrate on anything until I check the online directory for the listing "Monakey." As I sit down I realize, happily, that I haven't thought about Dustin and Amy all afternoon.

The computer room is really just an alcove situated between my room and Faith's. I pull my eyes away from Faith's door. Regardless of the fact that I can't stop thinking about her death, about the cause, or the possibility of suicide, I'm not going back in there.

The sound of the Friday Night Movie jingle trails up the stairs. I spread my schoolbooks out on the desk, just in case Mom heads up to bed and looks in on me.

Opening the online directory for Sharon, Oregon, I type in "Monakey."

No entries found. I try "Moanakey," "Moanakee," "Mona-kee," plus other variations. Still nothing.

I click on the Google icon and try four or five spelling combinations. "Monachie" and "Sharon, Oregon" nets a few results. I quickly tab over to my other open window and type this spelling into the local phone directory. Still nothing. So if there's some homeschool student in our town with that last name, he must be unlisted.

Clicking back to the first Google entry, a Portland online newspaper article comes up. The small write-up talks about a car being hauled from Trundle Valley Lake, which is only an hour or so away, with the body of Mrs. Annie Monachie still in it. The article is dated three years ago and cites the tragic incident as a suicide.

The word "suicide" brings a sick feeling to my stomach.

I click on the other two listings, but they reroute me to the same article. There's no address, no phone number, and no pictures. Just some dead lady.

chapter SIXTEEN

onday morning, I've almost forgotten about Dustin and Amy when I round a corner and see them leaning up against a locker kissing. I gasp, but I'm far enough away that they don't hear me. I can't seem to turn my eyes away though, as Dustin moves from her lips to her ear with the exact same form he always used with me.

The thought makes me feel sick, grossed-out, like he's kissing us both at the same time. Amy giggles when his hand slides down her side. I can't stand looking and yet I can't stop. It's not until I hear Clancy's voice that it jolts my attention away.

"Hey! Enough, you two. Miss Cooper, do I have to warn

you about this again?" Mr. Clancy goes on about Principal Voth and I smile inwardly, glad that the whole world isn't behind this happy couple. After they're escorted toward the school office, I notice the eyes of all my schoolmates. Not staring after Dustin and Amy, but instead with their eyes on me. Were they watching me watch them? My face heats up. I drop my eyes and head for my locker.

When the first bell rings, I hustle to Ms. Lamberton's office. She offers her same warm smile, obviously thinking I'm struggling emotionally over my sister again.

"There's a homeschool student I'm trying to get a hold of. The Monachie kid?"

When her face straightens, I realize that's probably not a great reason to miss first period.

"I mean, I think he knew my sister and I just want to talk to him about her."

"You can talk to me about her, Brie." She reaches a hand across the desk. "That's why I'm here."

I look down at her hand. "I know I can. You've been really great, it's just he . . ." *He what? He's cute, so I think he'll be a better listener?* "I wonder if he knows things about her that I never got to know." Probably untrue. He did bring carnations in full bloom to her grave, after all. But Ms. Lamberton looks like she's mulling it over.

"I'd like to help you, Brie, but I can't give out personal information on the homeschool students. If you'd like, you can write him a note. Next time he's at the school I can make sure to get it to him."

I stare at the desk and wonder if I should bother. The guy has run off on me twice already. But even so, something about when our eyes met makes me think it wasn't because of me. I scrawl a quick note with my name and phone number, and pass it over. Who knows if he'll actually call, but it's all I can think of to do.

Plan R: Follow Mr. Clancy's lead and stare at the ceiling until the mysterious guy's name, address, and phone number miraculously appear.

At lunchtime, Tessa leans against her locker when I approach. I'm always tentative about going to mine if she's around. She still scares me. But she appears happy today. Not smiling—she never actually smiles—but her lips are twisted into a kind of smirk.

"Hey," I say.

"Hey. How's it goin'?"

"Good." It sounds fake as it comes out of my mouth. "Not great, actually. I'm trying to find this guy and they won't give me any information on him at the office."

"Who's the guy?"

I eye her. She pulls a black Sharpie out of her pocket and starts writing notes on the inside of her arm.

"Just some guy I saw at the cemetery."

She stops writing and studies me.

"He was at my sister's grave and when I went to talk to him he took off. Like, ran away."

Tessa nods. "And so he goes to school here, but you can't find him?"

"No," I say. Then I explain the whole homeschool thing. It feels good to be honest with someone. "I can't find a phone number or address for him anywhere. I don't even know his first name."

"You want to find this stuff out?"

"Yeah," I say. "Of course."

She shrugs. "Easy."

At four o'clock, Tessa and I are leaning against a post by the offices when Ms. Lamberton leaves for the day. Once she disappears through the main doors, I follow Tessa across the hall. Secretaries still mill about, so we duck all the way to the other end of the clear glass window. Ms. Lamberton's office is the last one.

Of course the door is locked, which makes me think our

big plan is done, over with, kaput. But then Tessa pulls out a Visa card.

Crazy. From Tessa's wardrobe, I'd never have thought she has access to money. She wears the same loose-fitting black jacket, with a black turtleneck underneath, almost every day.

After instructing me to watch the hallway, she gets to work, fumbling and swearing several times before I hear the click of the door.

"Come on," she says.

I've never done anything like this and my heart beats like the bass drum from our pep rallies. Probably just as loud, too. "What's this kid's name again?"

"Monachie," I tell her and spell it out the way I found it on the Internet, figuring that's the only spelling I know to be an actual name.

She ruffles the papers on Ms. Lamberton's desk, sliding and dropping books off to the side. I hold out my hand to quiet her, but don't say anything. She knows what she's doing a hell of a lot more than I do.

"There's nothing here with the name 'Monachie' or even the word 'homeschool'," she says.

"Crap. Maybe it's filed away somewhere."

Tessa ignores me and boots up Ms. Lamberton's computer. "What do you think Lamberton's password would be?"

I shrug, but Tessa rattles off words. "Guidance, friend, caring, listening, kids . . . dog."

"Dog?" I ask.

"Yeah, who's the dog in this picture? Have you ever asked her?"

I think back. I had commented on the picture the first time I was in her office. "Appy?" I say.

She plugs in "Appy," and sure enough, it works.

"Right on the desktop," she says, after only a few seconds. "Homeschool Exams." She clicks on it and scrolls through the list.

A sound in the hallway makes me freeze in place. I slowly put my ear to the door, hearing Principal Voth. His voice grows louder. I can't make out much of what he says, but I do hear the name "Hilary," which I remember is Ms. Lamberton's first name.

"We gotta go!" I whisper to Tessa, but she's absorbed. "Tessa! We gotta go now. Shut that thing down."

Principal Voth's voice pauses a few feet away. I'm praying he ducks into the main office. When I feel Tessa behind me, I crack the door. With one eye, I see Mr. Voth standing outside the large Plexiglas window to the main office, leaning through the opening to talk to someone.

I give Tessa a nod and tiptoe out of the office. There's

no sound behind me and I wonder if she held back for some reason. But then her hand lands on my shoulder, turning me around. She grabs my arm, and we walk straight for Mr. Voth.

Then straight past him. "Hey, Mr. Voth," Tessa calls out over her shoulder. She's just as casual as I've ever heard her.

"Hi, Tessa," he says back.

I feel like I haven't breathed in days.

"So what did you find out?" I ask when we reach our lockers.

"Phone: 555-0175," she spouts. "Address: 3459 Maple Court." She smiles. Like, really beams.

"Holy crap! You memorized all that?"

"Yeah, I'm pretty good with numbers."

"No doubt. Can you do that again? I gotta write this down."

She rattles off the address while she pulls a paperback book out of her messy locker, then shuts the door before the rest of her books fall out. When she goes to repeat the phone number, she stumbles and gets mixed up on the last part. I write down the two versions she comes up with, but decide the address will probably be a better bet.

"And what's the guy's name?" I ask.

Her eyes snap away from me. "I gotta go." She clicks her lock on.

"No, wait." I run after her when she practically races down the hall.

"Look, haven't I given you enough?" Her tone is defensive.

When I get beside her, I can see that her unusually happy face has turned back to a scowl, and all at once I understand. She can't remember, and doesn't want to admit it.

"No worries," I say, even though I really, really want to know his first name. "I have more information than I even thought possible."

She barrels out the door and lets it slam behind her.

At home, I plug the location into the computer, and sure enough, it is an actual address. Over three miles away, mind you, but it does exist. After printing out a map, I look it up on Google Earth, so there'll be no mistaking it.

Mom and Dad turn in shortly after nine these days. I wait until their light goes out, and then tiptoe down the stairs. In my backpack, I have the address, bus route, and five bucks in change. I'm still not sure of my plan. Knocking on a stranger's door at ten p.m. doesn't exactly sound like the ultimate in safety. But I need to see where he lives. And maybe I'll leave him a note right at his house in case it's a while before he comes back in to see Ms. Lamberton.

The bus is nearly empty for the ride over, except for the

wino in the back. I don't know if he's eyeing my backpack for money, or if he's just doing the pre–pass-out seven-mile stare.

At almost ten o'clock, I exit the bus, walk two blocks, and arrive outside the address on my notepaper. It's a two-story place, spelling out suburban middle class. A garage and a pathway on either side of the house leading to the backyard complete the picture. The porch light, along with one light on the upper floor, are the only signs of life. I sidle up beside a tree across the street.

Now that I'm here, I want to do something. But should I go up to the house and ask for their son, whoever he is? I really wish Tessa had remembered the name, and I search my imagination for what name would suit him. But I can't think of any. He doesn't look like any other guy I've known.

Before I make a move, a car pulls into the front drive and a second later the upstairs light snuffs out.

The old white Honda's brakes make a crunching sound as it stops. A tall girl with light brown hair gets out of the car and for a second I think I recognize her profile, but then she turns away.

She grabs some grocery bags out of her trunk and puts them down briefly to fix her pant leg. That's when I get a glimpse of those wide eyes. It's Reena M. Black. From Facebook. Probably from Faith's home group, and now from the house of the cute guy who was visiting my sister's grave. I guess that explains how he knew Faith. But why is her last name Black and his Monachie? Unless that's what the *M* stands for.

Reena heads for the house, but stops and checks their mailbox on the way. I figure she must be expecting a delivery because she slides her hand in twice and double checks that it's empty. I march across the street to talk to her, but the front door thuds shut before I even get halfway. The porch light goes out a second later and the house appears totally black. I check my watch and it's almost ten thirty. Not an acceptable time to knock on a stranger's front door.

Peering down the side path, I see a garden swing in the backyard. A beat-up red bike leans against the wall near the corner. It has the old-fashioned straight handlebars and a seat that looks off center and really uncomfortable. Faith's voice is noticeable in my head again, but I'm glad. It's been so long since I've really noticed it and it drowns out the thumping of my heart.

I scan the house again, and a curtain shifts in an upstairs window. Standing under a streetlight, I suddenly feel very exposed. I inch into a shadow and grab for the zipper on my backpack. I rip off a piece of notepaper and crouch in the driveway to write, "Call me. Please," followed by my home and cell numbers. As much as I want to talk to the guy, I'd be almost as happy if his sister called. She knew Faith. I'm pretty sure she knew her well.

After pinning my note under the windshield wiper of the Honda, I take one more glance up at the window and the curtain moves again. It's a creepy feeling like I'm being watched, and now I just want to get out of here.

I pick up my backpack and run all the way to the bus stop.

chapter SEVENTEEN

*W*hen I get home, it's after eleven thirty.

I tiptoe in. My mind's been racing with all sorts of possibilities that someone's following me since I saw the curtain move in that upper floor window at the Monachie house.

I place my keys on the hall table right beside the phone when it rings. I snap it out of its cradle in half a nanosecond. No one ever calls this late. Except possibly Dustin—drunk. Or Amy—broken-up. But if they ever did call me again, it would be on my cell. Maybe it's a wrong number.

"Hello," I whisper.

"Stay . . . away . . . from . . . my . . . house." The voice sounds stern, but young. Male.

"Who is this?" I cup my hand above my mouth to shield my volume.

"You know exactly who this is. Just leave us alone."

"Leave you alone?" I whisper, suddenly defensive. I think back to the moment we shared in the hallway and wonder if I read him wrong. The thought brings a flush of embarrassment to my cheeks. "What's with my sister's grave? What's with you running away every time I see you? It seems like you're the one—"

"I mean it. Just let it go. You don't know what you're sticking your fingers into." He softens slightly; I hear it in his voice. The sternness is a definite act and I don't think I did misread him.

"Okay, okay. I'll do what you want, but please, meet with me once. Just once. Then I'll leave you alone. I promise."

Silence. For a long time. Did he hear me? Should I ask him again?

"Fine. Tomorrow, three o'clock. Grant Park." And he hangs up.

When I set the phone down, I hear a noise and look up the stairs. Dad stares down from above. I've already gotten my shoes off, thankfully, but I'm so close to the front door and so far from the kitchen where I might have been getting a drink of milk or something. I wonder if he suspects I've been out.

"You okay?" He grumbles, still half-asleep.

"Yeah, fine. Dad, I—"

He holds up a hand. "Get some sleep, honey." He skulks back to his room without another word.

The next morning, Dad stops me on my way out the door.

"Who called?" he asks.

"Huh?"

"On the phone last night. Just before midnight. Who called?"

"Oh, uh, no one. Wrong number."

He nods. "There were a couple of hang ups before that. Did they wake you?"

Huh? "Oh, yeah, they did." I'd accidentally left my cell on silent, but there were three missed calls on there, too. I try to come up with something to make my lies sound a little more believable, but when I look up, Dad's eyes are scanning this morning's newspaper and he walks for the kitchen, the conversation already forgotten.

When I get to school, Tessa waits at our lockers, looking anxious to talk to me. Tessa Lockbaum. Anxious. Unreal.

"So did you go there, or what?"

I feed my books into my cavern of uncompleted assignments. "Yeah, I went there, but calm down. Nothing really happened."

"You chickened out, didn't you?" She huffs and rolls her eyes before I even have a chance to answer.

"Kind of. But I did leave a phone number."

She glances up.

"And he *did* call."

Tessa Lockbaum turns downright eager on me. "What did he say? Tell me."

Of course if it was about a normal crush, it would never garner this reaction from her. Something's weird, haunting, mysterious. That's what's hooking her. I gloss over the details and can tell she's hinting for me to tell her which park I'm meeting him at, but I don't. This guy runs away from me enough as it is. And Tessa's wearing her dog collar today.

chapter EIGHTEEN

Plan S: Find out why this guy is bent on staying away from me.

He's standing at the fountain when I get there. At least he chose a park close enough to the school that I could walk. He looks pretty nonthreatening—a little on the skinny side, wearing jeans, a sweatshirt, earphones tucked into his ears, and his red-checkered Mack jacket. Not exactly stylish, but this doesn't surprise me. He is homeschooled, after all.

His hands rest on the cement ledge of the fountain. He has strong-looking hands. Faith's humming grows louder in my ears, or in my head, or wherever it emanates from, when I approach.

"Hey." I edge up beside him at the fountain, but don't

look directly at him when I say it. This whole meeting feels very covert.

He reaches down and switches off his MP3 player. "What do you want from me?"

He gets straight to the point, doesn't he? I want him to look at me so we can share a connection again, but he keeps his eyes straight ahead. "Well, your name for one. I found out your last name. Should I just call you Mr. Monachie?" I snicker, but he doesn't even crack a smile.

"Alice," he says.

"Huh?" falls out of my mouth, loud and rude. I snap it shut.

"Alice," he says again. "That's my name."

Alice for a boy. Okaaaay. "Like Alice in Wonderland?" I force a deliberate laugh. The tension is killing me. *Lighten up already!*

He shakes his head. "No, my full name is Alistair. I hate it. *A-L-I-S*." He spells it for me, very slowly and methodically, like I'm in first grade.

"I'm Brie," I say, in my same chipper tone.

"Like Brianna?" he asks after a pause, and I realize that we are having an actual conversation. Just not the kind I'm used to. Even before Dustin, I knew how to flirt. I cracked jokes or giggled at the ones boys told me, and there was just an understanding that I liked the guy. My methods didn't seem to be working here. At all.

"No," I say, trying harder. "More like as in Camembert. You know, the cheese?" I feel like a flailing stand-up comic.

A hint of a smile breaks at the side of his mouth.

"Brie," I say again. "That's all I ever got. My sister got the holy, religious name. I guess my parents knew she'd be her and I'd be the cheesy one." I'm about to leave it at that, like I usually do, but something compels me to tell him the truth. "Actually, I have an Aunt Brie. She's battled with a list of different cancers. More than once, the doctors told her she wouldn't live."

"And she did?" Now he looks at me, but I can't meet his eyes. Not on this subject.

"Yeah, still is. So, really, I guess the name has kind of a connotation."

When I tilt my head to finally look at him, he's turned away again. I stare at the side of his face. His skin isn't acne-covered like most guys my age. In fact, it appears completely unmarred. Baby soft. I want to reach out and touch it, run my hand along his perfect cheekbone.

"Listen," I say after way too long of a silence. "I'm sorry if I make you uncomfortable. I just noticed you knew my sister. I'm trying to learn more about her and thought you could tell me what you know. Then I'll leave you alone," I add, testing him to see if he still wants that. Hoping he doesn't.

He mulls it over for a few seconds. "Well, I don't know much about your sister. Actually, I never met her."

I study him to see if there's a joke or some hidden meaning in his words. "Right," I pronounce in a stern tone. "So you hang out at graves of people you've never met." I nod. "Makes sense."

"It's not that . . . you don't . . . Look, I was there because I felt bad. I don't know, my sister knew her." His pinched face shows the same kind of confusion I feel.

"Can you tell me anything?" I feel like this is another lost cause and resignation tinges my voice. Maybe no one really knew Faith, not even Celeste. Alis and I both stare at the water.

"My sister Reena was friends with Faith."

I already knew this, but I let him go on.

"They were meeting most nights with a group of girls and one guy in my sister's room for a few months, you know, before."

I look up in surprise. Home group. Maybe there is something to learn here. "So if they were at your house almost every night, how could you have not met Faith?"

His face tenses again. "My sister, she's, um, pretty secretive."

He picks at the edge of his jacket. "I didn't answer the door or anything."

"And what went on in her room?"

He scratches his fingers along the cement barrier to the fountain. "There was always lots of singing. Worship singing. Shouts of hallelujah, yelling things to God, stuff like that. At first they went to different churches, but then Reena came home one night saying she couldn't hang out with those 'lukewarm Christians' for another second. She didn't want their habits rubbing off on her. I thought that meant she'd just stop going, but next thing I know, our house is worship central."

So definitely home group. With something finally making sense, I suppress a smile. "And your parents didn't care about the noise or anything?"

The question makes him flinch, and suddenly I remember the article about Annie Monachie, found dead in a car.

Could that be his mom? I divert my eyes for a second to think about this, but Alis turns away from me and takes a few steps toward the trees. I glance down and see what looks like the end of a pocketknife sticking out of his back jeans pocket. For a second it makes me catch my breath. But no, he doesn't seem dangerous.

"Sorry." I say, trying to rein him back. "Let's stick to the subject of Faith. You said you never met her, but you must have seen her, right? I mean, she was over there so much." I can sense that he knows more. I just need to pull it out of him.

"Sure, I saw her. But when they started taking over the living room, I stayed out of the house during meetings. Reena liked it that way." He reaches near the cement wall for his backpack. "That's all I know."

"But I still don't get it." He starts to walk and I follow. "Why did you show up at her grave?"

"I don't know," he says. "I guess I wondered—"

"Wondered what?" I hope he's not going to bring it back to the possibility of suicide.

"I just wondered what happened that night." He stops in place and looks from side to side, as though deciding which direction to bolt. "I wonder why they even went to The Point."

His last line stills me in place. I don't want to picture their decision to go up the mountain. "Who else was there?" I force out.

He twists his lips to the side. "I don't know who was with them. Sorry. I remember Faith because she's the only one who ever stood up to Reena. The only one who ever argued with her."

The way he says it, he sounds like he admires my sister. And okay, maybe I do too. Reena seems older and sounds a little controlling, but Faith still stuck up for herself. This feels like one of the first good memories I've had of Faith since she died. The first piece that I know is really her. A wave of assurance washes over me. This sounds like the sister I remember—arguing over the finer points of religion.

"I guess it wasn't so much guilt," Alis goes on. "More like I wanted to understand."

I move in front of him and put my hands on his shoulders. "That's exactly it!"

He just shakes his head, like he's already decided he's done with this conversation.

Being so close to finally getting some answers, an indignant feeling rises up in me. "I guess I'll have to ask Reena, then—"

"No!" He grabs my wrist and his hands are even stronger than they look. But I don't pull away. His strength makes me feel grounded, and I know he's not going anywhere, at least not this second. "The deal was, you leave my family alone, remember?"

I remember. But why is he acting so protective? "Well, you have no idea what it's like, what I'm going through. To have so many questions."

He stares at me for several seconds before he lets go of my wrist and replies quietly. "I do know." He clears his throat and looks away and I feel like such an idiot. "You can ask as many questions as you want," he goes on, "but you won't find closure. You'll only find more questions. I don't know anything else about your sister." He backs away. "If I did, I'd tell you."

This time he doesn't run and I don't follow. He picks up his bag and marches purposefully away from me.

On my walk home, I try to process. Maybe he understands more than I gave him credit for. And maybe he's right. So far everything I've tried to do to find some kind of closure, to fill this emptiness, hasn't worked. Maybe it's time for a new tactic. If only I knew what.

One thing I figure out by the time I get home: I will leave Alis and his family alone, even if it means missing out on the one guy I've felt this kind of connection with. But I promised, and he seems like a good guy. He doesn't deserve me making trouble for him.

Dad arrives home early from work, nodding without saying hello. Something's wrong. He moves dishes around the kitchen as though they're Frisbees. I cringe with every rattle, but don't move from my curled-up spot on the living room couch.

"Where's the cheese grater?" he mumbles. "Huh, mold again."

Mom walks through the front door a few minutes later. She gives me the same nod without eye contact on her way to the kitchen. Dad's nattering continues, about nothing being in its place and not being able to find what he needs, but as expected, Mom doesn't offer any rebuttal.

"Grater's in the cupboard under the sink," I say, pushing my way through the swinging door.

Dad stops in mid-sentence, now on to the subject of the church ladies group Mom used to attend, but hasn't since . . . well, since before. Dad glances at me for the briefest of seconds. "I found it, honey, thanks." His tone is so calm toward me. I don't know what to make of it.

He turns back to Mom. "Brie met with a pastor, and look how well she's doing."

Whatever he's bringing me into, I already know I don't like it.

"You need some fellowship, Gina." The way he talks to her—a demanding tone, not the way they used to discuss things—I know it's only a matter of time before they call it quits. Get a divorce. This is so polar opposite of my parents.

"Yum, looks good." I pick up a can of green beans off the counter. We've never, ever, eaten green beans out of a can.

"I-I can't." Mom stares at the beans and starts sobbing.

I shove the can behind my back. "No, Mom, please. I didn't mean—"

"You know they're not going to push you to talk about anything," Dad goes on. "But I'm driving you there tonight. You're not staying home in front of the TV again."

I wonder what happened to make Dad freak this way. Did he suddenly just decide that it's time for Mom to get over her daughter dying, and that's that? And shouldn't the solution be for *us* to talk about it? She collapses into a chair and drops her head in her hands.

Dad walks toward her like he doesn't even notice how she's shutting down. "It's almost six and—"

"Can you just shut up?" It's not until my eyes land on his that I realize what I've said to my dad. And how loud I've said it. But he only registers shock for a second, and then turns back to Mom and opens his mouth to say more.

"Dad. Stop. Can't you see what Mom's going through? She's not ready for some women's gossip group." I stop, not because I think I'm wrong, but because I don't think we should talk about Mom like she's not even here. "Shouldn't she have some say over her own life?"

"Brie, stay out of—"

"I'll say what I mean, Dad. And somehow I think that's what God meant for us to do."

Dad glares at me, probably ready to throw all my ungod-liness right back at me. But I can't quit. All these pent-up emotions are bursting out of me. "Why don't you read your Bible?" I ask, not even believing it's coming out of my mouth. "What about love and gentleness and patience. What about mercy, Dad? What about mercy?"

His mouth opens slightly, but he doesn't say a word.

"You think you're helping by sending a charity truck around to get all Faith's stuff when she was barely gone a week?" I throw a hand up in the air. "Stop rushing everybody!"

His glare pulls together and now he looks downright con-fused. I crack open the can of beans and dump it into the pot on the stove just to be doing something, anything, to get out my frustrated energy.

"I didn't call any charity," he says quietly.

I turn and search his face, but don't see any evidence of a lie. Clearly Mom didn't call them, and I sure didn't. Since I don't know what else to say to that, or why it even matters, I grab a pair of scissors out of the cutlery drawer and spin for the door I'd come in from.

I head up the stairs and straight into Faith's room. Do charities read the obituaries and send trucks all on their own?

When I open the door, the first thing I see is the pile of boxes just inside. The same pile that made my gut ache the last time I was in here. But everything else looks the same. Now I eye the pile and wonder: Could Faith have called the thrift store before she died too, not wanting to leave Mom and Dad with any extra burden? That just seems way too planned out.

I reach toward the top box tentatively, and slide one point of the scissors along the line of tape. The flaps fold open, and the first thing I see is a pair of high-waisted jeans I'd told Faith to get rid of ages ago. They made her look so bottom heavy. Digging under those, there's a dress from her seventh-grade band concert. It takes me only seconds to realize these are all old, unwanted clothes.

Marching for her closet, I swing open the door.

It's just as messy with clothes as it always was and her favorite pair of capris lies balled-up on her shoes at the bottom.

For the first time in months, I breathe all the way into my stomach and don't sense the slightest bit of bile. The sense of relief I feel is so strong, my eyes fill with tears.

Faith was not planning to die. She just wanted to get rid of some old clothes.

chapter NINETEEN

Plan T: Ask Tessa for help.

I don't plan to break my promise to Alis. Not exactly. But the next day at school I enlist Tessa's expert advice on how to move on from my sister's death.

"Distraction," she says. "That's exactly what you need."

I eye her skeptically. What could possibly distract me from all my questions?

"It'll be easy," she adds.

Everything's easy for Tessa. Sure seems like a good trait in a friend right now, since my whole life seems about as difficult as extracting gum from my hair.

"After school, meet me here. We'll get the car," Tessa says.

That's where I stop her. "You have your own car? Wow. I don't even have my license."

But she just smiles.

Uh-oh. Something tells me she doesn't either.

I spend my classes trying to divert myself from the possibility of going to jail for stealing a vehicle and driving without a license. I don't perform this diversion by catching up on assignments. Oh no, not me. Since I can't concentrate on a single word in my textbook, I doodle instead, writing down my questions.

1. Is Celeste hiding something or is she just upset?
2. Why didn't Faith ever bring Reena home?
3. Am I ever going to be able to think about anything else?

Tessa waits at our lockers at the end of the day. She's not the type to hold up for anybody, so I know she's really into this.

"So if you don't have your license, obviously you don't have a car. How are we doing this again?" I follow her onto a school bus and we sit at the back. "Where are we going?"

"To pick up the car, shithead. Wow, you don't catch on too quick, huh?" She's having lots of fun with me. Well, good. As long as I can be entertaining, I guess that's what matters.

"And whose car exactly are we driving without a license?"

"*We* are not driving. You think I'd trust my life with you behind the wheel?" She scoffs as the bus pulls away from the curb. "Don't you worry your pretty little head about it, Brie."

We get off the bus outside a row of apartment buildings on Fifth. She walks purposefully and I follow.

"I need to call home," I say. "You know, the big-time accountability program I told you about?" I haven't pulled my phone out though, mostly because I don't know how to talk to Dad after what I said to him in the kitchen last night.

"Yeah, so?" She eyes me.

"I guess I should just call." I reach into my purse and grab my phone. Just after I dial our home number and hit send, Tessa snatches the phone from my hand and walks on ahead.

"What are you—" I race to catch up, but she's already talking into it.

"Hello, Mr. and Mrs. Jenkins. This is Hilary Lamberton from Sharon High School."

Tessa doesn't sound anything like Ms. Lamberton. But she doesn't sound like herself either, and she's not using any four-letter words. I keep pace with her as she goes on.

"Brie's been trying to do some extra credit work to get caught up and I'll be helping her this afternoon with a project."

I make a motion of turning a steering wheel with my hands.

"I'll give her a ride home when we're done." Tessa leaves a phone number, which I have no idea if she made up on the spot or what, and hangs up.

"Wow. Thanks."

She passes back the phone, just as we arrive at the base of one of the buildings. Then she stops and tells me to wait while she heads inside.

The apartment buildings are old and worn, and the one that has been repainted stands out in a Cinderella-and-her-ugly-stepsisters sort of way. Two cute twentysomething guys amble up the front steps of the building Tessa entered. That makes sense. It looks like it could be cheap housing for college students. I wonder if Tessa has an older boyfriend in there somewhere.

Half an hour later, I'm snapping my history book shut with eyes at half-mast when she reappears. I follow her around the corner into an alley. It doesn't feel safe here, with piles of garbage and cigarette butts every couple of feet and I automatically feel wide-awake again. A guy with long, scraggly hair crouches under a fire escape, picking through a beat-up shopping bag, but Tessa crunches a granola bar and kicks at rocks like she hangs out here every day.

Soon, she stops in front of a newish Volkswagen and

holds up a set of keys. She hits a button and the locks click, taillights flashing.

"Is this your boyfriend's?" I ask as I slide into the passenger side.

"I don't have a boyfriend," she says. Nothing else.

No, really, don't bother telling me anything about what we're doing here. If the police catch us, I'll just tell them I hit my head and don't remember who you are. No worries. "Is it your mom's?" I try again.

She shakes her head, and I figure that's all I'm going to get. Then, just as I turn my attention to the outside window, she says, "Dad's."

Score one for Brie. "He doesn't mind you taking it out?"

Tessa scowls at me. Right. Her dad has no idea. This is not increasing my confidence any.

"Why do you think it took me so long to get out of there?" she says.

I swallow down my misgivings and ask her where we're going.

"It's a surprise," she says, not meeting my eye.

Of course it is. But I must admit, she's doing an admirable job of distracting me so far. The silence that follows brings on a new bout of nerves though, and I search for a calming topic, or better yet, something that will give me a hint of where she's taking me. "So what do you do in your spare time?" I ask.

"Nothin'." She turns to shoulder check, as though she's much too busy for my question.

Good. As long as we can have a lively conversation, that should keep us both awake.

"I'm taking an art class at the Y," she adds after a long span of silence.

The combination of her sudden voice and her voluntary information make me stutter. "A-a-art? You do art?" It really shouldn't surprise me, since the only class we share is Art with Mr. Poindexter. Of course she stays at the back of the classroom with her head down, so I rarely notice her there. I never knew she was serious about it.

She laughs. "No, I don't do a-art. I paint. Dad works from home, and I like to get out as much as possible."

"What do you paint?" I'm imagining the morbid graffiti on the back of the local movie theater.

"Mostly landscapes. But the class is for portraits. I really suck at those."

"Yeah, well, I suck at poetry, but I still write it," I say, trying to show my support. I run my hand along the rim of the window, waiting for her to say something. "It's good for me, I think. Makes me stronger somehow."

Tessa nods. "Like the one at the funeral? You're right about that."

I wonder what I'm right about. The fact that I suck or the fact that it makes me stronger, but I don't have a chance to ask because she turns in to a strip mall and the first thing I see is the liquor store, right on the corner.

Great. Looks like we'll be adding to our underage infractions. But she drives past that, and the pharmacy, over toward the movie theater. Just as I start to let out my breath, a flash of familiarity catches my eye.

"Hey!" I say in an excited whisper. "There's Reena. Alis's sister. The one I told you about."

Reena gets into her Civic across the parking lot and Tessa idles in place watching her.

"Whoa, she's a quick one," Tessa says when the white car whizzes past in the opposite direction.

I nod, following Reena's car with my eyes until it turns a corner, out of sight. I sigh, ready to turn back and make an effort at focusing on the latest movies, but Tessa's already pulling a U-turn.

"Wait, no," I tell her. But my voice is quiet, and obviously Tessa can tell I don't mean it. Seconds later, she burns around the same corner where Reena disappeared.

"Well, just don't try too hard to keep up." I grip the sides of my seat. But I can already see the white Civic and we're gaining on it.

"Oh, no, you don't, honey," Tessa says when Reena's car moves over into the next lane. I think it's hilarious that I, her supposed friend, get nicknames like "shithead," while endearments like "honey" are reserved for total strangers. "You're not getting away from us that easy." Tessa swerves across lanes with one car between the Civic and us.

"You're too close. She'll see us!"

Tessa shakes her head. "She's not seeing nothin'. She's barely seeing the road. Look at that girl wail."

I lean toward Tessa to get a better view. Reena sways back and forth, and in her rearview mirror, I catch a glimpse of her mouth in an opened, almost-pained expression, her eyes practically closed.

"She's a singer, huh?" I say.

"Well, you're the one who told me about all that hallelujahing."

Finally, Reena pulls over at Bertram Nursing Home complex—three low buildings with rows of perfectly trimmed shrubs dividing them. Tessa slows down and heads into the same lot, but takes a right where Reena took a left.

"What do you think she's doing here?" I ask.

Tessa shrugs. "Who knows. Maybe a grandparent or something."

That makes sense. It looks like the same type of building my grandma lives in. Plain, drab, old people in wheelchairs decorating the front entrance. "So I guess we just wait around and see where she goes next?"

"Suit yourself," Tessa says.

"What, you think I should go in there? Bombard their little family reunion, put Reena in a headlock and interrogate her about Faith? Her grandma'll have a heart attack on the spot."

Tessa chuckles.

"Besides, I'm sticking to my promise. I told Alis I wouldn't bother her."

We sit and stare at the automatic doors for several minutes before Tessa says, "Of course, *you* don't have to bother her."

I look at her, raising my eyebrows.

"Let's go in pretending we're Lilibeth and Gertrude Bonapart." She laughs at her stupid names. "Alis isn't here. He never has to know." Tessa talks like she's got it all figured out, and it's oh-so-easy.

At least she isn't planning on going in alone. I can imagine the whole staff hitting the floor and raising their hands.

"Right," I say. "They're sure to take us for a Gertrude and Lilibeth. I might as well go in there pretending I'm Annie Mo—" I stop. I haven't told Tessa about Alis and Reena's mom, and I'm not completely sure I want to yet. "I mean, let's just use some normal names. Like someone from school."

Tessa's already out of the car. "Okay, come up with another name, then."

But I am excited. It could work. Or maybe Reena will recognize me as Faith's sister and actually want to talk to me. Maybe Alis has it wrong.

Barely through the sliding doors, I spot Reena. She stands behind the big open administration area, talking to a couple of nurses. She holds a clipboard and the nurses nod back to her in a way that makes me think she not only works here, but she's their boss—that they'll do anything she says—which is weird because she looks like she couldn't be more than a year or two out of high school.

Still, she looks friendly and I feel more and more convinced that Alis was overreacting about the need to stay away from her.

Two hallways break off from the administration desk, with a lobby beside us. Before I've gotten my bearings, I hear a musical female voice coming toward us.

"Excuse me. Can I help you find something?"

I look up. It's her.

"I'm, um, just here to visit someone," I say, only turning an eighth of the way in her direction. My heart speeds up as I wait for her next words. I wait for her to say, "Hey, aren't you Faith's sister?"

"Oh, okay. Do they know you're coming? What's the name?" She walks closer and must be wearing heels, because I hear their *clickety-clack* on the linoleum.

It takes me a second to process her words, since they're not what I expected. In the meantime, Tessa jumps in.

"Lori," she says, extending her hand. Reena places her clipboard on the table beside me and shakes Tessa's hand. "And this is Annie."

"She means my grandma's name, stupid," I say to Tessa, bumping her on the arm, hard, and trying desperately to break the tense silence. I can't believe she just named me after Reena's dead mother.

"Oh yeah, right." Tessa turns back to Reena. "This looks like a great place." She walks toward a couple of men playing chess and Reena's eyes scrutinize her. As Tessa goes on about how much my granny must like it here, I scan Reena's clipboard for the first name I can find.

"Ivorson," I blurt, because Tessa's started making fun of an old man who's fallen asleep in his wheelchair. Reena turns to me. "Sorry. I, um, we're here to see Doris Ivorson. Uh, my grandmother, she doesn't know—"

"Oh." Reena brightens. "You're Mrs. Ivorson's granddaughter?"

I nod, because I have no idea what else to do. I feel a grin cross my face and an ease come over me as Reena's wide eyes meet mine. She seems so friendly and I wish Tessa hadn't given fake names. Reena may be someone I could really talk to, even if she is a bit on the religious side.

"Don't worry about it, Annie, is it?"

The reminder of my fake name makes my lies feel so obvious, like they're written right across my face. But she goes on, apparently not noticing.

"I've been visiting her twice a week for months, and she doesn't know me, either. But I still think it's important that you're here. Everybody needs to feel loved." She nods, with a look of assurance. "Come on, this way to the Alzheimer's wing."

I feel like I can't help myself and follow her down the hall. I'm not sure if it's her voice or her eyes that are pulling me along, but since the whole feeling is so peaceful, it's hard to fight against. I'm about to meet my new, Alzheimer's-inflicted grandma and I'm hardly nervous. I should be. I know I should be, but there's something about Reena.

Tessa hangs back. "I'll give you some time alone and come in a few minutes." But she stops outside a door labeled "Pharmaceutical Supplies." Tessa's voice helps me shake off the slight daze I'd fallen into.

Tessa. Pharmaceutical supplies. Right, so instead of hearing Reena's memories of Faith, we'll get busted for ripping off drugs from old people. Perfect.

When we round the corner into Mrs. Ivorson's room, I prepare my first line.

"Hi Grandma. It's me, Annie."

The frail lady lies on her bed, watching a soap opera on a miniature television. The tiny room is just big enough for her single bed, a dresser, and one other chair. It smells like old people, kind of like dust, but not the kind that gets stuck in your lungs. Reena walks into the room behind me and shuts the door. I'm not sure if her hand slipped on the knob or what, but she opens it and shuts it again.

The old woman hasn't looked over, so I reintroduce myself.

"Jesus!" she replies.

Reena holds her hand in front of her mouth and at first I wonder if she'll scold Mrs. Ivorson for her trespass, but then I see the smile creep out from behind Reena's hand.

"We've been talking about him every day," she whispers to me. "She's starting to remember his name really well."

"Wow, that's so great," I whisper back. "I didn't know if Grandma knew him anymore."

"Praise the Lord!" Mrs. Ivorson says and raises both hands up toward General Hospital.

"Did she ever go to church?" Reena asks.

"Um, yeah. All the time. When she was . . . you know."

Reena nods her understanding. "Which one?"

"Huh?"

"Which church did she—do you go to?"

"Oh, I'm new in town. I mean grandma's been here for, uh—"

"Six months."

"Right, six months, but I just moved to town after my parents split up. Moved here from Canada." Amy's story slips off my tongue like it's my own.

"Oh, I see." She stares at me expectantly and I feel myself starting to fall into a daze again.

Oh yeah, church. I snap myself out of it. "I haven't . . . found a church since I've been in town."

She raises her eyebrows.

"I mean, I've been to a few, but all the churches around here just seem so . . ." Alis's recap of Reena's church life comes back to me. ". . . lukewarm."

Her smile widens, and her eyes light up with a secretive

look. I can't stop my feet from shuffling, so I walk over to where Mrs. Ivorson lies on her bed. After easing down beside her, I scoop an arm around her and say, "Hi, Grandma. I've missed you."

Reena doesn't leave. She just stands there watching us.

"So what's he up to?" I say to my pretend grandmother, motioning to the guy onscreen. Her eyes don't leave her soap opera. She's very serious about this. "Who's he cheating on now?"

"Yes." Mrs. Ivorson nods. "Yes, he is."

I don't know what else to say to this woman. Why is Reena still standing there? "Mom says she'll be up on the weekend," I continue. "And she says to give you a hug for her, too." I reach over and give Mrs. Ivorson another one. This time she smiles, turns, and kisses me on the cheek.

Progress. Okay, maybe I can do this. "So, Grandma, it seems like you've been getting to know this nice nurse pretty well."

"Oh, I'm not a nurse," Reena says, as if I'm suggesting she's the local garbage collector. "I'm here preaching the Gospel. Talking to those who want some hope. I do it a couple times a week."

"Really? That's so . . . giving of you." And I thought *Faith* was a Bible-thumper! I think back to the nurses at the

209

reception area. How they seemed so subordinate to her. I feel her staring at me waiting for more, so I add, "There are so many in the churches who just don't seem to know how to serve," quoting Dad.

She turns her eyes to the window and is silent for several seconds. Did I say it wrong?

"So, Annie. We have this group. I don't know, you seem like our type. Of course I have to talk to the others. . . ."

I jump up from the bed, more out of nervousness than enthusiasm. "Oh, okay. Uh, yeah. I'd love to!"

The words tumble out, even though I know I'll have to retract them somehow. I mean, I assume Celeste would be there. But still, I can't help being excited by the prospect of spending more time with Reena. Spending more time with the friends who really knew my sister.

I keep my eyes on her hands as she pulls a paper off the bottom of her clipboard and says, "What's your last name again?"

I only pause for a second, then give her a fake one and my cell number, glad I still have that generic voice mail greeting, stating only my number. Now doesn't seem like the best time to tell her about my lies. Besides, it seems easier somehow to get to know her as someone else. Someone who fits with her. For the moment, I need to come up with an excuse to get out of here before I say anything else stupid.

"I have to get home before dinner to walk the"—as I'm about to say "dog," a jolt of panic hits me that maybe she knows Faith had a dog—"um, rabbit."

"You have to walk your rabbit?"

"Yeah." I nod. "He's really overweight. Just, um, around the yard."

She crinkles her forehead.

It's not *that* far-fetched. I wave and slip out the door.

When I meet Tessa back in the Volkswagen, it feels like my lungs are on fire. How long have I gone without breathing? Tessa stares at me and taps the steering wheel, waiting for the story.

I take a quick glance in the backseat and thankfully don't see any stolen pill bottles.

Looking over at her, I say the words slowly. "I think I just accidentally joined her home group."

chapter TWENTY

b y the end of the week I still haven't heard from Reena. I'm zoning out at my locker at lunchtime when Tessa slams her hand against the door beside me.

I can't stop the flinch, but compose myself quickly.

Without looking at me, she puts her books away and asks where I'm going to eat lunch.

"Uh, I don't know." I usually go to the cafeteria and perch on the end of someone's bench these days, keeping my eyes to myself, but I'm quite sure if I walk in with Tessa Lockbaum, the ends of all the benches will suddenly be overrun.

"You want to go to Wendy's?" she asks.

It's only a block away. I slip my hand in my purse and feel a few stray pennies at the bottom.

"I'm buying," she says, as if she can read my mind.

I nod. "Sounds good." But then over her shoulder I get a flicker of familiar dark hair and red checkered jacket in the sea of students. It couldn't be . . . Alis?

Oh, right. He's probably here to take another test. I turn away to slide my books into my locker since I said I wouldn't bother him anymore. But when I look to see if Tessa's ready, he still stands there, leaning against a locker less than twenty feet away, staring at me. I wonder if he somehow heard about the senior center.

"Hey, Tessa," I say. "Can we take a rain check on lunch?"

She follows my eyes, and then shuts her locker with a bang. "Yeah, sure. Whatever," she says and tromps right through my line of vision and down the hall.

Uh-oh. Definitely offended. I cringe, feeling caught between running after her and staying to talk to Alis.

She disappears around the corner, as have the majority of the students who were here a second ago. I inch toward Alis, leaving my locker wide open. His mouth is a flat line of non-emotion.

"Here for a test?" I ask.

He offers one nod. I feel stupid, my heart rate going berserk over his cuteness when he so obviously isn't here for me.

"Oh yeah?" I'm hoping he'll open up the conversation, but he stares blankly at me. Feeling uncomfortable, I turn back toward my locker. I should have gone after Tessa.

"But it got rescheduled," he says suddenly, like he finally remembered how to work his mouth. He gestures to Clancy's classroom. "Sometimes it works out at lunchtime, sometimes it doesn't. But I thought maybe we could talk."

Since I'm already facing the other direction, I head the twenty feet back to my locker. I feel like I need a few seconds to settle into the idea of this. Strengthen myself in case he found out about my run-in with Reena. Though the more that I think about it, Reena seems the more levelheaded, or at least the more relaxed, of the two of them. Alis makes me so tense and I wonder with his strange overreactions the other day if he's the one I should be avoiding, cute or not. I close my locker door and turn to him. His eyes flit away from me, like I suddenly make *him* nervous.

"Okay." I walk back toward him, studying him to see if I've got it wrong.

"Can we go somewhere a little more private?" he asks.

I raise my eyebrows, an automatic reaction, even though I know he doesn't mean it like that.

"My sister will be here to pick me up, and I don't want her—" He shakes his head. "Never mind."

"Oh. Yeah, sure." My breath quickens and I'm not sure if it's from his nerves or my own.

He motions his head to the side and leads me toward the history classroom. "Mr. Clancy's at a meeting in the office."

He pulls the door open and we slip inside. I back into Clancy's desk and lean against it while Alis turns to face me.

"Listen, I wanted to say I'm sorry. I've been thinking about you and your sister a lot, and I just . . . I guess I want to help you. I mean, if you want to find out more about her."

"I do!" I jump to my feet. "Thanks, Alis."

He picks at the edge of his jacket. "Look, I'm not very good with . . . I mean, I haven't been around people my age in years, and now . . ."

No friends for that long? Not that I have any real friendships to brag about at the moment.

"I, uh, I've been homeschooled for a long time," he adds.

He's sincere. Either that or he's the best actor on the planet. "Don't they have social clubs and stuff for homeschoolers?"

"Yeah, they do, but . . ." He looks down and scuffs his feet. "Ever since Mom died . . ."

"Yeah." I try to peek under his bangs to see his eyes but

they're half-closed and shaded by his long eyelashes. "I read about that."

"It was a long time ago." He turns away to the blackboard, as if he's reading Clancy's long list of history notes. "Reena and Dad haven't been the same."

I try to figure out what this has to do with my sister, but I sense that maybe I shouldn't ask and search for a better question. "Is your dad depressed?"

"I don't know what he is." Alis leans on the desk beside me, bringing him a few inches closer. "Dad's on the road a lot, so we don't see him much."

"Who lives with you?"

His eyes move back to the history lesson on the board. "I can trust you, right?"

Well, no, not to tell the truth, but with other stuff, yeah, probably. "Of course."

"My dad's been a trucker for years. When I was little, it was mostly overnight trips. After Mom died, he started taking longer trips though. Said we needed the money."

He stands again and walks over to the blackboard. Picking up the eraser, he turns it over in his hands.

"I think he just needed some time to himself. He wanted us to move to another state to live with an aunt we've never met, but Ree went ballistic."

Alis puts the eraser down and digs his hands into his pockets.

"So did your aunt move out here with you then?"

He shakes his head. "Reena came up with this elaborate idea to start an online homeschooling program. She printed off pages and pages of info about it, convinced our dad how responsible she was and how she could not only teach herself, but teach me as well. And then when our aunt said she couldn't take us in anyway—"

"So, what? You guys live completely on your own?"

"Reena's almost eighteen now," he says, as if that explains everything.

But I do the math. If his Mom died three years ago, Reena would have been only fourteen. Alis must see something in my reaction because he jumps in on my thoughts.

"No one really knows. The school board sends things home for Dad to sign, but Reena perfected his signature right after Mom died. Dad was determined to stay out of town as much as possible, and Reena was set on staying in our house."

"Wow." I'd like to say it must be great to not have anyone to answer to, but somehow I don't think that's the case. "It must be . . . lonely." It's not until the words leave my mouth that they hit me and I feel that automatic connection again with Alis. I can relate, wishing for parents who would be part of my life in a real way, not just consumed with their own emotional troubles.

He nods and turns back to face me. "I knew you'd understand. Reena warns me all the time not to tell anyone, and especially not to get into trouble."

Suddenly it all makes sense, why he was so frantic to keep me from his family. "So that's why you wanted me to stay away?"

"Yeah. I don't know, maybe it's an overreaction, but we just need to keep everything quiet. At least until Reena's birthday. She'd kill me if I screwed things up for her."

Reena seemed so friendly, and again I wonder if Alis's perception is off, but I nod as though I understand.

I see a flash of dirty blond hair through Clancy's window. It's her. But she hasn't looked this way yet. I drop down into a student chair in the front row and tilt my head low toward the desk. I don't want Alis to get in trouble, not to mention Reena finding out about my lies.

"It's just with my family," he goes on, but he's having the hardest time getting the words out. I feel bad for him, and want to interrupt and make him feel better, but I know Reena could open the door any second. "Ree and I have learned to count on each other—"

"Hey, let's talk later," I say. "You should probably get

going." I move to the side wall so I won't be seen when he opens the door. But then I notice his face. He looks hurt. And maybe scared, now that he's told me all these secrets. "I'd like to talk to you more," I say, and it's true, because in all this we didn't end up talking about Faith at all. Now that the conversation has opened up, I do have hope that we will, though. "Can you meet me later today? After school?"

He gets the blank look again, but only for a second.

"Okay," he replies, and then suggests a meeting location out behind the football field. I come up with a quick excuse of why I need to wait for Mr. Clancy and watch Alis walk out of the room, off to meet his sister.

I spend the rest of the afternoon once again unable to concentrate on my schoolwork. I've had about two good days of classes so far. Not nearly enough to get me any passing grades.

I sidle up to Tessa's desk in art class that afternoon. "That was Alis," I tell her, expecting her to be excited when she understands. "And we scheduled another meeting for later."

"A meeting?" She glares at me. "A date, you mean."

"We're taking a walk." I wave her off. "No big deal."

"Obviously he's tracking you down for a reason, and I don't think the reason's your sister." She looks me up and down.

My face heats up at the suggestion. For a second I think she's jealous. Of me, of him, I don't know. But then it hits me what this is all about. I'm not inviting Tessa along, letting her be a part of the "investigation," so she needs to make it my fault. But I really can't picture Alis opening up in front of Tessa.

"What are you talking about?" I try to dismiss it.

She shakes her head. "It's a good thing you're cute."

"So, what? You're saying he likes me?" Again, I feel a flush to my cheeks.

Her right eyebrow raises in agreement.

"Come on, Tessa. He's just looking for a friend. He's lonely."

"I'll bet he is." She reaches to the empty desk beside hers, grabs a piece of black construction paper, and folds the edge of it.

I ball my fists and force some strength. "Give me a break. Look, we're just friends." I head for my desk.

"Right, just friends," she says from behind me. "Because that's what friends do. Dupe each other and secretly spy on their siblings."

All I can think of the rest of the afternoon is whether or not I should tell Alis about the nursing home. It almost seems too late now. The first person he thinks might possibly be someone he can trust betrays him within the first week.

chapter TWENTY-ONE

Plan U: I need to tell him, I do.

Alis stands exactly where he said he'd be, near the break in the fence across the backfield. He is a good-looking guy, I'll give him that. But I'm not in the market for another boyfriend, thank you very much. Besides, if I have to pick a family to get cozy with, the Monachies aren't exactly at the top of my list.

"Hey," he says when I'm close enough. "I'm glad you came."

Even though I feel a bit of weakness in my knees at his voice, I force a strong and casual tone. "I said I would, didn't I?" But after the words leave my mouth, I feel a rush of guilt, because it implies I keep all my promises. "Your sister's not around, is she?"

"Nah. She's at work."

"Yeah? Where does she work?" I feel like such a fraud, playing dumb, but I have to find a way to tell him gently.

"Well, it's not really a job. She helps out over at a nursing home on the East Side. You know the one?" He makes a rolling motion with his hand like he wants me to fill in the blank.

"Um, no," I blurt, and I don't even know why.

He leans his back against an intact piece of fence and eyes me. "Really?"

My face heats up. "Well, I mean, my grandma's in one." This part, at least, is true.

He turns to walk down the trail leading away from the school.

Great. He knows. *Stupendous job of being up front and honest, Brie.*

I rush to catch up. "I kind of ran into your sister by accident."

He stops and swings around, his face suddenly pale.

"She doesn't know who I am or anything," I add quickly.

He doesn't move, just stares at me. "Where did you see her?" His tone sounds angry, nervous, but at least he's giving me a chance to explain.

"I was, uh, visiting someone at the Bertram Senior Center." Okay, well, maybe not complete honesty, but at least I'm coming close now. "I saw Reena at the front desk, and I recognized her from Faith's Facebook page, and also from—"

"When you were outside my house." Alis says the words before I can, like he's in too much of a hurry for this story.

"Anyway, we sort of got to talking," I say. Alis shoots me a look like his heart just stopped. "I mean about religion and stuff. Not about Faith." I can't figure this family out. Is he really this afraid of her? "When she asked my name, I gave her a fake one, and I really don't think she recognized me. She didn't come to Faith's memorial service, did she?"

He shakes his head. "Reena didn't want anything to do with you or your family. At least that's what she said. Didn't want to meet you because you weren't a believer and didn't want to attend a service at a 'lukewarm' church. I can never tell what she's really thinking or how she'll react."

He gets quiet after that and I'm not sure if he's mad or just wants to get away from me. He keeps leading the way through the trail, which becomes denser with leaves and branches. Unfortunately, from my view all I can concentrate on is the silver nub sticking out of his back pocket. His knife. And I wonder just how stupid this is to be following this armed guy who may or may not be angry with me.

He stops and peers through a portion of brush where I can hear the rush of a stream. After stomping out some of the lower branches, he tries to break one right up near his face to get through. It's thick though, and he struggles with it.

Before I can think, my mouth opens and I confront my fear. "Why don't you use your knife?"

He glances over his shoulder, his eyebrows raised like he didn't quite hear me. But then a second later, he reaches for his back pocket and I suck in my breath.

When he pulls it out, I can see that yes, it is a knife. Dad has one that looks almost identical that he keeps in his fishing kit. Alis flips it over a few times in his hands and then pulls at one side of it. When that does nothing, he flips it over and tries the other side. A serrated blade pops out.

I try to relax at the fact that he doesn't seem to even know how to use the thing. Alis doesn't strike me as the type to carry a knife in the first place. But I study his profile as he saws away at the upper part of the branch.

"Why do you carry a knife?" I force out, a wobble still in my voice.

"My mom gave it to me for my last birthday before she died. Since she's gone I like to carry it around." He passes it to me, which settles my nerves dramatically. And he doesn't seem angry anymore. Not at all.

I immediately recognize the inscription on the side as a Bible verse Dad's read to us before. "The weapons of our warfare are not carnal," I read aloud.

"Not sure exactly what it means, but it was a big deal to Mom when she gave it to me. Probably would've been more appropriate for Reena. She's more of a fighter."

"So your mom was pretty religious, huh? That must be where Reena gets it." I stop and cringe. "Oh, sorry, are you religious too?"

He laughs. "Not especially. I have more questions than anything."

"Yeah, me too." It's probably my turn to open up a bit more. I bite my lip, trying to decide where to start. "I guess the most likely answer is that Faith committed suicide. There are verses highlighted all over her Bible about martyrs and sacrifices and stuff, but I always thought she was too trusting, like she'd be willing to wait for God's timing on things."

"Hmm," Alis says. "That seems more like *my* sister to not want to wait for things."

"Yeah?" I'm surprisingly relieved that he changed the subject back to Reena.

"She has obsessive-compulsive disorder."

"Really?" OCD had always been kind of a joke around school. I didn't think of it as an actual affliction that real people suffered from.

"It wasn't so bad when we were younger, but when she turned about thirteen, it got pretty severe. We all went to church, but Reena suddenly got extra involved. My parents stopped going because they thought they should rein her in, but she went the other way and started reading all sorts of religious books and watching those evangelism shows all day on Sundays. Maybe we all would've been better off if my parents had kept her in a church setting after all."

"Why? Did something happen?"

"Well, yeah." We make it to the stream and he stares down into the water for several seconds before going on. "My mom drove over a curb and into a lake. We all thought it was an accident, until we found her suicide note at home. Actually, it wasn't much of a suicide note. More like a love letter. To Jesus."

I can't think of any kind of response. I'd always thought of my own family as crazy, overboard religious, but they suddenly seemed like the median of spiritual mediocrity. "But I thought your parents weren't that religious. Not like Reena?"

"That's what I thought too, but Reena explained to me that Mom had been suppressing her feelings about God for quite a while."

I nod, trying to connect all these new details with the girl I'd met in the senior center.

"Reena's rituals got kind of weird after Mom's death. She tried to teach me stuff about the Bible in homeschool, but

I asked questions on so many things that she didn't want to answer, and eventually she said something about not wanting me to taint her beliefs. She never brought up the lessons again and never invited me into her special group. She locks me out of her religious life just like she locks me out of her room."

I can tell he feels jilted by his sister. It makes sense, since she's all he has.

A few seconds later, he regains the evenness to his voice. "That's why I was so glad when the group started meeting at our house. I thought they'd help Reena sort out any delusions she had about God. Especially your sister. Even though I wasn't allowed into the meetings, I could tell Faith stood up for herself and what she believed. I knew she'd be good for Reena."

But was Reena good for my sister? I couldn't help but question it. Faith always thought she could help everybody. But how much had Reena changed Faith? "Do you think Reena could, um, hurt anybody?"

"Uh-uh. Not Ree." He jerks his head to me. "Wait, you don't think—"

"No," I say. Even though I'm not completely convinced about anything at this point, his quick reaction does calm my suspicions a little. Reena might keep him at arm's length when it comes to her little spiritual group, but otherwise they seem pretty tight. Alis would know if his sister were some kind of bloodthirsty psychopath.

I shiver, and he must notice because he places his hands on both sides of my arms and rubs them.

His hands feel warm and nice, but I remember Tessa's scowling face and suddenly feel determined not to think of him like that. "We should probably head back soon."

He turns, slides his arm around me and pulls me close to him as we start back for the school. A millisecond later, he drops it. "Uh, sorry, I didn't mean . . ."

I wonder what he *did* mean, because something about it felt more than just brotherly. "No, it's okay," I say. He shoves his hands deep into his pockets.

The crunching of the leaves under our feet is the only sound for a long time. But a comfort grows between us. After all he's told me, I feel stupid about the one little lie I told him.

"Look," I say. "I don't know anyone in the Bertram Home."

He glances over at me, then ahead to the path in front of us.

"I saw Reena downtown and followed her because I wanted to feel closer to Faith. I wasn't going to talk to her, really I wasn't, but—"

"Don't worry about it," he says. Then he looks at me. "I

trust you," he says. "I don't know quite why, but I feel like we can understand each other."

He's right. I know he is. And it feels so good, necessary even, to have someone who understands me right now. "You get where I'm at with my sister, then?"

He nods.

We get back to the school, and Alis says he'll call me if he can, and suggests we meet on Monday when Reena's working. He'll walk me home from school.

While I watch him walk away, I consider my new social circle. Alis. Tessa.

Who'd have thought?

chapter TWENTY-TWO

*m*r. Poindexter's Art room is more like an
experimental color lab than an actual
classroom. Rainbow paintings are slath-
ered across every wall.

Tessa and I don't share the intent of Art class or anything.
She's private about her creations. Now I realize she seats herself at the back between two empty desks because she's so
serious. I sit in the middle because I'm so not. I approach art
like my poetry. I just kind of smush color on the page and if it
looks like something recognizable by the end, yippee.

Because I can't make sense of the angle I'm supposed to
draw my still life at today, I play around with words instead.

First my name, then anything I can come up with to rhyme with it. One reason I'm thankful for my cheesy name: Brie, sea, tea, bee . . . the list goes on and on.

My mind wanders to Alis. Does anything rhyme with Alis? Hmm. Oh, wait. Malice.

Uh-oh.

Mr. Poindexter walks my way so I flip my paper and draw a big oval with a squiggly line through the center. It looks nothing like the artifact at the front of the class. Looks more like I'm in the third grade. But Poindexter doesn't stop, not even a glance in my direction. I haven't produced anything awe-inspiring so far this year. I'm sure he doesn't expect that to change.

By the time the next bell rings, I've added a bit of color, but it still looks like something Celeste's little brother could have drawn.

This thought makes me realize I still haven't heard anything from Celeste. Not that I'm surprised after the way she acted at Starbucks. Tessa heads my way, so I quickly flip my drawing over and place my hand on top to hold it down.

"How was yours?" I ask.

She tilts her head with a half scowl, staring at my desk. I follow her eyes to the back of my paper.

"I knew it!" she says. "You're hung up on the guy."

I'd written my name and Alis's about a million times, trying to come up with rhymes.

"It's not what you think," I start to say.

But she's already gone.

The next day, I avoid Tessa for most of the morning. Of course, I'm also trying to steer clear of Amy, Dustin, and Steph, and it would be more than I could possibly expect to avoid them all.

I'm taking a shortcut past the library toward my history class when I catch sight of Dustin's sandy-colored hair and red Stanford sweatshirt leaning against a wall near the library doors. I keep my eyes straight ahead, but hear a giggle from his direction. A giggle that's not Amy's.

Part of me wants to look and feel the satisfaction of seeing him cheating on her. But the other part of me wonders if I could be reading things wrong again. I decide I'd rather live in my bubble, think that maybe I'm not the only one Dustin's ever been a jerk to, and move on.

That afternoon when I finally do run into Tessa, she wears a pink turtleneck under the black trench coat she takes off at her locker. Soft, baby, never-consider-using-a-four-letter-word pink.

"Nice shirt," I say.

She shoots me a look, warning me not to say another word.

"So, this Alis guy is pretty cool," I say, "but that doesn't mean I like him."

Her eyes don't show the anger I expect. Instead, they light up. She's almost as interested in my life these days as I am. "So what'd you talk about?"

"I wasn't going to, but I told him the truth. About everything."

"Huh." She drops her backpack with a thud in front of her locker. "Was he pissed? Did he ditch you again?"

"No. He seemed to get it. I think he understands why I can't just move on."

She shoves her backpack inside and shuts the door, not bothering to extract any books.

"We mostly talked about Faith. And his sister. Just some weird stuff about their meetings and—"

"Weird stuff?" She grabs my books and throws them into my locker. Shuts the door and clicks my lock on. "Let's go to Wendy's. We have to talk about this."

"But I've got English."

She doesn't even look back.

And the truth is, this is all I want to talk about anyway.

Wendy's is deserted, so we sit in a corner where we can see the parking lot through the windows. She asks me questions about my conversation with Alis, and I do my best to answer her. But because Alis trusted me, I only give her half truths about their family situation.

Tessa catches on that I'm being evasive. "Come on. What is it? You're obviously into him."

"Why am I obviously into him? I'm not in the space where I need any of that crap right now." The more I talk like this, the more I'm convincing myself. "Will you get off me about it already?"

"'Not in that space.' *Phtf*. It's written all over your face, Brie. You want him."

"I don't *want* him." But my face heats up at the words. Well, *maybe* I don't.

"You're shittin' me." She takes a sip of her coffee. "You're shittin' yourself."

The pink obviously isn't working for her. "You know what? This is not a good time. Who cares if I want him, or like him, or even just think he's cute." My face feels like it's three hundred degrees, but I grip my chair and go on. "My sister just died. Can't you get that? I have plenty of reasons to not be in the right space, for your information."

She doesn't say anything for a while. At least thirty seconds. Then, "Sorry."

"It's okay," I say. I think it's over, that she's finally going to leave it alone, since that's what any normal person would do.

Her lip twitches into a smirk. "Fine. But if you're going to be friends with this guy, it's time I got to meet him."

I nod, thinking that's it, and that's a fair demand, but she goes on.

"And you have to convince him to help us break into Reena's room. I want to see what she's hiding in there."

Want to what? Alis will never agree to that. But I force a smile and nod again, figuring I'll come up with something to pacify her later. At least I have two people on my team now. Even if the team might be a bit of a job to bring together.

chapter TWENTY-THREE

*m*y parents are both still at work when Tessa pulls up in our driveway just after four the next day. I'm getting used to her behind the wheel. So far, she hasn't put us into any life-threatening situations. Considering her lack of instruction, she drives pretty well.

She honks, but I'm still layering my clothes to avoid wearing a jacket. When I open the door to her knocking only minutes later, she looks like I'm wearing on her nerves already. I jot a note for Dad, explaining I'm going to a friend's house. I include Tessa's cell number, just in case.

"Good to go," I say cheerily.

She rolls her eyes.

I still can't believe Alis agreed to let us come over. He didn't even put up a fight about Tessa coming along, or about her lock-picking plan. He must be curious about Reena's room too.

Tessa checks her watch twice on the way to the car. I wait for her to suggest we synchronize. She loves this covert stuff.

My heart beats techno-fast on the ride over. I take calming breaths. "When do you have to get the car back?" I have to talk to keep my mind off things. Even sneaking into Faith's room made me nervous, and I sure didn't have to worry about *her* walking in on me.

Tessa shrugs. She's not exactly making this conversation flow.

"Do you think your parents suspect you drive it?" I try again.

She glances over with a raised eyebrow. I'm not sure what the look is all about, but I'm a lot less concerned about that than I am about her keeping her eyes on the road.

"It's just me and my dad," she says. "And I guess you don't know him." She faces forward again.

What am I supposed to say to that? Of course I don't know her dad. She made me wait outside her stupid apartment! But her words make me wonder if she was hiding something in there. Like me staying outside wasn't just a matter of convenience or keeping me at arm's length.

I test the waters. "You're right. I don't know anything. What's your dad like?" After her tone, I know better than to ask what happened to her mom.

Tessa taps the steering wheel. We go through a couple more intersections before she says anything. "You want to know what my dad is like, huh?"

I don't bother answering, since it sounds rhetorical.

"Come over tomorrow after school," she says. "You'll see."

Plan V: Breaking and Entering 101.

A few minutes later, Tessa drives right past the Monachie's cul-de-sac.

"You missed it!"

She shakes her head. "Come on, think, Jenkins." When she calls me Jenkins, it gives me the feeling I'm growing on her. "We don't want what's-her-face to recognize this car. We need to keep it hidden. Just in case."

Just in case what? I want to ask. But I bite my lip to keep my dumb questions to myself.

We walk a block and a half back toward the house, and then Alis separates from the shadows, and waves from the side of the house by the garden swing. We skirt around the corner in his direction.

"Come through the back," he whispers when we get close enough.

I awkwardly gesture at Tessa. "Alis, this is Tessa. Tessa . . . Alis."

Tessa's eyes dart back and forth between us. Then she studies Alis and his preppy polo shirt. Eventually, they both nod at each other. Alis stares down at her skull belt buckle. This is not exactly a friendship waiting to happen.

He opens the sliding glass door off the porch and we enter his small kitchen. Tessa takes a slouching position against the sink and Alis leans on the kitchen table. I hover between them.

The yellow walls with rose wallpaper bordering around the upper perimeter could've been in style a decade or two ago. The paint on the cupboards is chipped and the whole room feels much older than it had from the outside.

Tessa glances between the clock and her wristwatch.

"Synchronizing?" I joke, trying to break the awkward silence.

She scowls. "I'm setting my alarm for five-fifteen."

"We better get a move on," Alis says. "I've been trying to pick the lock on her bedroom door, but . . ." He shifts like he wants someone to interrupt. "Maybe you'd be better at this sort of thing," he says to Tessa.

"Me? Why?" she says in false shock.

"Well, no. I mean, I just thought—" He shoots me a look, and I'm about to take the brunt of this one when she pushes past him.

"Shut up." She leads the way. I can tell she's joking, but by the look on Alis's face, he has no idea. I follow them up the stairs, wishing I had a better idea of why we are even here. I always thought it was more a girl thing to sneak into a sibling's room. Then again, Alis seems protective of his sister and I wonder if he worries about what her group is into after what happened with Faith. Maybe he wants to make sure Reena doesn't plan on following in Faith's footsteps.

Along the stairwell, I notice tiny nails in the walls, but no pictures. Not even one. "How long have you guys lived here?" I ask Alis.

"Most of my life. We moved from the other side of Salem when I was three."

Tessa swings doors open one by one, poking her head into each room and not bothering to ask which one is Reena's. She'll find it herself.

Alis scoots past her. "It's this one." He rattles the locked knob and gives Tessa a warning look.

Tessa fiddles with something in her black jacket and pulls out a foot-long rod of metal. She gets down on her knees and sticks it into the keyhole. Alis eyes me, and I give him a nod to let him know she won't bust Reena's door. He still looks doubtful. We turn our eyes back to Tessa, but it seems to take forever. She pushes and looks relieved, then leans in closer and fidgets some more.

"Are you . . . Do you think you'll be able to?" Alis ventures.

She glares up at him. Holds out the rod. "You wanna try?"

He takes a step back.

Thirty seconds later, a click sounds. "All yours," Tessa says to Alis. She knocks him on the leg with her wand so hard I hear the *snap*, but if it bothers Alis, he doesn't show it.

He reaches to try the knob. When it turns, a smile tugs at the side of his mouth.

Alis holds the door open, and Tessa and I walk through. He follows behind us. I lean into the wall, thoroughly creeped-out by my first glance at Reena's hidden world.

Taped around Reena's walls are papers with Bible verses— that much I expected—but there's also what I could only describe as hate messages, strewn among them. AN EYE FOR AN EYE, in big bold letters. VENGEANCE IS MINE. HATE YOUR MOTHER AND FATHER AND SISTER AND BROTHER . . . EVEN YOUR OWN LIFE.

"What is this?" Tessa asks. "Some kind of labyrinth of deep-seated confusion?"

Across the length of her ceiling is a large hand-drawn,

half-painted picture of a cross. If not for what's attached to the cross, I would love to lie back and admire the artistry. But the unmistakable likeness to Reena overlapping the ornate drawing causes my eyes to shoot away and down to the floor. At least her brown shag carpet is nothing unusual.

When I hear Alis gasp beside me, I glance up. He's taking in the whole room at once. I wonder how recently Reena did all this.

"Let's get to work," Tessa says. She, obviously, is over the shock.

I want to ask Alis if he's okay, if he wants me to do this instead, but when Tessa starts yanking open drawers, he crouches by her bookcase, running his thumb along the spines of her small library. Many of them are Bibles, and again I wonder why one person needs so many. I follow him over and lean down beside him.

He pulls off a hardcover book of photography. It's coated in dust and I hold back a sneeze.

"This was my mom's." He fans through the pages, and now I do sneeze. I turn my head, so as not to get any spray on his heirloom.

He removes a card from the middle. A piece of notepaper slips out, which he scans, and then slides under the cover of the book. Without acknowledging it, he flips back to the card and opens it. "An old birthday card. For my dad."

I peer over his shoulder at the card addressed to Henry. The whole left-hand side is covered in cursive writing and signed *I love you. Annie.*

"This is from your mom to your dad? Why does Reena have it?"

He scans the writing and shakes his head. "Just memories, I guess."

"Are you okay?" I whisper. He doesn't answer right away, and I put my hand on his shoulder.

"Check these out," Tessa says, holding out a pair of silky full-fit underwear from Reena's drawer. "Looks like something my grandma would wear." Tessa cackles, which for a second seems like it's aimed right at Alis and his pain. When I look at him, his jaw is tense.

"Come on, Tessa." I scoot over, take the underwear, and shove it back in the drawer. I wonder what she's even looking for. Did she really suggest we break in here so she could check out Reena's undergarments? "Please stop," I add when she reaches for the next drawer.

She glares at me.

Turning away, I head over to the window to avoid her bullying eyes. But that's not any less scary, since the second-story view makes me jittery. At home I keep my blinds closed and my bed as far from the window as humanly possible for this very reason. I put my hands up on either side of Reena's large window frame to catch my breath, but the latch is loose and I shriek when it suddenly gives way under my hands and the cold outside air blasts against me.

In less than a second, Tessa grabs my arm and jerks me away from the window. "Will you shut up! You scared the crap out of me."

I snap my mouth shut and glance at Alis apologetically, but he's just staring down into another book. I'm afraid he's on the verge of telling us both to get out, so I turn the opposite direction for Reena's nightstand while Tessa pulls the window closed.

I take measured breaths and try to focus. Under Reena's bedside lamp, I find a rectangular pad. My hand catches on a hook of paper, sticking out from it. I place the lamp on the floor out of the way, and pick up the rectangular piece.

When I flip it over, the papers attached on the back side fall loose toward me. "Hey, look," I say. "A calendar."

The first thing I notice is it's still on September. There are notes in almost every square, with times listed. Most say seven o'clock, but there are a few as early as five. There are also a few acronyms scattered on different dates. Most of them read *YE*.

I feel Alis's breath over my other shoulder. The only

noticeably different square is one near the bottom. September twenty-fifth, the day that Faith died. It says OR. *Talk to Faith.* When I flip to October and then November, the pages are empty.

"Faith?" Alis says from behind me. I turn back. He looks as serious as I feel, but I can tell in his eyes that he doesn't have any more answers than I do. If anything, just more questions.

"I bet these are those home group meetings," I say, pointing to the times. It's all I can do to distance myself. I try to think of the whole thing like a puzzle and not like the key to the last moments of my sister's life.

I look up from the calendar to Reena's strange room decor and shake my head. "It's like she's in some kind of cult."

"No," Alis says too quickly. Defensively. "It's not . . ." He stops. "We have to go soon," he whispers.

The truth is, I want out of here way more than I want to keep looking. My stomach feels queasy. I try to give him a look that says it's okay. That whatever this is, my sister was wrapped up in it too.

He doesn't see me though and turns to make his way to the door with fists clenched.

"Wait!" Tessa is crouched down near the bottom drawer of a file cabinet, flipping through an open file. "I thought this was all just homeschool shit, but look."

Alis and I both kneel beside her. The first thing I see is a page of stickers at the front of the file. Five more of the same yellow ones Faith and Celeste had on their dashes. Several more in orange, red, and black. Tessa starts reading from another page.

"Yellow Entry Level," she says. "It says they need to memorize these eight Bible verses and prove their lives to be pure." Her eyes scan the page for anything else of interest.

I can't believe she's found explanations of what this home group is all about. But somehow the whole thing sounds a lot more normal than I'd expected.

"Orange Level Two," Tessa reads from another sheet. "Otherwise known as The Martyrdom Level."

"It says that?" I pull the paper down so I can see it too.

"Look at all those verses," Alis says. "There's got to be at least thirty."

"Do they all have to do with martyrs?" I ask.

Tessa scans the sheet. "I think so."

I pick at the carpet under my knees. "Faith had one of those yellow stickers in her car." I can't help my mind going to the possibility of her having an orange one somewhere else. Somewhere I hadn't seen.

"But if there were four levels, how could they actually martyr themselves at level two?" Tessa asks. And this makes sense. I start to relax a little, but the room is so silent, and when Tessa's watch beeps, it sounds like a fire alarm.

"Crap, we gotta go." Tessa pushes all the papers back into the file. "We have to keep this."

"No!" Alis tries to grab it from her. "She'll know. Reena's meticulous with her stuff. No way."

Tessa grits her teeth, so I quickly grab it from both of them. "Listen, I know there's more in here, but we'll have to come back." I pass it to Alis.

Tessa turns and stalks away, thudding down the stairs like she's three hundred pounds.

"She's a little hard to get used to," I tell Alis. "Thanks for letting us do this."

He offers a half smile, then bends down to tidy up the mess of papers Tessa left. "You better go."

I back toward the hallway, wanting to stay and make sure we're okay, but also in a panic to get out. Not coming up with anything else to say, though, I finally turn and rush to catch up to Tessa just outside the back door.

We cut through a path in the backyard to get to her car. It's twenty-five after by the time we leave. I let out my breath when we finally drive away from their cul-de-sac.

Tessa's still pissed, I can tell by the way she keeps her face away from me. I try to think of a way to calm her down, but she opens her mouth before I can come up with anything.

"You need to get back to your homework before your teachers start getting on your case," she says, surprising me with her sudden change in temperament. "One of us might go to college, and at the moment, it's looking in my favor."

I wonder how she knows I'm behind on schoolwork. And that all of my teachers have been giving me a break. Personal experience, I suppose. But now that we're getting some answers about Faith, even if some unexpected answers, I actually think I could concentrate on a bit of homework. Tessa hits the brakes just outside my house. "Call me," I say.

She nods. "No meetings coming up on Reena's calendar, huh?"

That's when it strikes me. Alis says Reena hasn't had any meetings at the house. Not since the night of Faith's death.

"But she invited me to a group," I say. "The meetings must still be happening."

"Yup. You're right. That means we just have to find out where."

chapter TWENTY-FOUR

for most of the next day, I look for Tessa and can't find her. She doesn't show up at her locker and I wonder if she's skipping. I can't help thinking that it could be because she doesn't want to bring me home after school. I already told Dad, and he seemed pleased I was going to a friend's house.

But on my way out the front doors at the end of the day, there she is, waiting for me. I start to ask her where she's been, but she interrupts with, "Don't ask."

Okayyyy. But she motions with her head for me to follow her toward the bus. That's a good sign at least. I board behind her and sit in silence while she stares out the side window.

The bus pulls up in Tessa's neighborhood and we get off. We walk into the lobby of her dark apartment building. The walls in the hallways aren't the usual light cream or beige colors you normally see, but murky forest green instead. And the doors to each apartment are an old, scuffed-up brown.

I follow Tessa to apartment number thirty-two and she slides her key into the lock.

The inside isn't any brighter than the outside. The walls within my vision are a dark navy blue. The pictures on the walls—large family gatherings, smaller family portraits—cram into one another, almost overlapping. Many are similar, four people in the same burgundy-and-white outfits, like they're all from the same photo shoot, but somebody doesn't want a single one to get wasted in a drawer.

"This is your family?" I whisper. It seems deathly quiet in here, and I figure her dad must be taking a nap if he's home.

"Yup," Tessa says.

I look at her, just for a second, and then back at the pictures. My breath catches. Tessa and her sister who was hit by the truck. Corey. Tessa, maybe in kindergarten, seriously looks like a fairy princess. So happy. The blond is such a far cry from her current jet-black look, I can't get my head around it.

"Come on," she says, and pulls me down the hall. I doubt anyone in our whole school has ever been in this apartment and it feels weird, scary even, that she wants to bring me here.

A slight humming sounds when we get farther into the apartment, but this time it's not Faith. It's a deeper hum that I might mistake for a household appliance, but then it changes octaves.

We turn the corner into the living room, and I get my first glimpse of Mr. Lockbaum. He sits at a computer desk with his back to us. It's late afternoon, but he wears a gray robe and scuffed black slippers. His hair, sticking up like a punk rocker's, looks like it hasn't been brushed yet today.

"Hey, Dad. This is my friend, Brie."

The casual words stun me. I guess I thought I'd never hear them.

Mr. Lockbaum cuts his humming, switches off his computer screen, and spins on his stool to face us, beaming.

"A friend? Oh, Brie. It's so good to have you here." He stands and reaches over to place both hands on my shoulders. He's not a big man, more like a teenager who never filled out. I would have expected Tessa's father to be much tougher-looking. "Are you girls hungry? Why don't you go play in Tessa's room, and I'll make you up a little snack." He backs toward what must be the kitchen. "I'll call you when it's ready."

Play in Tessa's room?

"Watch this," Tessa whispers, so only I can hear. Then, "That's okay, Dad." She walks for the kitchen. I'm not sure what she's doing or expecting, so I stay glued to my spot. "I'll just make us a couple of grilled cheeses."

Mr. Lockbaum rushes for Tessa, arms outstretched. Maybe grilled cheese is code for something in this house?

"No, no, no," he says. "You keep away from the stove, honey." He eases Tessa out of the doorway and back toward me. Then he gives her a pat on her head, which looks strange since she's almost as tall as he is. "I'll call you two when they're ready." He disappears behind the door.

"Holy cow," I whisper. "What's up with him? He won't let you near the stove? Did you start a fire or something?"

Tessa laughs. Loud. "It's okay," she says, taking in my wide-eyed glance toward the kitchen. "He can't hear us, and even if he could, it wouldn't matter." She walks in the other direction. "My dad thinks I'm six. Seriously. Like first grade."

I can't believe my ears. Tessa seems so casual about it all. "Wow." I follow her toward the other end of the apartment, but part of me wants to head straight for the main door and get the heck out of here. "Um, shouldn't he be in counseling or something?"

"Tried that. Only made it worse. He's easier to live with this way, we decided."

"Who decided?"

"Me and Mom. Before she left."

And I think *I* have problems. "So this is still from your sister? Still from Corey?"

Tessa opens the door to what I assume is her bedroom, but not the bedroom I would've expected from her. Not in a million years. A row of teddy bears lines the shelves of one whole wall. The pink on the walls is the exact shade of the turtleneck she wore to school that one day. Her bed has a lace-covered canopy. A canopy!

"Are you sure it's just your dad who thinks you're six?" It slips out.

She shakes her head, not an ounce of offense on her face. "Uh-huh. It's Dad. I used to try to update my room, but he changed it back when I was at school. Or made it even more sickly sweet." Tessa snickers like this is old news that she dealt with a long time ago. "I put a lock on once. He hired a locksmith. I took the teddy bears down to the courtyard and lit a fire when I was twelve. He went out and bought a whole new set the next day. Money we don't have."

While Tessa tells me all this, I can't keep my eyes off her black clothing and jewelry and eyeliner, such a stark contrast to the room around her. Is this her only way to try to bring her dad back to reality? "What about your clothes? Doesn't he try to change them to little frilly dresses?" I think of the dresses in the pictures near the door.

She opens her closet, and the row of pink and purple frills makes me gasp. She shoves a step stool among the hanging pastel jumble. As weird as all this is, something keeps me from running out of here and finding a new set of friends.

She climbs the step stool and her head disappears for a few seconds. A light emanates from the top of the closet and she steps down. "Have a look." Her hand points up to where she came from.

Holding on to the top of the rickety step stool, I move slowly up its three steps. Before my head is through the opening in the top of the closet, I see piles of folded-up black clothes. The one pink sweater. Stacks of notebooks. Makeup.

The stool shakes a little and I let out a small yelp.

"Oh, come on," Tessa says, and groans.

At first I think she's reprimanding me for the noise, but then I remember how little she seems to worry about noise in her apartment. When I cautiously back down the steps, I can tell by her one raised eyebrow directed at the step stool that she's chiding me for my fear.

Of course she doesn't know what it's like to be afraid. Of anything, it seems.

"It's everything I own," she says, motioning back toward the attic. "This"—she spreads her hands out in front of her—"is all Dad's. I'm worried about next year after high school, if I want to move out or whatever. But I guess we'll have to cross that bridge when we come to it."

She says it lightly, but her forehead crinkles and I can tell she's thought a lot about it.

"So obviously your dad has no idea you borrow his car." I drop my voice a bit to say this, even though Tessa hasn't dropped hers the whole time we've been here. Her dad doesn't want to find anything out. I'm starting to get it.

"Dad has no idea I leave the apartment," she scoffs. "I used to go out the fire escape, but now I just take the front door. I don't know what he tells himself. That I'm going over to a friend's. You know, for a playdate. Who knows." She pulls a pack of gum out of a dresser drawer and hands me a piece. "Doesn't matter. Dad doesn't drive much anyway. Just to get groceries. He'll never miss it."

I drop down onto her bed, under her canopy, in stunned silence. Could my family turn out like this?

Plan W: Make a lunch date.

"Did you get back into Reena's room?" I ask Alis when he walks me home the following week.

"No." His face tightens. "But I saw her leave with the folder on Sunday, and she didn't come back with it."

"Oh." I'm disappointed, but I know it's not Alis's fault. Reena would definitely have noticed if we'd taken the thing.

It's cool and wet, but thankfully not raining. I wrap my arms across myself. "Is she acting any different? Like she suspects you of anything?"

"I don't think so." He nibbles his lip, but I have the sense he's not worried about himself. He's worried about what exactly his sister might be into.

"Can you meet me for lunch tomorrow?"

"I guess," he says. "Why?"

"I think we should put our heads together and figure some of this out." I don't tell him that "we" involves Tessa. It will take all three of us to figure out what our next move should be with Reena, and Tessa seems the most objective about it all. "Wendy's? Eleven-thirtyish?"

He nods. "I'll tell my sister I'm going for a walk. We can't be too long."

First thing the next morning, I ask Tessa, "What are you doing for lunch today?"

"Dunno. Wanna go to Wendy's?"

Perfect. I nod. "There's just one—"

"Hey, did you hear that Amy and Dustin broke up?"

I stare at her. I had no idea she even knew who they were. Why is she telling me this? And how would she have this information? I want to feel satisfaction at the news; I should feel that way, but all I feel is numb.

Before I can snap out of my daze to ask Tessa any details, Mr. Poindexter walks by our lockers and pulls her aside. Tessa looks happier, brighter, when she talks about art. They're still chatting when the first bell rings for class.

I decide I'll have lots of time to ask her about Amy and Dustin later. And I'll tell her about Alis on the way.

When the lunch bell rings, I head straight for my locker. No Tessa, but a note flaps off the front of my door.

I'll be late. Meet you there. T.

So, fine, Alis will have to be a surprise. I scoot out the front doors and across the street by myself.

Alis sits on the far side of the restaurant stirring a Frosty.

"Hey, stranger," I say, even though I saw him yesterday.

"Hi." He smiles, but his lip twitches like he's nervous.

"Trouble getting away from you sister?"

He shakes his head. "Not really. It's just . . . I've never had to sneak around this much."

"Yeah, I know. It comes so naturally for Tessa. She—" I

stop, realizing I should probably give him a heads-up. "She's meeting us here too."

He looks at me blankly for a second, like he doesn't understand.

"I really think we need her help." I touch his arm, and for a second I feel a rush of electricity. He must feel it too, because he stops scowling.

"I found something," he says, and pulls a piece of folded notepaper from his pocket.

I recognize it as the one I'd seen him pull out of the photography book in Reena's room. "What is it?"

He unfolds the paper and places it flat on the table. "I told you about my mom's suicide note, right?"

By the time he finishes his sentence, I've scanned enough of the note to realize that's what this is. I hold my breath in alarm.

"I found it the other day, and just wanted to read it again." He stops and blinks down at it a few times. "But the thing is, Reena's been homeschooling me for a few years now. I know what her writing looks like."

I feel a sudden rock in the pit of my stomach.

"She did a pretty good job of forging it, but there were a couple of slipups on the *y*'s."

"Wait, you're saying you think Reena forged your mom's

suicide note?" I'm stunned, but I realize how much worse this must be for Alis. I place my hand over his.

He stares out the window. "I know why she did it. She loved our mom. She wanted her to look like a hero and I don't think Ree could process the idea of an accident, why God would take her."

"Still," I start, but there's nothing else to say.

"What's he doing here?" Tessa blurts from behind me.

I jump in surprise and pull my hand away while Alis snatches the notepaper and stuffs it back into his pocket.

I motion for her to sit down. But sliding halfway off his chair, Alis looks like he's about to bolt. He probably thinks I'll tell Tessa all about the forged note.

"Listen, the reason I wanted to talk to you both is to figure out what to do next." My words come out so quickly that they sound jumbled. "Look, I know you two aren't exactly best friends," I go on. "But you're both so much smarter than me with this stuff. Can you please just give me half an hour? I won't force you to sit together again, I promise."

Tessa leans back in her chair and crosses her arms.

"I don't know," Alis says, worry in his eyes. "It's my sister we're talking about."

"Your sister's a whacked-out crazoid," Tessa says, half under her breath, but we both hear her.

"No!" I grab Alis's arm before he can get up. "She's not crazy, we just need—"

"Maybe she is," he says, without emotion.

We sit there silently for a minute, and even Tessa doesn't say anything.

I start quietly. "Okay, when I talked to Celeste at Starbucks, she swore Faith never would have killed herself." Alis frowns when I say this, so I stare at him and wait.

"Starbucks," he says slowly. "Reena has a friend at Starbucks who used to bring her these fancy coffee drinks."

"Yes, Celeste! That's Celeste." I grab Alis's hand.

"Oh, isn't that cute," Tessa says. I pull my hand away.

"Yeah," Alis says, ignoring Tessa. "But she hasn't had coffee in a while now."

Looking over at Tessa, I can tell her mind is piecing something together. I explain to Alis how Celeste was Faith's best friend and recount the attempts I've taken at speaking to her since Faith's death.

"Somebody needs to talk with that girl," Tessa says, finally.

After all that thinking, this is what she comes up with? "Yeah, but I already tried. She won't say anything."

"I can't go near her," Alis says. "She's seen me plenty of times at the house. If it gets back to my sister—"

"No, dumbasses. I mean me. I'll talk to her." Tessa shakes

her head. "Boy, it's a good thing there's someone around here with their brain turned on."

I ignore the slight. "But seriously, Tessa, don't you think she'll recognize you from school?" My eyes scan her for emphasis. "Even if she doesn't, no offense, but Celeste wouldn't talk to someone like you."

"Like what?" Tessa smirks. "Calm down. I mean I'll go in undercover. She'll never know me. Trust me on this one."

I start to catch on when she tells me, "I probably need to borrow some clothes."

"What makes you think she'll talk to you if she wouldn't talk to me?" I say.

"Because. I know what to ask."

chapter TWENTY-FIVE

y Wednesday, Tessa still hasn't given me any
clues about her plans, other than that she needs
Alis's MP3 player. Apparently mine's not good
enough, because it doesn't record.

I skirt behind the school at lunchtime, through a football
practice on the backfield, and find Alis leaning up against
the fence.

"Hey," I shove my hands in my hoodie pockets.

"Hi." He smiles. "You didn't bring your friend."

I look toward the school, then back at Alis. "You have
to give Tessa a chance. She means well. Sometimes she just
doesn't know . . . etiquette."

Alis snickers, the closest thing to laughing I've heard from him. "That's an understatement." He reaches into the pocket of his red checkered jacket. "Anyway, here's the recorder she wants."

I take it, but my hand rests on his for a few seconds and I don't want to pull it away. He's so warm, and I suddenly realize how nice it is to trust someone. He doesn't pull away either.

"I'll give her a chance. For you," he says. He moves a little closer and squeezes my hand around the device.

I smile, wanting to tell him that Tessa doesn't matter, that I don't care what she thinks of him, or anyone else at the moment. But before I open my mouth, a football flies just over Alis's head and bounces beside him with a thud.

With the stomping of feet in our direction, we quickly drop hands and step apart.

"I better go anyway," Alis says, just before two guys barrel between us.

"Okay." I back away, disappointed. "See you soon."

I'm sticking my books in my locker after school, when I see my ex–best friend walking toward me, her broad smile stretching her face tight. Her hair is not straightened or curled, but just falls across her shoulders in frizzy waves. In a split second, I know the rumor Tessa told me was true. Why else would

Amy be wearing that fake, embarrassment-covering grin?

"What are you doing here?" I ask, point-blank.

"Um, I've missed you," she replies in such a saccharine tone it makes me want to spit.

"Huh. Well, I can't say I've missed you." I turn back to my locker. "I've got other friends."

Just then, from across the hall, my peripheral vision catches a flash of black.

Tessa cuts right in front of Amy and slaps her hand on her locker beside me. Amy stops in place, about three feet away, and stares in horror.

"So I got some stuff to do," Tessa says, completely ignoring Amy, "but I'll pick you up at your place around four."

Amy backs away, her eyes wide.

"She's a better friend than you ever were," I call over my shoulder.

I'm lying in front of the TV, nearly asleep, when Tessa's special *thud* sounds at the door.

But confusion strikes when I open the door to a girl with soft, silky hair. It takes me a minute. Maybe I'm still sleeping.

I pinch myself and definitely feel it.

"Move it," the girl says in Tessa's voice. "We've got work to do."

My mouth opens, but nothing comes out. Maybe from the hair, or it could be from the lack of charcoal makeup. Her skin is, well, skin color. I really would not have recognized her on the street.

"Wow. How did you do this?"

She rolls her eyes at me and tromps for the stairs. "I took a shower, stupid."

I follow her to the upstairs hallway. "This is mine." I open the door to my room.

I've never thought of my bedroom as anything special. A few knickknacks from my childhood decorate the place, but mostly clothes and makeup. Watching Tessa scan each item, I suddenly feel very superficial. There's really nothing of me in here.

But then I wonder, who am I? What would I display around my room to make it more "mine"? Tessa's so sure of who she wants to be, and even thwarts everyone else's opinions to be that way. I don't know enough of who I want to be to pin one of my favorite poems on the wall. I don't have a favorite poem.

"Well, let's get at it." Tessa throws the pink top—the one she'd worn to school—onto the bed, then opens my closet without asking. "I need pants." She holds out a hand and looks up at the ceiling, like I'm taking far too long.

I dig in a drawer and pile a slew of sweatpants onto my bed, not wanting to come out and say that she'll never fit into most of my other clothes.

"Here, try these." I hold out the biggest pair. They're navy blue with our school emblem and SHS across the butt.

She scowls. "I'm not walking in there dressed like a bum."

I can't help sizing up her current wardrobe at that.

"Jeans. Give me some jeans."

If I ever feel up to arguing with Tessa Lockbaum, I'm going to choose a more valuable subject than clothes. "Okay." I pull a pair out of my bottom drawer, not even bothering to look for the size.

She snatches them from my hand and heads for the door.

"To the left," I tell her. To the bathroom.

While she's gone, I fold up my sweatpants and shove them back in their drawers. Fine, she doesn't want to wear sweats? Go ahead, find something else. Anything you like.

"These'll work," she says in the doorway.

I spin, and for the second time today, my eyes nearly explode from my head. I must be in some kind of alternate reality. Not only do my jeans fit, they look much better on Tessa.

"Wow. I never thought . . . I mean, how come you always wear such baggy clothes?"

She shrugs.

I cross my arms and lean back to take in the whole look. "You look great."

"Makeup," she says. "You can help with that, right?"

"Sure." I grab my small array of makeup and transfer it from my dresser to the bed.

Tessa sits across from me, tilts her head slightly upward and closes her eyes. I've never put makeup on any face other than my own. In fact, with Amy's lifetime aspirations, I'd always been the apply-ee, never the apply-er.

Just the basics, I tell myself. *Make it even; that's all that matters.*

The way Tessa sits, so still and silent, makes me nervous. When Amy applied my makeup, I wouldn't shut up. In fact, she'd tell me over and over again, "Be quiet. You're making me mess this up." Then I'd start laughing. She'd start laughing. Makeup would be everywhere and we'd have to start over.

"What are you stopping for?" Tessa asks. "Are you done?"

"Uh, no. Just distracted. Sorry." To give myself a bit of a breather, I get up and head to my dresser. I have a brand-new green eye shadow I bought just before Faith died that I haven't opened yet. For some reason, I just let it sit there. Every time I look at the paper bag, it reminds me of how much my life has changed, so I couldn't seem to touch it.

But it's time. I take out the small eye shadow disk and move back to the bed.

"Okay," I say a few minutes later, when I've applied the last swipe. I can't believe she sat still for so long. "Here's a nice lip gloss. Put some on and I think you're good."

She leaves her eyes closed. "Can you put it on?"

Um, okay. Can I help you put your shoes on too? Maybe she is six. But I keep my mouth shut, tug on the applicator and run it along her lips.

"You're done," I say while I pack up my pile of makeup. "Check it out. The mirror's over there." I point above my dresser.

"We better get going." Standing and turning the opposite way, she heads for my door, her black clothes bunched in a ball under her arm.

"What? You don't even want to see how you look? What kind of a girl are you?" I laugh, but Tessa already clunks down the hallway. I chase after her. "Hey!"

She holds up a backhand toward me. "Just leave it alone, okay, Brie?"

The way she says it, it feels like the first time she's ever asked me for a favor. The first time she's admitted to something she can't quite handle—though I can't wrap my brain around why a little bit of makeup would do that to a person.

I'm so caught up thinking about it that I don't notice where she's walking. Suddenly, her hand is on Faith's doorknob.

"That's Faith's room," I say, a little too loud.

"Uh-huh." She doesn't stop turning the knob. "You don't go in here much, right?"

"No. Never." She moves through the door. I inch down the hall in complete disbelief that she hasn't even asked permission. "Well, just once."

"Same here. With Corey, I mean."

The way she talks about her sister, it's like she's so distanced. So healthy. When I reach the door frame, she's touching her way around Faith's room. Her eyes scan every inch, like she's in awe of the place. Like she has some kind of fascination with death. So okay, maybe "healthy" isn't the right word for her. She reaches out, touching the walls, the carved detail on Faith's desk, the bedposts.

"Do you think Faith really knew something about God?" she asks.

I scoff. "Yeah, she knew plenty about God. I've told you this." The tension of being in here makes my words sound rude.

"No, I mean, do you think she knew the real God. What he's really about?"

I don't quite get what she means, and shrug in response.

"What's this?" She reaches for a horn on Faith's bookshelf.

"It's called a shofar." I want her to put it back down, but I figure the sooner I can explain it, the sooner she'll move on. "I remember the name because when I used to go to church with my family, I'd joke whenever she was taking it along. 'Sho far, sho good.'"

Tessa runs her hand along the rounded bonelike instrument.

I can still see Faith's small hands wrapped around it. "She used it back when she was on the church worship team."

"For, like, music?"

"Not exactly. I don't know, it was weird. Like when she really sensed something in the spirit realm, she blew it. There was something spiritual about it. I'll give it that." I reach over and take the shofar from Tessa. "It has only one note." I place it gingerly in the exact spot where it came from.

I head out of the room, expecting Tessa to follow, when I hear her say, "Can I have it?"

I keep my back to her, letting her words ring over and over in my head. She doesn't interrupt with "Oh, never mind." Or "Just kidding." We stand there with the silence stretching like a rubber band between us. Someone has to let it snap, and apparently it's not going to be her.

Would Faith have wanted this? That's the most important question. Mom and Dad haven't been in Faith's room for a long time—I'm sure they don't remember a single thing in here. I've been in here once in over a month. Faith would rather have seen her things used by somebody than left to sit around and rot. Especially the shofar.

"Okay," I say, finally.

"Okay?"

"Yeah. I guess." But I can't stay to watch. I take the stairs two at a time to the bottom. "We better get a move on, though. Shut the door behind you, okay?"

Thirty seconds later, I glance at Tessa on her way to the car. She doesn't have it. Just her balled-up bunch of clothes. Was she testing me to see what kind of friend I am? Or did she recognize my hesitance?

Either way, I'm relieved. I force it out of my mind on the drive to Starbucks.

"Did you get the MP3 player?" she asks as she bends her rearview mirror up to the ceiling of the car.

Why is she so afraid to look at herself? She looks really good. But I don't press her and just follow her lead on the conversation. "Check."

"How many gigs does that thing hold?"

I pull it out of my pocket and turn it on. Before I look at the capacity, I can't resist scrolling through Alis's playlists, just to see.

"I never would've pegged Alis as the girl-band type." I laugh and keep scrolling. "I mean, eighties tunes, that seems like him. Even rap. It's amazing how much variety this guy's got on here."

"What'll it hold?" she says, in an aggravated tone. "I know you wanna find out all about your little boyfriend and everything, but maybe we could save that for later, huh?"

My face heats up and I scroll back to find the menu. "Thirty-two," I say, finally. "Only four and a half used."

We park at the far side of the strip mall. I reach for the handle.

"Where do you think you're going?"

"Shouldn't I find a good hideout near the building?"

She scoffs. "It's, like, thirty degrees out there."

I glance down at my layered look. Maybe she's right. The car would be warmer.

"Besides, this thing should make the range we need."

She reaches into her backpack and pulls out a sculptured Winnie-the-Pooh ornament, adjusts something on the back and sticks it on her dash. Then she slides what looks like a tiny white walkie-talkie into her left inside pocket.

"Hopefully you'll hear everything, but we'll get a recording just in case." That's when she takes Alis's player from my hands and slides it into her other pocket. Now that the pockets are equally weighted, they don't look odd at all.

"You sure we should do this?" I ask. Celeste can be so skittish, and I know what Tessa's like.

She blows off my question and double-checks Winnie the Pooh. "Volume's on the back if you need it."

Without another word, she steps out of the car and marches toward Starbucks. I hear the scratching of her feet against the pavement and pebbles as she goes, and it's only after she's twenty feet away that I realize the noise is coming from the little Pooh-bear on the dash.

I'll have to remember to ask her where she went to spy training school.

When she first gets into the coffee shop, I'm convinced I won't be able to make out a thing. There're muffled voices upon voices and all I can catch are the odd words. "Meeting tomorrow . . . breakfast at nine . . . lazy, rip-off mechanic . . ."

Five minutes pass, and I close my eyes, leaning back. Suddenly, I hear Tessa's voice, loud and clear. "Can I get a tall Americano, please?" At least I think it's Tessa. She sounds, well, sweet.

"Anything else with that?" It's Celeste.

"Um, let me think." A pause, and I hear the murmuring again. "A brownie," she says.

"Six eighty-seven."

Some clinking of coins. We hadn't talked about money.

I hope Tessa has enough. "Hey, did someone just call you Celeste?"

Did someone? I didn't hear it. Maybe Tessa's making it up. Or maybe Pooh here just doesn't have enough range.

"Yeah, that's right."

"You don't know Reena, do you?"

My hands start sweating and I reach forward to turn up the volume, even though I can hear it just fine. The only sound for several seconds is shuffling of papers, coins dropping. Then, "Um, I don't know anyone—"

"I met this girl, Reena, and she was telling me about this group," Tessa goes on. "Said I might want to come in and chat with you about it. That was months ago, so I'm glad you're still here."

Another pause. Celeste clears her throat. "I don't know of any group. If you want to talk about it, you should talk to her."

"Well, that's the funny thing." I'd love to see Tessa right now, but she's out of view. "She gave me her number, but I lost it."

"Excuse me." Another voice. "Are you almost done? I'm kind of in a hurry."

Murmuring.

"Aren't you a Yellow Entry Level? Reena said you'd be ready to move on to Martyrdom soon," Tessa says in a loud voice and I nearly choke on my breath.

Clanking noises sound through Winnie the Pooh, like a bunch of coins have been dropped.

"I—I don't know anything," Celeste says. "Go talk to Nathan." She sounds almost like she's going to cry when she offers to help the next customer.

A minute later, Tessa pushes through the coffee shop door with her drink and brownie and strides for the car.

"Yup, that girl's definitely hiding something. Pretty freaked, too, if you ask me."

"I'd love to have seen her face when you mentioned martyrdom." This is only partly true, because I've never heard Celeste like that and I can't help worrying about her. But still, she's obviously not being up front.

"Who's Nathan?" Tessa asks, staring across the parking lot at the supermarket. "She waved over that way when she said his name." Tessa points to the store.

All of a sudden, I remember the boy in Reena's Facebook pictures, the one with the stupid supermarket buttons all pinned to his shirt. "Hang on," I say. "The boy with the pins!"

By the contorted look on Tessa's face, I can tell I'm not making any sense.

"Just drive across the parking lot," I tell her. "I need to check something out."

chapter TWENTY-SIX

i stroll up and down the cereal and canned-food aisles, walkie-talkie in my pocket, looking for the Facebook kid who had worn the Albertsons Market buttons. In the cheese section, I take an extra ten seconds to study my namesake in the cooler. What's my first question for this guy if I do find him?

After walking the perimeter of the store, I head for one of the cashiers at the front.

"Can you tell me if a guy named Nathan works here?"

"Yeah, but I think he was off as of a few minutes ago." The dark circles under the cashier's eyes make me suspect she's been working a double shift.

"Okay, thanks." I back away and check my watch. It's five after nine, which is the time I'd told my parents I'd be home in my note. Disappointed, I head for the sliding glass doors.

Just as I'm about to step on the automatic doormat, a blond guy emerges from the staff door along the side wall with a black backpack slung over his shoulder. He looks about nineteen or twenty. Cute. He wears a name tag, but I can't see it from here. If his hair was spiked up, I figure he could be the same guy from the Facebook pictures.

He almost bumps into me as he walks, head down, for the door.

"Whoops." I step back before he hits me. Focusing on his name tag, it takes several seconds to make out all the words: ALBERTSONS. PROUD TO PICK YOUR PRODUCE.

No name.

"Can I help you with something?" he asks, and I realize I'm staring at his chest.

"Um, do I know you?" I conjure some sudden confidence when Tessa's headlights flash through the doors.

A smile edges onto his face. "I don't think so. Have you shopped here before? I'd remember you." The words slide off his tongue like butter into a nonstick skillet.

A player. Right. My angelic sister hung out in a group

with a player. "I don't shop here much. My mom does," I say. "I'm sorry, I didn't catch your name."

He extends a hand. "Nathan."

Bingo. When I reach my hand to his, his fingers slip into mine like a glove. He's a pro hand-shaker. And maybe I'm just nervous, but he doesn't seem to let go as soon as he should.

I pull my hand away and he readjusts his backpack over his other shoulder. As he switches it, I catch a glimpse of a round red sticker pasted to the back. It has the same scribbly cross design, but with two large words above and below it, easily readable from a distance. LOVE. SERVE.

"And you are?"

It occurs to me all at once that the phrase sounds like an echo. Probably because he repeated it while I zoned out on the sticker.

"Annie," I say, my alias coming to me quickly. "That's a cool design." I point to the sticker. "Where'd you get it?"

He ignores my question and says, "Well, Annie, are you just starting or just finishing?"

"Um. Just finishing."

He looks down at my empty hands.

"They didn't have what I needed."

He glances out the front window. "You driving or walking?"

"Walking," I say.

"Let me walk you. You shouldn't be out by yourself at this time of night."

Right. Much better to be with a total stranger who's just been hitting on me. A honk sounds, and I look outside. Tessa zooms along the front windows, flashing me a thumbs-up sign while Nathan has his back to her. She drives across the parking lot and idles at the far side in the direction of my house.

I doubt she can still hear our voices unless Pooh-bear has bionic powers, but at least she's within view.

"What do you see?" Nathan asks, following my eyes.

"Oh, nothing. Just thought I recognized somebody." I shake my head. "It wasn't them." I shove my hands into my vest pockets, but when they hit my stash of electronics, I quickly pull them out again, not wanting to mess up the recording. Though I'm not even sure the point of the recording equipment. We can't trust our own memories? I decide it must be Tessa going overkill on all the cloak-and-dagger stuff.

"Which way?" Nathan asks, and I direct him to where Tessa's car has now disappeared.

"You don't have a car, either?"

"I do," he says, and then points behind us in the parking lot. "Right over there, but walking is good for the soul. I think

279

too many people rush from place to place and automobiles just breed busyness."

Great. This guy's a total creep. He could have just offered me a lift, but no, he wants to walk with me. Probably lead me down some dark alley. "So you don't like busyness," I say. "What do you like?"

"God. Women. Love," he says so automatically I wonder how many times he's been asked this before.

The three words repeat over and over in my head. The first and the last seem to go together, even resemble my sister's views. And with the word "Love" I immediately think of the red sticker. But "women"?

"So you're, like, a Christian, right?" This seems like the quickest way to get some answers. Plus, I'm not sure I'm interested in his view on women.

He nods. "Not the same as most, though."

Why does that not surprise me? Though I'm not sure what "most" Christians are like anymore. Mom kidnaps statues of Jesus. Dad ignores his pain, running back to church like nothing bad ever happens. Then there's Reena: preaching to senile senior citizens and painting a personalized crucifix on her ceiling. But I have to ask. "What do you mean, 'not the same'?"

"God is all about love," he says. "Most people have a hard time with that concept. Try to put so many rules on everything."

I think back to the pages of Bible verses in Reena's file folder. "What kind of rules?"

"Well, what do you believe, Annie?"

This catches me off guard. But if he was in the same group as Faith and Reena, I should probably play up the fervent religious thing. "I love God," I say. "I'd do anything for him."

He stares at me, and I feel a sudden need to study my sneakers.

"So what do you think He wants from you?"

I try to let Faith's words flow through me. Her humming is still so clear, but her words, I can't find them anymore. "Well, he wants me to pray and sing to him. And always think about him." I cringe. It sounded nothing like Faith.

Nathan shakes his head. He must be able to see right through me. "No, that's not it. He doesn't. It's just about the love."

The way he says it makes me think of hippies stumbling out of a smoke-filled van.

"Well, yeah," I add. "Of course, love and all that, too."

"No." He stops in front of me and takes both my hands in his. "*Love.*"

I'm not sure what to say to that. Trying not to be obvious, I scan the streets around me. I can't see Tessa anywhere.

I squeeze his hands and smile, trying to give a back-off

281

signal. But he looks into my eyes and I feel like I've already given him the wrong idea.

A second later, he turns and starts walking again. He doesn't let go of my right hand, and since I'm so relieved he didn't try to come any closer or kiss me, I don't retract it just yet. A little rejection at a time.

"You see," he goes on, as if our little moment hadn't happened, "most church leaders ignore the Scriptures that don't suit them, adding their own narrow-minded spin on things. And of course, there's more good instruction out there besides the Bible."

Besides the Bible? This sounds like the polar opposite of something Faith might have said. Though I could see it with Reena maybe.

"You remind me of someone," I say.

"Yeah? What's his name?"

"Well, actually, it's a girl. You don't look like her or anything." I try to force out a casual laugh, but it doesn't help the tense knot in my stomach. "She runs this prayer-group thing."

He stares at me so intently that I have to just blurt it.

"Her name is Reena Monachie."

His quiet reaction scares me at first, but then he readjusts his backpack and clears his throat. "You know her?"

I swallow. "I met her once, when I was visiting my grandma."

"At the senior center?" His voice lightens.

"Yeah. You know her?"

He nods.

I suppress a smile. "She was telling me about her group. But then she never called. Do you know anything about when they meet?"

He stares around at the trees for a few seconds. "The group . . . isn't really happening at the moment."

"Oh, that's too bad." I rub a sweaty hand on my jeans. But he must be lying or not part of it anymore. Reena told me she was going to invite me to a meeting. "I've been looking for something like that. Do you think it'll start up again?"

He looks me up and down, and I feel like my figure might be the deciding factor. "Maybe. I'll talk to Reena. Does she have your number?"

"Uh-huh." I try to keep my voice calm, even though the sudden progress makes me so nervous and so excited at the same time.

"We'll give you a call when we get set up again." The way he says "we" makes it sound like he and Reena run the group together. He winks. As we turn the corner into my housing development, Nathan's eyes settle on the large, engraved ARLINGTON HEIGHTS sign. "You live in here?"

"Yeah. You look like you've been here before." I quickly calculate a different route in case it looks Faith-familiar.

He gnaws on his lip. "Yeah, my girlfriend used to live in here."

My mouth drops open, but only for a millisecond. There's no way it could be Faith. She didn't bring boys home or date. Ever. In fact, she didn't believe in dating until she was ready to get married. The sudden realization that she never would marry now seems so sad. I push myself back to the moment to get my mind off of it.

"Girlfriend? Really? But she doesn't live here anymore?" I say it as casually as I can muster. When he doesn't respond, I add, "Did she move away?" I lead him past the turnoff for my street and onto the next one.

"Um, yeah." He nods, but his voice is hesitant.

I stop just before the driveway of the house behind mine. Through their open yard, I can tell my parents have turned in. Only the porch light shines. "I live over there." I point the opposite direction. "But my dad, he's kind of—"

"No, I understand." He squeezes my hand. I still feel odd, letting him hold it, but if that's the worst he tries, I'm not going to break out the pepper spray over it. I squeeze back and he gets a glint in his eye. A small smile breaks.

"I should probably go." The trees in the neighbor's yard

move in the wind. Even though my house is dark and Tessa's car is nowhere in sight, strangely, I feel like I'm being watched. Protected.

Nathan leans in, which catches me off guard. I snap my head to the side, so he ends up planting his lips almost on my ear.

"Thanks for walking me," I say, backing away. "I'll drop into the store again soon. And tell Reena to call me."

He lifts his hand for a casual wave. By the time I fall into the shadow of our neighbor's house, I turn to look for him and he's halfway down the street, jogging in the direction we came from.

Looking both ways, I ball my hands into fists. I can't believe Tessa left me on my own with that guy! What if he didn't stop with a kiss on the cheek?

On my way up our front steps, something catches my eye behind Mom's rosebushes. A few feet closer, and the flash of red is unmistakable.

Alis's bike.

"Alis," I whisper-call around the side of our house. When he doesn't answer, I try the other side. I look inside and around Dad's van, but I can't find him anywhere.

I don't want to shove the bike in the garage where he can't get it in case he's still around somewhere. Instead, I push it a little deeper into the bush so it can't be seen. Then I circle the house once more, calling his name.

Finally, I give up and head inside. When I shut the door behind me and see movement in the dark, a scream comes up my throat and almost leaves my mouth.

"Oh, Dad. Hi." I wonder how long he's been standing there waiting for me. Seeing the worried look on his face, I sense his pain. I feel so sad for him, and so horrible for all the sneaking around I've been doing.

"Good night," he says. He touches my back and heads up the stairs to bed without another word.

I stand there, stunned. If he's so worried, why doesn't he yell at me or do *something* about it?

chapter TWENTY-SEVEN

the next morning, Alis's bike still lies buried in our rosebush. I wonder if something happened, if he came to try and find me for some reason. Maybe he heard about Reena planning another meeting. Or what if she found out about our snooping in her room? I take a slow breath to clear that thought. But why would Alis leave his bike behind?

When Tessa shows up at her locker, I turn and give her as hard a glare as I can muster and then angle into my own locker to grit my teeth.

"Wow, someone woke up on the wrong side of the Midol," she says.

I don't reply. Maybe she thrives on hanging out with strange guys in the middle of the night. Doesn't mean I'm stupid enough to.

She goes on as if nothing's wrong. "So I guess I pictured your family as the huggy/kissy type. The curt 'good night' was a curveball."

I turn and scowl at her. "What?"

"Your dad. He doesn't say much, huh?" She pulls a binder from her locker. "Hey, can I get that receiver back? I don't want my dad going out and buying another one." She holds out a hand.

My mind quickly fills in the blanks. The Pooh walkie-talkie. Which is still in my vest pocket at home. I make a show of patting my pockets anyway. Tessa must have stayed with me right until I got in the house.

"'Course, I shouldn't be surprised. Your boyfriend doesn't say a hell of a lot either."

She's lost me again. "You saw Alis? Where were you?"

"The guy walks like a cockroach on uppers. Found him halfway down Marshall."

Marshall. The street adjacent to mine at the end. No wonder I didn't see her.

"I give the guy a ride home and all he does is scowl the whole way. I thought we were making progress." She shakes her head and shuts her locker. "At least he said thanks."

"You gave Alis a ride home last night?"

"That's what I said, isn't it?" She clicks her lock on and walks away.

I dig out my books for first class. Hopefully Alis will call after school, and translate all that into English.

Through the day, I'm surprised that Steph and other ex-friends actually make eye contact with me. It's nice to walk through the halls no longer the school pariah. But at the same time I know it's so superficial. They'd all so easily turn against me again.

When the last bell of the day sounds, I reach into my purse and scroll the ringer volume on my cell up.

"Miss Jenkins," Clairvoyant Clancy bellows over the stream of students leaving his classroom.

I nod and wave, but don't divert my path toward the door.

"I'd like you to stay for a moment, please," he calls.

With my back to him, I purse my lips, and then turn around with a forced smile.

"I'm concerned about you catching up with the rest of the class," he says.

He's not the only one. And maybe it would help keep my focus if I had a teacher watching over me. I nod.

"I think we need to come up with a plan—," he says, but he's interrupted by the sound of John Mayer. Coming from my cell phone.

Clancy stares at my purse and then up at me. I have no idea what to do. Cell phones are so not allowed in classrooms. I cringe as the music starts up again.

"I'm really sorry, Mr. Clancy. It was turned off during class, I swear." He doesn't respond, just crosses his arms and taps his foot. Taking this as a sign that he wants me to get it over with, I turn my back and flip my phone open to my ear. "Hello," I say in little more than a whisper.

"We have to talk," Alis says. Yes, the words are serious.

"I, um, can't. Not right now—"

"Oh, no, go ahead, Miss Jenkins. Please," Mr. Clancy says sarcastically.

"Can you call back in a while?" I inch away from Clancy's desk and talk even quieter. If Alis is calling so quickly after the school bell, something must be up.

Alis doesn't say anything, and after a few seconds I realize he hung up.

When I turn back to Clancy, he's writing in a notebook. He doesn't look up after I slip my phone into my purse. Or after I approach his desk and clear my throat.

"Um, Mr. Clancy?"

He looks up like he doesn't know where the sound could be coming from, then glances around until his eyes rest on me. "Oh, right. You have some time for me now, Miss Jenkins?"

I can't stand his patronizing tone, but I swallow my pride. "I'm sorry, sir, but it's not what you think. Someone's helping me—"

"If they're not helping you get caught up on your history assignments, I don't want to hear about it."

I bite my lip to hold in any further explanation.

"Now, listen, Brie. I've tried to be patient. We all have." He motions around him, as though the rest of the teachers from the school are sitting right there in his classroom nodding their heads in agreement. "A tragedy in the household is a big deal, for certain, but none of us can help you if you're not at least making an effort to get back on track. Colleges, I'm afraid, won't be as sympathetic."

I duck my head to my chest, nodding. I know he's right.

"I'm not asking you to give your essays publicly with the rest of the class. But you have to at least write them, Brie. You have to do something, show some effort in order for me to give you a passing grade. I've made a list, but we need to start working through this after school. It doesn't seem to be happening at home, and I'm sure you have a lot of good reasons why. . . ."

He has no idea.

"But I'm determined to make sure you get through this. Now, why don't you turn off your cellular phone and have a seat in the front row."

I slide into my seat and open my books. He takes a seat beside me.

After an hour, he lets me go and I'm surprised how much actually went into my brain with him hovering over me. Maybe this won't be such a bad idea.

Tessa's nowhere to be found in the school afterward. She's probably at home having cookies and milk. Alis hasn't called back, so I know Reena must be home with him.

If it was important enough, wouldn't he find a way to call though? Or maybe he called Tessa.

I shake my head at the thought, remembering the way they looked at each other in Wendy's. Of course he wouldn't have told her anything.

I have no choice but to wait it out until either Alis or his sister finally calls.

chapter TWENTY-EIGHT

friday, Alis doesn't show up to walk with me, but when I arrive home from school, his bike is gone. By Saturday morning, I still haven't heard from him.

By nine a.m., my parents haven't woken up. For Mom this has become normal, but I wonder if her depression is rubbing off on Dad, since he's almost always up by seven.

I flip on the TV and don't bother to turn the channel from cartoons. My cell sits beside me on one side, with our cordless on the other. My stomach lurches every time I think about breakfast. I'm so queasy that if I'd actually slept with Dustin, I might suspect pregnancy. That thought makes me even sicker.

The first time I hear a honk, I ignore it. The second time,

I grumble about the time and turn up the TV. The third, I go and look out the window. Mr. Lockbaum's Volkswagen idles in our driveway.

When I swing open the front door, Tessa gives me a head motion to get in the car.

Since I'm still wearing my pajamas, I hold up a *one-second* signal and then race up the stairs. After throwing on the first pair of sweats I can find, I shut my bedroom door quietly, hoping my parents will think I'm still in bed. Two minutes later, I slide into Tessa's passenger seat.

"Where to?" My voice is gravelly, even though I've been up for almost an hour.

"The cop shop." Tessa looks over her shoulder to back up, but avoids eye contact.

"Like, the police station?"

She nods. "Yeah, I'm turning myself in for stealing my dad's car, and I'm bringing you down with me."

I stare at her, but her mouth remains in a straight line. Tessa can be so off-the-wall sometimes. What if that *is* the reason? But then I catch the hint of a smirk.

Is it a power thing or what? Why do I always need to beg just to get the tiniest bit of information out of her? I sit back in my seat and cross my arms over my chest. *Fine. Don't tell me where we're going.*

Three traffic lights, and she doesn't say a word. Finally, she turns onto Dorchester and pulls over by the library, which is located right behind the police station. I stare at her.

"Come on." She reaches for her door handle.

I don't move.

"Come on," she repeats. "You want my help with this or not?"

I flop back in my seat.

"Fine," she says. "I'll do it myself, but I doubt I'll get anywhere, since I'm, like, no relation at all."

No relation? I look at her.

"They'd probably say something if they knew it was the sister asking, but whatever." She gets out of the car, starts walking for the path that cuts behind the library, and doesn't turn back.

"Hey!" I slam the door behind me. Questioning the cops hadn't crossed my mind. I didn't think they'd tell a teenager anything. Of course I'm not Tessa, the teenage terror. "Wait up."

Along the path, she fills me in. "I called in early this morning, said I was a relative wanting to talk to the person who investigated Faith Jenkins's death. It took them a long time to find any info. Said they've got way too much paperwork.

"Anyway, they finally came up with this Malovich dude.

He's supposed to be at headquarters all morning. I said I—or actually I gave them your name—would be stopping by."

A shiver runs up my spine. "Do you think they'll tell *me* anything?"

"Don't worry," she says. "I'll do all the talking."

This relieves me and scares me at the same time. When we get through the front doors, Tessa stares the receptionist in the eye and says we're here to see Mr. Malovich. The woman behind the counter chuckles, but only for a portion of a second. Nobody makes fun of Tessa and the lady seems to pick up on this quickly.

"That would be *Detective* Malovich," the receptionist says. "Is he expecting you?"

"He's expecting my friend here, Brie Jenkins." She gives me a little shove forward.

The receptionist tells us to take a seat and picks up the phone. We can't hear a word of her murmuring and she doesn't look in our direction for nearly fifteen minutes.

"This is a waste of time," Tessa says, standing.

Just then, the receptionist calls my name. She doesn't appear to be expecting Tessa to follow, but being a pro at thwarting people's expectations, Tessa barrels her way in front of me anyway.

Detective Malovich is the pock-faced cop who I met in

our living room. His stubble makes him look like he's been working through the night, but when he smiles now, everything changes. He has a nice smile.

He holds a hand out to Tessa, because she's the first to enter the room. She shakes his hand, hard, and then motions to me. "This is Brie Jenkins. She's still pretty broken-up about her sister's . . . demise."

I cringe, not because of Faith, but because of the melodramatic tone Tessa uses.

"Yes, I remember you, Brie," the detective says. "Have a seat."

He faces Tessa. "So what can I do for you, Miss . . ."

Tessa ignores his leading, not about to give her name. "Brie wants to know exactly what happened to her sister."

Now he looks at me. "Have you talked to your parents about this?"

"Her parents are a mess," Tessa interrupts. "How long would it take for you to talk about your daughter if she died?" She clucks her tongue once. "Or maybe you don't have kids."

When I catch Tessa's attention, I shoot her a warning look. She doesn't have to be so rude.

"Actually, I do," the detective says, and turns a photo frame on his desk to face us. A boy and a girl, elementary school ages. I see a resemblance in the eyes, but not in their silky smooth skin. "And I don't think I can imagine how I'd feel if something happened to one of them."

I'm impressed with his calm demeanor. He's not about to let Tessa have the upper hand.

He goes on. "The reason I ask is because I've gone over this information with your dad, Brie. The final report was sent to him a couple of weeks ago."

So Dad got a report and didn't bother to show it to me. I wonder if he showed it to Mom, or if he's just pretending it doesn't exist. Or maybe he got the report that day he was freaking out on her.

"Were you up there? Where she died?" I ask.

"I was there. After." He nods. "I can't go into the details without your parents here, but there was a call from a couple who live in the vicinity." He glances down at his notes. "Soon after, we caught up with a boy who was up the mountain with your sister."

A boy? My mind immediately goes to Alis. But no, he must mean Nathan. I bite my lip.

"We were able to get a couple of statements, one at the site and one later at the station." The detective shifts some papers aside to find another one underneath, "I'm afraid I can't give you their names, but they both gave us the same basic rundown of events."

"Which are?" Too anxious, I force myself to take a deep breath. I don't need names. Besides, I'm pretty sure I know who they are. Nathan and Reena, since Celeste was at another church that night.

He lets out a slow breath, and I can tell he's already said more than he should. But then he drops his eyes and starts to read again. "Faith Jenkins, your sister," he says in a softer voice, "went for a walk alone. She seemed sad, but neither of the witnesses knew why. Ten minutes later, they heard a scream. When they made it to the other side of a big boulder, Faith's purse was there, but Faith was gone."

I sit there for a long time looking down at my hands. To Tessa's credit, she's quiet. A warmness fills my cheeks, and I reach up to brush away the tears.

A rap on the door makes me jump and I reach for a tissue while Detective Malovich stands to meet his receptionist. A minute later, when his door clicks shut again, I look up to see the Detective scooting back around his desk and Tessa readjusting herself in her chair.

A long silence follows, and I know it's my job to break it, if I indeed have any more questions.

"Did she kill herself?" I ask in a whisper.

Detective Malovich clears his throat. His eyes rest on his notes like he's studying for an exam, like he doesn't quite know the questions or the answers. "We did rule it as a suicide."

I suck in a breath. Now that he's said it, now that I know Faith had so many secrets, I feel like this has to be the answer. I wrap my arms tight around my stomach. "And is that what you think, Detective?"

Even though I don't look at him, I sense him nodding. "Yes," he says. "Yes, I do."

Tessa and I don't speak all the way across town. When we're almost at my house, she asks, "Are you ready to talk about it?"

I'm not sure exactly what there is to say. But maybe it'll help, and she would know this better than anyone. "Yeah," I tell her.

"So I couldn't read the whole thing, but I did get the gist," she says. "Nathan's report was just like Malovich said, walking away sad and all that. And he definitely thought it was suicide."

I look up and clue in. She read the witness reports.

"But Celeste's. First of all, it was dated September twenty-sixth, the next day—"

"Wait—Celeste? But she wasn't there. She was at the church youth group."

"Well, apparently that's not what she told the cops." Tessa

parks a few houses down from mine and stares at me. "Anyway, her report was really vague. Like, it didn't say anything about Faith being sad, just that she went for a walk. Celeste's report is pretty short, but Nathan's describes every detail and goes on for pages."

"What about Reena? What did hers say?"

Tessa shakes her head. "There were only two witnesses. That's what Malovich said."

"But she had to be there. Alis said she was. Celeste and Nathan must be covering for her for some reason. We need to talk to Celeste again," I say.

"If Celeste will lie to the police, she's not going to talk to us, Brie." Tessa starts her engine, my cue that it's time to get out of the car. "What we need to do," she says, "is talk to Reena."

chapter TWENTY-NINE

Plan X: Okay (deep breath). Find a way to talk to Reena.

I don't hear from Alis all weekend, and by Monday afternoon I'm sick with worry that something's happened. But then I spot him out behind the school in our usual meeting place. Today, he doesn't lean by the fence. He stands, feet apart, like he's not planning on being there long.

"Oh, good," I say, picking up my pace toward him. "When you didn't call back, I was worried that—"

"I just came by to get my MP3 player back." His tone is abrupt.

"Oh." I look at my feet and study them, but I have no idea how to fix whatever's wrong. Did something happen with

Reena? Something he doesn't want to tell me about? I pull the player out of my pocket and pass it to him. He snaps it out of my hand.

"Did something happen?" I ask.

He scoffs a little, and then straightens his face. "No, Brie. Don't worry about it, okay?"

When he turns away, I run up beside him. "Alis, what's wrong? Please tell me."

Some kids wander out toward our side of the field. Alis moves deeper into the trail and I shadow him.

"Look," he says. "I guess I had the wrong idea or something. I just thought . . . I shouldn't have expected . . ." He stares down at my hand, and I remember when he held it. Then my memory morphs into Nathan and I get a flash of Alis's bike.

It all makes sense.

I run ahead so I can turn and face him. "This is about Nathan, isn't it?"

His eyebrows pull together. "Nathan? Is that his name?" He tries not to look at me, but I keep my eyes trained on his.

"Nathan is this guy from Reena's home group."

His scowl doesn't change, so obviously this isn't news for him.

I try to get the rest all out at once. "And he was on the

mountain when Faith fell, and then I found him at the grocery store and he wanted to walk me home. I thought he might tell me more about how he knew my sister, but then he stopped talking and he was holding my hand and I thought it might help, but I didn't want to, Alis. I didn't want him to hold my hand, or kiss me—"

I stop at the stunned look on his face. He must have missed that part.

"On the cheek," I add. "He kissed me on the cheek and said a bunch of strange stuff about love, and being Faith's boyfriend, and honestly, as much as I wanted to know about my sister, I couldn't wait to get away from him."

Alis stares at the trees above us. "Really?" he asks, turning his eyes back to me.

"I like you," I say, and even though I want to check over my shoulder and make sure Tessa's not somewhere lurking, I add, "A lot."

His face softens. For a few seconds neither of us knows what to do, but then he scoops up my hand in his and leads the way toward my house.

I wouldn't have minded if he'd waited there a little longer. If *he'd* kissed me. But I don't say anything. My heart's in overdrive right now, and I think I need to change the subject.

Alis beats me to it. "So tell me everything about what you found out."

I tell him about Celeste and Nathan and Detective Malovich.

"Wow, you've had a busy weekend," he says.

"Yup. So what about you? Were you locked at home, or just feeling slighted by your idiot girlfriend?" I snap my mouth shut, not even believing I said that.

"Reena was home all weekend," he says, not reacting to my words. "So I couldn't get out or use the phone."

Even though I've gotten used to the weather getting cooler, it's drizzling out today and a sudden sneeze hits. I grab a Kleenex from my pocket.

"Why don't you wear a jacket?" he asks. "It's been raining all day." He sounds slightly annoyed but I have a feeling it's not about my lack of jacket. It's about finding a way to get close to me.

"Have you ever had a girlfriend?" I ask, trying to let him know it's okay.

He slides his arms out of his Mack jacket. "You're changing the subject. Here, put this on."

He holds it behind me and I stuff my thick-sweatered arms into each side.

"You didn't answer my question," I say.

"You didn't answer *mine*," he says. "And no."

Shouldn't surprise me, I guess.

"Don't you own a jacket?" He looks away.

"Yes," I say. He stops in place and stares at me. He's wearing a long-sleeve cotton shirt with a Quicksilver logo across the front. It's starting to show dark dots of misty rain. He must be freezing. "Yes, I own a jacket, and I've also had a boyfriend, but neither have brought me any real comfort."

He suppresses a smile. When we walk again, his arm comes up behind me and rests on my shoulders. My breath catches. Alis's arm around me feels much more important than Dustin's ever did.

"So Reena must keep a good watch on you if you haven't had many friends."

"I haven't had *any* friends," he says. I feel him pull away a bit, so I bury myself deeper under his arm. Besides, I'm wearing his jacket. He'd freeze without me.

"Well, sometimes I think having lame friends is worse than having none at all."

"Is Tessa a lame friend?"

I think about this, but it doesn't take long. "No, she's a good one. Maybe the first good one." Funny how I can say this so easily to Alis, but I could never, ever, say it to Tessa.

"Were you ever friends with your sister?" he asks.

306

"Sure, when we were young. We set up tents and camped in the backyard, fought over toys, same as most kids." I take a big breath and let it out slowly. It's still a hard subject, but I'd rather talk about it with Alis than anyone. "I think it was the religion thing that really pulled us apart."

"Hmm. Same here."

"The stupid thing is, I think Faith still wanted to be my friend. I was the idiot who couldn't get past how sure she was about her beliefs." Saying it out loud makes it feel even more true, and I feel another wave of guilt wash over me.

"So you don't believe in God, then?"

I shake my head. Add a bitter laugh. "Oh, I believe in him, all right."

He smirks. "Right. You just don't like him."

I bite my lip to keep from agreeing. This conversation is hitting a deep, sore spot in me and I'm not totally sure if I can go there. "Faith wanted to . . . wanted to stay home on that night. The last night. I was too busy making up lies for my lame boyfriend to notice." I pause, not wanting to actually say it. But I have to. "I pushed her into going."

"Oh, Brie." His words rip open the sore spot inside me and a small whimper escapes my mouth. He pulls me closer, wrapping his other arm around me too. "I'm sorry."

I bury my face in his shirt and can't tell if it's the wetness from his shirt or from my tears that I feel on my face. When he squeezes me tighter, my body pulses with each cry. I've never felt this safe, like I can really let go. I don't want the feeling to end, but at the same time, it's jumbled together with my pain. I can't separate them.

I force a deep breath. Then another.

After a few minutes, we start walking again in silence, sticking to back roads in case Reena gets off early. It takes me a long time to feel clearheaded again. Almost at my house, Alis stops at the corner and pulls my hand to stop me.

"I wasn't sure if I should say anything, but, well, I guess whatever you said to Nathan worked. My sister's having a meeting tonight."

"Tonight? At your place?" I pull out my phone and look at the display, but I haven't missed any calls, which means Reena doesn't plan to invite me. I frown.

"Yeah. She said this morning that I should find some-where to go. That's kind of like code for 'Get the hell out before my meeting.'"

"So why didn't you want to tell me?"

"I don't think you should be a part of this, Brie. I don't know what's up with my sister, but—"

"Do you think she's dangerous?"

"No," he snaps. He's being defensive again, probably

because of own his confusion over this. It *is* his sister, and what if he thinks *she* might take the martyrdom thing seriously? Or what if Nathan's the one who's pushing that agenda? We don't really know what we're dealing with here. Alis shakes his head, staring at the ground. "I just don't know what to believe anymore."

"Look, Alis, I think the only way to feel better about any of this is to figure out what's really going on." His head doesn't move to look at me. "I'm not afraid."

"Well, maybe you should be," he says, louder. Angrier.

I'm having a hard time figuring out if he's protecting her, or me, or himself. Or maybe he's just scared of the unknown.

"I'll try to listen in tonight," Alis says. "I promise I'll tell you if I find out anything." I've never seen him so tense, and I know this is not up for discussion.

"Okay," I tell him.

He looks at me like he's not sure if he should believe me. I slide out of his jacket and offer it back to him before he leaves. As he walks down my street, I watch his back, knowing it's definitely not okay. I can't sit at home while the only group that knows the truth about my sister meets in Reena's room.

I just can't.

chapter THIRTY

*a*t the front closet I pull out the warmest jacket I can find, a blue and gray snow jacket of Faith's. She got it on sale at the end of last winter and I don't think she ever got a chance to wear it. It feels strange to slip my arms into it. Even though we were close to the same size, it feels way too big for me. I wonder if I should wear it, if Mom would freak out if she saw me. But I can't seem to bring myself to take it off.

Forty-five minutes later, I stand at the end of Maple Court, hunched behind the minivan in Alis's neighbor's driveway, wondering how much Alis will hate me for doing this. I thought about calling Tessa on the way, but couldn't bear the thought of Alis finding not only me outside his house, but Tessa as well.

Reena's white Civic is nowhere in sight.

"I thought you might show up." The sudden voice beside me makes a little yelp escape from my mouth.

"Shhh," Alis says. "It's just me."

I turn to him, but flit my eyes away. "I, um . . ."

"Uh-huh. I know." His calming voice entices me to look at him, and his caring eyes relax me even more. "Or I don't know, really. I don't know what you must be feeling or what I should do about Reena, but I've been sweating over it since I got home and I think I do need your help. I'm not very objective these days, but I just couldn't handle it if something happened to you."

I bite my lip. It feels good to know he cares so much. This makes me want to help him even more. "Listen," I say. "Let me do this. Why don't I find a place to hide, see what I can overhear, and this way I won't even have to join their group." I think about the Pooh-bear walkie-talkies and wish I had called Tessa. "You don't have to be involved anymore. I could just—"

"I am involved, Brie. It's my sister." His angry tone resurfaces. "Come on," he says, grabbing my hand and heading behind the house of the driveway we're in.

I don't argue. We duck behind Alis's garden swing, across the back lawn and through a side door into the garage.

"Reena could be home any minute now."

So definitely no time to bring Tessa in on this.

"You can hide in here," he goes on. "I'll go into the house and act like everything's normal, then come out to meet you when it's time for Reena's friends to show up."

"Got it. So where does Reena think you go when she kicks you out?"

He shrugs. "I used to go to the corner store and play video games. One time I guess I lost track of time and she had to come looking for me. She grounded me from the TV for two weeks. I'm sure that's where she assumes I always go."

"Your sister grounds you? No way." I snap my mouth shut, hoping I haven't embarrassed him.

"You don't know my sister," he says, without a hint of a blush. "Trust me, she gets her way on things." Alis eyes Faith's jacket, up and down.

"What? It's warm," I say.

"No, it's good." He reaches for the doorknob to the house.

"You know, you don't have to do this," I say. "Not tonight."

He stares at the wall beside me for a few seconds, and then meets my eyes. "Yeah. I do."

When he walks through into the house, I scan the garage

312

using the beam of fading daylight that streams through an upper window. It's pretty spotless, other than the dust. A pair of garbage cans sits in the corner. That's pretty much it.

Alis brings me a blanket and I make myself a comfortable little snuggle area on the step near the door. I swish the blanket around me, almost knocking over a small tool kit with a transparent lid that rests on the far side of the step.

A few minutes later Alis drops onto the stair beside me. "She just called. To make sure I leave the house. Says they'll be here soon."

After all the afternoons I've spent outside without a jacket, it suddenly feels very warm. I throw off the blanket.

"Where should we listen from?" I ask.

"Right here's good." He motions to where he came through from the house. "We can open the door a crack without getting caught, I think."

"You think?" I look toward the door, worried.

"It'll be okay." He wraps his hand over mine.

When I turn back to face him, I realize how close he is.

"It will, Brie. We'll get through this together."

I slowly let out the breath I've been holding.

"We have a few minutes," he whispers and a smile tugs at his lips. All this time, I'd been thinking how much he must hate me for putting him in this position with his sister, but his voice is soft, lulling, and I don't think he's capable of hate.

Something about Alis makes me feel like I can't pretend. I can't put on a face as though I'm confident. A strand of his dark hair falls in his face and he pushes it back. He nibbles his lip, and I want to tell him I'm nervous too.

He slides an inch closer and looks down at my lips. I've had lots of time to pull away, he makes sure of that. But I haven't moved forward, either. I force myself toward him ever so slightly.

With a sudden forward motion, he knocks into my nose. "Sorry," he murmurs, then tilts his head and tries again before I can say anything.

When he presses his lips into mine, they're warm and soft, and I immediately know this is different than any kiss I've had before. It's new and naive. But gentle. Caring. He puts a hand on the back of my head and steadies me. His lips angle slightly until he finds a good fit and his tongue finds mine. I slide my hands along his sides and up his back, feeling much like this is my very first kiss too.

We stop momentarily to rearrange our arms. He puts one around my lower back and pulls me closer. I feel his warm breath when he brings his lips toward mine again.

When he pulls away, his hand is on the side of my face,

touching along my cheek, down to my chin, my lips. I keep my eyes closed, feeling a warmth and tingle that goes all the way up my spine. It takes me several seconds to come to my senses when a rumble sounds in the driveway.

"She's here," he whispers, his face still close.

He slips an arm from around me and cracks open the door behind us. Through the small opening, I can see a sliver of their living room—a striped gray couch sits against the far burgundy wall. When I get a flash of Reena traipsing across the small line of my vision, I hold my breath. She sings a worship song I don't recognize.

The doorbell rings and Reena's singing cuts out. The pitter-patter of her feet tap toward the front door and then I hear another female voice.

I recognize the voice immediately. Celeste. She enters the living room wearing an oversize pink sweatshirt and faded jeans. Not her usual put-together look.

"Thanks for coming," Reena says to her and the way she angles her head from side to side looks like she's trying to catch Celeste's eyes. "I think you'll be glad you did."

"I'm only here because I want some answers," Celeste replies, staring down at her feet.

I move a little closer to the door.

"Don't worry, we'll get to that." Reena ushers Celeste out

of sight and into the living room. "Okay, we won't wait for Nathan."

Reena's voice carries like she's walking around with a microphone. Celeste seems to be mumbling questions, I can tell, because Reena's giving answers.

"Of course I want to talk about it! It's *you* who's been turning tail, like Peter after Christ was arrested. It was a great thing she did!"

Alis strokes my hair. I expect to be uncomfortable when he looks at me now that we've kissed, but I'm not. I can't hear Celeste's response.

"Good. We'll get into more of that later," Reena says. "But I called you here for something else. I have some exciting news."

"Look, Reena," Celeste butts in, and I'm surprised at her boldness. Alis raises his eyebrows, apparently surprised too. "I'm out, okay. I just need to know what happened to my best friend."

"Calm down," Reena says in a soothing voice. Even though I can't see them, I picture her wrapping an arm around Celeste. "It will all make sense, if you'll just listen. We need four, our best four, to complete our circle of energy." She pauses, probably indicating somehow that Celeste is among her best.

"Yes, that is exciting," Celeste says. I can tell by her tone she's humoring Reena. "But what does this have to do with Faith?"

"You don't understand. You're not there yet. That's why we have to go back to the mountains."

"Well, I'm *not* going unless you tell me about Faith!"

Alis's eyes are so wide, I'm afraid they're going to fall out. I'm surprised too. And proud of Celeste.

Reena crosses out of sight. I can hear her at the hall closet, opening the folding door and closing it again. Then she repeats the motion. I turn to Alis.

"It's a stress thing," he whispers.

After a few more rattles of the closet door, Reena marches back to the living room. "Look," she says, and I can't believe how calm her voice is now. Her anxiety methods obviously work. "Sometimes these are spur-of-the-moment decisions. When some of us hear from our Higher Power, we don't want to wait."

So she's saying Faith did martyr herself?

Alis leans in close and says, "There's usually more of them. It's weird that there are only two." I know he's changing the subject, but for a second or two, it helps. Sweat trickles down the side of my cheek. How did it get so hot in here? I guess he notices the heat too, because he pulls away in a hurry.

But when he does, he knocks the small tool kit off the step, and it topples to the floor with a clank. We jump away from it in one quick motion as if it sent electrical shocks through both of us. We huddle together, counting the seconds.

chapter THIRTY-ONE

*n*ine, ten, eleven . . .

The door swings open above us. A bright light gleams from the middle of the room and feels like an interrogation light—aimed directly at Alis and me.

Gasps erupt from the shadows behind the door. Then, "What is going on?"

"Hey, Ree," Alis says. His voice sounds surprisingly light. "This is my friend—"

"Annie," I jump in.

"Yeah, this is Annie. We were just talking out here. You said out of the house, but the garage is fine, right?"

Celeste's eyebrows contort as she pokes her head past Reena's shoulders in the doorway. I shoot her a pleading look, having no idea how I could have even considered joining their group. I can't be two people at once.

Since Reena hasn't said anything, Alis goes on. "She's just a friend and it was only—"

"Shut. Up," Reena says, focusing hard on the wall behind us. Then she glares at me and sizes me up as if I'm a stranger, not the same person she met at the nursing home. And she certainly doesn't seem like the same sweet girl I met. "Where did you find this *friend?*" She turns her eyes back to Alis on the last word.

"From, uh . . . the high school," he says. "I was done with my test early last week and she was in the hall, and we just got to talking."

Reena snaps her head back to me. "And so you found out he was my brother and decided, what, to spy on me? Is that it?"

Not only does Reena's glare feel hot on my skin, but I can sense Celeste's laser eyes too. "No!" I say. "That's not it. Well, not exactly."

Reena crosses her arms.

Celeste steps forward, so I race on before she can speak. "Yeah, I heard you were his sister. And yeah, I wanted to find out more about you. But, no, I would never spy." I take a breath and force my most innocent face. "I told Alis I wanted to come over and get to know him. I really didn't give him a choice."

Alis's tense face softens. A thankful look.

"Um, hang on," Celeste says, holding up a hand.

"He intercepted me when I got here." I talk louder. "And said if I wanted to hang out, it had to be in the garage. I've been asking him questions about you and about your group, because I've been so excited since I met you. Then when you didn't call—"

Celeste looks back and forth between us.

"There are procedures," Reena says, banging her palm against the house door. Her eyes flutter back and forth. Clearly, she doesn't like being confused. She pulls the door shut and then opens it again. I wonder if she's considering my story. She turns slowly. "These things take time, and if you're so impatient, maybe you're not the type we're looking for."

"I'm sorry," I say. "You're right. I was impatient."

Celeste purses her lips, like she's not sure where her allegiance lies, which is crazy because clearly she and I are out for the same thing here: answers. But something still seems to tie her to Reena.

I know everything will change by tomorrow. Reena will

know all about my lies, so I try a last-ditch effort to play up my alias. "I heard there was a girl from our school who killed herself for Jesus. Was she part of your group?" I'm surprised how easy it is to get the words out. It's as if I'm talking about someone else. A stranger.

Celeste's eyes barrel toward me like a two-ton boulder.

"I want to join," I add.

Celeste steps in front of Reena and faces me. "What are you doing—"

"Annie," I finish her sentence, so she doesn't blow my cover quite yet. Reena may be willing to give some answers if she thinks she has devoted followers. It's my only chance. "I can only imagine being around a group of people who are so sold on what they believe. It's a dream I've had for years, and I—"

A ring of the doorbell cuts off my words.

"Great," Reena says, rolling her eyes. "Can someone please let him in?"

At first, no one moves, but then Celeste backs into the house.

Before I have time to process the ramifications of this new participant, Nathan stands beside Celeste in the doorway. They whisper, and it's impossible to know how much Celeste has told him, but when he spots me, he pushes his way through.

"Annie," he says, purely excited.

I let out a breath. He still thinks I'm Annie.

Reena glares at him. "How on earth do *you* know her?"

"I met him at the grocery store, and he seemed so on fire for God, so I wondered if maybe—"

"You wondered if he might be part of my group." Reena nods, but her tone doesn't sound like she's buying it.

"That's right. On my way home, I asked him if he knew you."

"You took her home!" Now Reena really loses her cool. I can't quite figure out why this is such an unforgivable sin, but I don't have time to mull it over. I need to change the subject.

"How do I get in the group?"

Reena studies me, but I divert my eyes, afraid of falling under her spell again. I expect her to head for the door and kick me out, but then she says, "There's an initiation first."

Nathan's lips fall into a straight tense line.

Reena blows out a breath, which turns her whole face into a smile. "Okay. This is fine. Fine," she says again, like she's convincing herself. "Let's take a little trip to The Point, friends."

She wants to take me up the mountain! I bite down on my tongue, trying to keep my cool.

"Hey, Ree," Alis says, his eyes giving away a hint of fear.

"Why don't we go into the backyard. The hill behind the house—"

"Get lost," Reena snaps, like a flyswatter on a fly.

Alis stares at Reena, but only for a second. He doesn't even give a cursory glance in my direction, but turns and walks straight for the outside door.

I wonder if he'll go for help somewhere or if he's still too confused and intimidated by his sister to know what to do. He hasn't got a cell phone, and I have a hard time imagining him going to the neighbors.

I'm now committed to go up to where Faith died, on the top of the friggin' mountain, with these people who were with her that night. And I willingly got myself into this. If I were Alis, I'd probably just want to get myself the hell out of here too.

Reena turns to Nathan, as if he hadn't heard any of her plans. "Annie wants to prove her trustworthiness. Her devotion." She turns her wide eyes on me for a moment.

Oh, no, I don't! Looking past her eyes, I change my mind. I don't want to find out the whole story about my sister. Not like this.

chapter THIRTY-TWO

i'm coming too," Celeste says.

She takes a step toward me. A protective gesture. I can tell by her pulled-back shoulders, there's no talking her out of this, no saving her from getting involved any deeper. She needs answers too. But when I glance down at her hands, they're both trembling.

"Oh. Good." Reena's voice trills up, as if it's a question. "You can move up to the next level while we're there," she adds, squinting like this is a test. When Celeste nods, Reena brightens and heads for the house. "I'll get my folder."

Nathan turns to the door leading outside. "We should get in the car."

Celeste and I follow, but almost at the door, Celeste juts her arm out to hold me back. After letting Nathan move a few steps around the corner, she whispers, "What are you doing?"

"Trying to get some answers."

"Go home, Brie," she says. "This is not a game."

"I know. My sister's dead, remember?"

She picks at her thumbnail. She probably doesn't know any more than I do, but feels just as responsible. Maybe more so.

"Were you there, then?" I ask softly.

She nods, not meeting my eye. "At first. I should have stayed with her, but I left . . . before." She stares at her feet. "I was scared because they were arguing so much. I thought we should just leave, but Faith, she didn't want to. Reena was suggesting all this crazy stuff and saying things that didn't make sense and Faith wanted to stay and set her straight." Celeste sounds like she's about to cry. "I went to that other youth group to clear my head."

"How come you told the police you were there when it happened?"

She shoves her hands in her pockets. "I don't know. Nathan came over that night and told me Faith had fallen. He said she had been really upset because I left. He didn't

326

tell the police that though, and said he wouldn't tell them as long as I backed up his story. It doesn't have to be anyone's fault, he told me." She swallows. "I felt so guilty and I didn't know what else to do."

"But you know she wouldn't have . . . you're the one who told me she never would have killed herself. Especially not just because you left. You know that."

She nods, but her eyebrows still pull together like she *doesn't* know. Not really. She's so confused I doubt she knows anything right now. "The next morning when the police came to my house, Nathan's words were the only ones I could think of. I found out later that Reena didn't even give a statement and now she's talking like—"

"Like what?"

She looks at me now. "You should get out of here now, Brie. I'm serious. Before your parents lose another daughter."

The saliva dries from my mouth with her words. "But I can't." I wait until I sense her understanding. "Do you think this is the only way to get answers?"

Celeste nods. "Reena opens up when the meetings get going." Her eyes show her worry, but now I think I'm starting to understand. She can't stop blaming herself until she knows the truth about what happened.

Nathan ducks his head back around the corner with his

brow furrowed. I hold up my purse in one quick motion.

"Found it," I call.

He turns back for the car and Celeste follows. I take one more deep breath before I round the corner behind them.

After slamming the door of the house, Reena checks and double-checks her mailbox by the glow of their porch light. She peeks around the side of the house and shakes her head when she walks back for the car. I assume she's looking for Alis, but can't find him.

Reena gets into the driver's seat of her Honda with Nathan beside her and Celeste and me squished into the small backseat. When I reach to buckle my seat belt, I see a swatch of red and black poking between my seat and Celeste's. I give it a tug, because it looks exactly like the material Alis's jacket is made of. When the swatch pulls away from me and disappears between the seats, I nearly scream, but bite my lip to rein it in.

I wait until Reena's on the road and diverted to take a discreet glance behind me. There's a knob to fold the backseat down on the outside edge of my seat, just like the one in Faith's Toyota.

The trunk. Alis is in the trunk. Which probably means he didn't call the police or anyone else for help. He thinks we can take care of this ourselves. I feel a sudden burst of confidence from this. He knows his sister better than any of us.

Of course, he probably thinks he has no other options.

"Why don't we put on some worship music," Nathan says, reaching for the dial.

He turns the volume loud, and he and Reena sing along. "Holy, holy, holy . . ."

Because I recognize the song from when I attended church with my parents, I make a show of joining in. When Reena glances back at us, Celeste follows suit.

Reena watches my mouth for a second, then turns to face the road as it begins to twist up the mountain. Luckily, it's pretty dark within the trees, so I can't see how high we're climbing. Still, my heart beats wildly in my chest. Sitting directly behind Reena's seat, I keep my eyes trained on her face in the rearview mirror. When she really gets into the music, she closes her eyes intermittently.

The good news is, she's paying little attention to Celeste and me. The bad news: We'll likely die in a car wreck on the way up this windy incline. Though, I must admit, that sounds better than making it to the top. The road splits in two several times, but Reena seems to know the way.

I lean slightly toward Celeste. "I'm texting for help," I whisper. She nods.

Reena's eyes dart to us in the rearview mirror. I jerk back

in my seat and fake the same pained expression she uses when she belts out lyrics.

Finally, the incline evens out and Reena parks. By the moonlight all I see are boulders and rocks in every direction. I can't see a cliff edge anywhere. Maybe she decided not to go all the way to the top. Maybe they're going to initiate me right here.

I can live with that.

Nathan steps out of the car first and Reena gets out and slams her door. When she moves to his side of the car, her face contorts like she's angry with him. A push to his chest confirms it. I wonder if this is still about him walking me home.

Celeste bends forward with her hands over her face. Even though I'm sure she's upset about all this, I don't have time to comfort her. I use the top edges of my purse to hide the glow of my cell phone. It has five missed calls, and suddenly I realize I forgot to leave a note for Dad. But when I scroll to the last one, it's from Tessa. I hit reply and frantically type a text message.

I barely get the word HELP typed in when Celeste sits up, her eyes wet. I start to type our location and seconds later, Celeste reaches for the door handle, I suspect to keep Reena distracted.

"Don't look in her eyes," she murmurs to me as she gets out.

"Brie." Alis's whisper from behind me makes me jump and the motion seems to remind Reena I'm here. She turns to the car to find me.

"Shhh," I say under my breath. My hand fumbles over my cell phone buttons and I hit all the ones in the general vicinity of send just as Reena bends into the car. I throw my purse to the floor and kick it under the seat.

Nathan leans in through the other door, about to say something.

"Get away from her," Reena snaps.

They share a look, and for a second I feel like I'm in the middle of a lover's spat. Was he not *Faith's* boyfriend?

"Come on," Reena says to me in a friendlier tone. I feel my shoulders start to relax, but I fight it. I keep my eyes from hers.

Somehow I get my legs beneath me and stand. The first thing I notice outside the car is the music. I haven't noticed it in days, but Faith hums again, loud and clear.

I've always known it's just a figment of my imagination, or a by-product of grieving or whatever, but now, I'm shocked at the volume and the clarity. The other thing that surprises me is how bright it is with no streetlights around. The moon looks so big and close up here. A constant reminder of how high we are.

Reena leads the way behind a boulder. "Let's go."

I glance back at the car. How will Alis get out of the trunk? In a split second, I realize that maybe he tucked his jacket through the seats for a reason. Maybe he wanted me to unlatch it for him so he could get out.

"I . . . uh, forgot my purse," I say, backing toward the car.

Reena laughs. "Don't be silly. It'll be fine. No one's around." She spreads her hands, as if to prove how absolutely isolated we are.

Celeste mistakes my hesitance for fear, and jumps in with "I-I'll go first. If that's okay."

"Yeah," Nathan says, stepping between Reena's car and me. "Let's do this."

Reluctantly, I follow Reena and Celeste behind the boulder. Nathan trails behind me. On the other side, we weave along a small dirt path leading us higher. Celeste sticks close behind Reena, but stumbles a little, and it gives me an idea. I force a slip and fall to the ground, hitting the dirt with the side of my shoulder and face to make it look extra convincing.

"Oh, come on," Reena says. "It's not that steep."

Nathan reaches to help me up, but when Reena glares at him, he backs off.

All three of them stay in place and stare at me, probably finding it hard to believe anyone could be so klutzy. "I guess the air up here is making me lightheaded," I say. "Maybe I should sit at the car for a few minutes."

Celeste's head snaps toward me. I know she's right. We have to go through with this now if we ever want some answers about my sister.

"It's up to you," Reena says. "If you're not eager enough for our group, then you won't be able to—"

"I am," I say. "Really."

I push myself up from the ground and hug Faith's jacket tighter around myself more from nerves than chill.

I can't make out much around me until we round the crest of the small hill. I gasp. I can see the whole world, or at least the Lite-Brite image of the township of Sharon. The dots of brightness wobble in my vision.

"So here we are," Reena says to Celeste. "You wanted to go first? You're sure you're not going to run away on us again, right?"

Celeste jitters her head side to side slightly, not looking sure at all. She takes slow steps toward the cliff edge. I want to reach out and grab her, pull her back, but she holds out her hands to each side about a foot away from the edge. All I can picture is the dream I had of Faith, arms outstretched, feet slipping off of rocks and into a dark abyss. And then of Faith's image changing to my own. I fumble my hands into my jacket pockets to keep them from trembling.

Reena opens the file she brought along, and I immediately recognize the multicolored papers that we'd discovered in the drawer of her room. The slight smile on her face tells me everything is going according to plan.

"All right, let's start." Reena glances back toward me. "She can't be in on this," she tells Nathan. "But I'm watching you. Keep your distance."

Nathan steps in front of me, blocking my view of the other two, and holds his hands out like an invisible force field. He guides me back a few feet without actually touching me until the back of my legs hit something solid. I look back at a large rock. Squatting down, I sit on it, hoping it'll give me a bit of a view past Nathan's legs, but he immediately crouches into my vision. It's more of a romantic gesture than a blocking one.

"Too bad." I try to smile coyly. "I was looking forward to seeing how it all works."

He whispers about how glad he is to have me here. I flutter my eyelashes, paying little attention to him and taking a peek over his shoulder. There's enough glow from the moon up here that I can see Reena holding her file folder out with one of those scribbly cross stickers on it a few feet in front of Celeste's face.

Each time Nathan stops talking to take a breath, I over-hear a few words of Reena's. "All your thoughts, all your cares and worries are emptying into the bucket in front of you."

I look down, and there's no bucket. She asks Celeste to repeat several Bible verses, and Celeste complies in a mono-tone. *Is Reena hypnotizing her?*

Great. I'm in this alone after all.

"The best part is," Nathan goes on, adjusting into my vision, "we'll see each other at least twice a week."

I fake a giggle, but the truth is, this does make me relax a little. If Nathan thinks I'll be around to see him twice a week, that seems like a good sign.

Celeste's voice, suddenly loud, interrupts us. "I offer my body as a living sacrifice. . . ."

I'm about to run past Nathan and stop Celeste before she launches herself off the cliff, but before I move, she cuts to another scripture. And then another. Celeste spouts Bible verses, along with their references like she's racing through a timed spelling bee.

I swallow. I've never heard Celeste so loud and so bold. She's so obviously not herself. When she stumbles over a few words, Reena steps in and tells her the proper ones, but Reena's nodding head tells me Celeste is doing just fine, even with mistakes. I don't know a single verse without a Bible sitting right in front of me, and suddenly I realize how easily Reena will break my charade.

"I must say, I'm impressed, Celeste." Reena turns to us. "Start the fire, Nathan. I think she's ready for the branding ritual."

I swallow. *Branding? With fire?* As much as I can see of Celeste, she hasn't flinched, not at any of this. I need to get her out of this somehow before she wakes up with burns all over her body.

Nathan nudges me off of the rock while Reena announces that they'll be going through the "Higher Scriptures" next. She starts reciting lines. Celeste waits for Reena to finish each one before repeating it back. I can't concentrate on any of the words as I watch Nathan grab small twigs and stack them in a pile. He digs matches, paper, and two long metal rods out of a backpack.

"Um, you don't use those on, like, people, right?" I whisper.

Nathan arranges the wood in a small teepee and then smiles up at me. He pulls down the middle of his shirt a few inches and I see it. My mouth goes dry. In the middle of his chest is a dark mark that looks like the scribbly cross from the stickers. It's blackened and looks like it's been there for a while. I wonder if it still hurts. Part of me wants to reach out and touch it, since I can't quite believe it's really there.

"Pain increases the energy in our circle," he says. "We have greater power."

I can't breathe and try to get my bearings while he adjusts his shirt back over the mark and lights the fire. My concentration is shot. Reena and Celeste's voices fade in and out of my consciousness, and blend together until I catch the phrase "higher power than God."

Celeste repeats the phrase without so much as a blink. I tune into the next one, a lengthy promise about committing to the Art of Martyrdom. Trusting your leader in all things, life and death. Trusting your leader above all other people and entities. I stare down at the long metal rods which Nathan now has heating in the fire.

Celeste repeats each word methodically. As they leave her mouth, I try to picture Faith saying those same words. But it's impossible to imagine. Faith didn't, would never have been able to repeat those words. Not without an hour and a half argument on the finer points of the meaning of such suggestions.

Unless . . . how strong is hypnotism?

I can't bear the thought. Could Faith have been branded too?

When Reena completes the page, she slides it into her

file. "Welcome, Orange." She says the word "orange" slowly, like it's more than just a color. Pulling out an orange sticker, she holds it up and hands it to Celeste. I wonder if Reena knows she picked the yellow one off of her dash.

While Reena looks down to rearrange her folder, Celeste darts her eyes to me. Or at least one of her eyes. The moonlight glints off her right one, which is turned in sharply toward her nose.

That must have been what Celeste had been doing bent over in the car—taking out her contact lenses. She can't see a thing! My heart jumps. Could she be faking the hypnotism?

Celeste turns back to Reena. "This is great," she says, and if I hadn't seen her eyes, I'd almost believe she is happy about the whole thing. She takes a step toward to Reena. "I did it. Everything you asked."

Reena narrows her eyes slightly, like she knows there's a "but" coming.

"Now can you please tell me about Faith?" Celeste says the words softly and sweetly.

"It's almost hot enough," Nathan calls out.

"But—"

"You're not done yet, Celeste." There's a bit of a clip to Reena's voice, and Celeste must recognize it too. She stares past Reena toward the fire and I can tell she's trying to keep herself composed, but I'm afraid her quickly blinking eyes are going to give her away.

I have to save her before they hold her down and brand her. "What about *my* initiation?" I say. And they all turn to me.

chapter THIRTY-THREE

*r*eena hands the folder to Celeste and walks toward me with her arm out, "Just step up here."

"Uh, no. I mean, I can't. Not up there. I'm afraid of heights. Petrified, actually." Just the thought of stepping closer toward the cliff's edge makes the sweat buds in my armpits rain like a monsoon.

"Annie," Reena says, consolingly. If she hadn't used my alias, I'd have forgotten it. "It's okay. We all understand. And we've all been there. But our group is about trust. First, you need to learn to trust God, and then you need to accept a human trust. . . . Us." I think about Nathan's words about pain. These are not people I want to trust. Ever.

Celeste knows about my extreme fear of heights, but I can't blame her for not stepping in. I really can't decide which is worse: falling off this cliff, or having a fire-soaked branding iron driven into my skin. But what if Reena tries to hypnotize me? I don't have the luxury of removing my contact lenses.

"How about this," I say, thinking fast. "I'll say all the verses, any that you want, but I could say them right here." I hold my arms to my sides like Celeste had. Now I know why she jumped in to go first. So she could show me how to fake it convincingly.

"No, not there." Reena shakes her head. "It has to be the *right* way."

Of course. The OCD thing. Everything has a system. But I can't move. I desperately want to help Celeste, to get some answers, but I just can't do it. Reena's face tightens with each passing second.

"Wait! What if I take just one step over that way." I motion toward the edge. "And you give me some inspiring words. Maybe about the martyr girl from your group. I'd love to hear how committed she was. And then maybe I can work myself up to take another step." I can't believe how easily the lie slides from my lips.

Reena stares at me, and for a long second I wonder if it was over the top.

"It'll be okay, Reena," Nathan says, still stoking the fire. "And we need her, right? We need four."

"Fine," she says, and blinks a few times in quick succession. "Take a step first," she says to me.

I try to do a little shuffle for my first step, since the area is small and the edge is only a few feet away, but Reena shakes her head. I take a deep breath and lift my foot, moving it forward, and then bring my other foot to meet it. When I see farther over the cliff's edge into oblivion, I wobble and Reena grabs my arm to help me regain my balance.

"See, it's fine," she says, as though teetering any closer wouldn't actually be a death sentence.

"So tell me something about that girl. Faith, right?" My voice is barely recognizable through my chattering teeth. I look at Celeste, begging for her to help me get through this.

"Yeah." She comes up beside Reena. "Inspire us, Reena."

Reena nods and stares down at the ground like she's trying to remember.

"Is this the spot where she died?" I push.

Reena's eyes widen, and I can almost see the scene running through her mind.

"She stood there." Reena points to the place where Celeste had been, but doesn't move her eyes. "And we talked through each of the Bible verses as she read them. The meanings, the histories, who wrote each one. She was a smart girl." Reena blinks, and a tear drips from her eyelashes. Then she remains quiet for several seconds.

"And the Higher Scriptures?" Celeste ventures softly.

Reena looks up at Celeste, her eyebrows contorted together. "I—I—"

"Another step first," Nathan interjects, suddenly standing away from the fire. "We can't forget about Annie here. This is an important night for her." He winks at me. Luckily, Reena's attention is still on Celeste and she misses Nathan's flirting.

I try to channel some of Celeste's acting abilities. "The more I hear, the more excited I am."

Reena stares at me now, waiting. Nathan's words clearly brought her back to her systematic thinking. I clench my teeth and take another step, making sure it's big enough to keep her from demanding a second one.

A rock shoots out from under my foot and topples over the edge. I'm close enough to watch it fall and jut off jagged peaks along its path into nothingness. Did Faith slip while she argued with Reena? Or had Reena actually hypnotized her?

"Wow." My jittery voice is nearly impossible to understand. "Tell me more."

"First, a Bible verse." Nathan smiles at Reena as though he's trying to earn brownie points.

She motions for Celeste to pass him the folder. "Why don't you do the next one, Red," she says to Nathan.

I remember the red sticker on Nathan's backpack. He beams at Reena addressing him by a color. When I look up to his eyes, they've gone glassy. I wonder if all it takes is the mention of someone's color to bring them into a hypnotic trance.

Nathan holds the folder up in front of my face so now a yellow sticker is right in my line of vision. He's going to hypnotize me. Only a foot from the edge!

"Just concentrate on the cross," he says, "And repeat after me. 'Fear the LORD and serve him faithfully with all your heart; consider what great things he has done for you.'"

I repeat it quickly, but keep my eyes an inch below the cross. Unfortunately, it's still in my peripheral vision, but I hope that won't be enough. As I say the words, I wonder what Faith would have thought of them. I decide she would have wholeheartedly agreed with this Yellow Level verse and that makes it easier for me to deliver.

When I'm done, I glance to Reena, and then Celeste. Nothing. I don't feel any different. I silently thank God. Since I only have one more step to go—a step I desperately don't intend to take—I know this is my last chance to get some answers.

"Tell me about Faith's last words," I say. Celeste shoots me a warning look, so I add, "For inspiration."

Reena's lips tighten.

"Did Faith say the Higher Verses?" Celeste asks Reena.

"You know how argumentative Faith could be." Reena's voice has moved back to wistful and she stares down at the rocky ground.

Nathan looks into my eyes and I try to hold his, because now I hear Reena whimpering.

"So that's why you needed to push her," Celeste says, soothingly.

"It all happened so fast. I didn't mean to . . ."

"You did the right thing," Nathan blurts. The sudden noise almost makes me lose my balance again. "Once you believe, you can't go back!" He moves over to Reena, slides his arm around her, and simultaneously pushes Celeste away with his other. "It was the right thing, Reena. She was straying from the truth, becoming impure. Like you said, it was the only way to keep the true vision—"

"The vision?" As I'm working this out in my head, I can't keep my mouth shut. I march toward them, not feeling any relief from being another foot farther from the cliff's edge. Heat rushes to my face. "You killed my sister for some vision?"

Everything stops. Even the slight breeze around us seems to still.

"Wait, what?" Nathan turns and grabs my arm in one

quick motion. Reena drops into a lump on the ground, her sobbing becoming hysterical.

My eyes flash red. So much anger and sense of injustice is rising up in me, I can't help but tell him what. "I'm Faith's sister." His grip hardens on my arm, but I don't care. "Let go of me." I try to yank away, but he's strong. I can't believe how he went from hippy love freak to this. Fear must come out in different ways.

He grits his teeth. "Your family is not going to ruin everything for us. Right, Reena?"

"I—I don't know," she says from her lump on the ground.

"You really think this is right?" I ask. "Send people off the cliff when they don't believe the same things you do? What happened to your big 'God is Love' philosophy, Nathan?"

Holding my arm, he forces me backward, toward the edge, and I scream.

"Get away from her!" Alis appears at the base of the trail, covered in white fluff, his pocketknife hanging from one hand.

He must have ripped apart the car seat to get it unlatched. Nathan spins and looks at him, then at Reena. "Why the hell is your brother here?"

Nathan lets go of me and rushes for Alis, grabbing the arm with the knife. Nathan has Alis by at least thirty pounds and it takes only a few seconds for him to shake the knife free. He throws it over his shoulder and we all watch it tumble over the edge.

"Come on, Black," Nathan says to Reena. "What's wrong with you?"

As in Reena M. Black? But with his words, something changes in Reena. She tilts her head up and wipes her eyes as though she's wiping all the emotion from her soul. She stands.

"I didn't bring him," she says in a hoarse but determined voice.

She glares at Alis, but he ignores her and turns to me. "Brie, run."

I turn to race past the dwindling fire and down the trail, but Reena grabs me from behind. I look over and Nathan has Alis. When they pull us back up to the small flat area, the first thing I see is that Celeste is gone, but I think Reena and Nathan are too busy to notice.

Nathan gives Alis a shove toward the edge. "They know everything now," he says to Reena. He pauses, then adds, "It's like you always say—you can't go back."

Reena's grip on me is tight, but she doesn't move. "It's my brother," she whimpers. Her emotional state seems to be bouncing back and forth between stoic and basket case. Part of her seems to want to give in to the hypnotic state, to stick to the rules, but she can't because it's Alis at stake here.

"It's the only way," Nathan says. "It will set them free." But he waits for Reena's agreement. She's still the leader and he's committed to following her word.

There has to be a way to talk her out of it. Should I sing and chant at the top of my lungs? Bow down and offer my undying devotion?

"This isn't what God wants, Ree!" Alis yells at her.

She scoffs and swings me around face-first toward the cliff. "What would you know about what God wants? God is good. Merciful. And I think he'll forgive you both, if you give yourselves now. With me."

Nathan's head snaps to Reena. "No! You can't. I need you!" His head swivels to the fire and then back to her. "I'll stay and cover for you. Like last time."

When I glance over my shoulder, I'm shocked to see Reena's face suddenly calm. Nathan focuses on her too, and an understanding seems to pass between them. His face goes white, but I don't know why.

"You'll have me," Reena says. "Forever now." She walks me toward Alis and Nathan. Toward the edge. I try to dig my heels in, but there's no use. Reena is too strong. "If we sacrifice my brother," she says, "we're all going with him."

chapter THIRTY-FOUR

nathan stares at Reena.

"Nathan . . ." And now she laughs. "Don't you see? This is the path to peace." Her voice is almost singsongy.

So her way out of this is to die? For all of us to die.

Nathan lets go of Alis and puts his hands up like he's under arrest. Like he's giving in. Reena takes a step to block Alis and me from any path other than straight down.

Alis moves slightly, like he's trying to shield me from the edge, but it's clearly a useless effort.

"You don't have to do this," I tell Reena, but she's still glazed over.

She takes a step forward so she's almost up against me. With one good swat, Alis and I would both go flying.

"I know you want to die, Ree, but is this how you want it?" Alis tries to penetrate her gaze with his own eyes.

"There is peace," I plead with her. "There's forgiveness. For everything." They're not my words. My sister didn't deserve to die, and this is what Faith would have said at this moment.

Reena's grip loosens on me, and her breathing accelerates, almost as though she's hyperventilating.

"It's okay, Ree," Alis says. "Somehow it'll all be okay."

I start to breathe, but behind Reena's head, down the slope of the mountain, I see a bluish haze. Or maybe red.

Cops. And suddenly, a siren blares, then cuts to a jarring silence.

Reena's head jerks toward the echo and she takes in the lights. "It's too late." She tightens her grip on my arm and grabs Alis with her other hand.

"Wait!" I say, trying to wrench out of her grip without budging my feet. "We should pray first. I mean, to commit this moment—"

But my words are interrupted by another sound. A loud, clear, eerie sound, echoing from . . . from . . . I don't know where. After a few seconds, I recognize it.

This time it's not Faith's voice. It's her shofar.

Reena's head whips around looking for the source. Her hand loosens on my arm, but I stay motionless. Soon it drops away and she wraps both arms around herself like she's in a straightjacket. And maybe she should be. The shofar is loud, but her sobs are louder. Without a sound, I inch along the edge of the cliff until I'm out of her reach. Alis follows my lead on the other side. Nathan is nowhere in sight.

The bellow of the shofar keeps sounding, like it never runs out of breath. Like Faith will not be silenced.

"Tessa," I whisper to Alis when he's close enough.

When I turn toward the path to make a run for it, I barrel into a big figure. Wearing a police uniform.

Plan Y: The truth, and nothing but the truth.

Four of them appear, one by one, and surround us. The last one, Detective Malovich, has Tessa by the arm in her pink shirt and my jeans. With her other hand, Tessa holds Faith's shofar.

"You're here," I say, but my throat feels like cotton. Two of the cops move over by Reena and murmur something to her. The echo of the shofar still seems to hang in the air over the scene like an eerie funeral procession. The other two officers lead Tessa and me back down to the cars, but Alis jerks away when a cop tries to herd him along.

"That's my sister," he says.

At first I'm surprised that he's defending her after everything that happened. But Alis has a bigger heart than she deserves. Maybe a bigger heart than anyone deserves.

"Are you okay?" the cop at my arm asks when we reach the cars.

I nod, and then he lets out a string of questions about how long we've been up here, who the others are, and how I know them. I exchange a glance with Tessa.

"Hey, Osterman," Detective Malovich says to the interrogating cop. He stands from his bent position near Reena's car and wipes off a bunch of fluff from her torn-up backseat. "We need to talk to her parents first."

My parents. The thought makes the knot in my stomach spread through my whole torso. How will they handle the whole awful truth, and the fact that I came up this mountain to get it?

Tessa's dad's car is angled in sideways ahead of the cop cars, looking like it slid into home plate. Obviously the VW won't be getting out until after the cop cars are gone.

Detective Osterman switches places and stays behind so Malovich can drive me down the mountain. After asking if the purse from Reena's backseat is mine, Malovich hands it to me with the top unzipped and opens the back door of the cop car for me. I'm surprised when Tessa automatically gets in behind me.

It's only after we're moving down the rocky, winding road that I notice my intense shivering. I turn and stare at Tessa beside me. "How did you know where to find us?"

"Well, gee," she says. "When I read 'Help . . . POIN . . .' I initially thought you might be hanging out at Mr. Poindexter's house trying to get some extra credit for art class. But then I remembered how bad your drawings were, so I decided it couldn't be that. Plus there was the smoke."

"So my text got through? I had to throw the phone."

"Hey, quiet down," Malovich reprimands from up front.

Tessa doesn't exactly take well to directives. "You could have at least told me how to dress," she murmurs a few seconds later. "I did the best I could to come incognito on short notice."

Her spiked hair does look a little silly with the preppy clothes, but I wasn't going to mention it.

"Sorry," I whisper. "But I'm surprised you called the police. Especially when you had your dad's car." I add this part so quietly that even Tessa can barely hear me.

She fiddles with the zipper on her boot. "Dad always goes grocery shopping on Monday nights."

Changing the subject again. Why am I surprised? I sigh.

She rolls her eyes. "But your cryptic message looked important. So I had to go." She picks at something on her boot and chuckles. "You'd think I could at least get across town before he reported it stolen."

"You didn't bring them on purpose?"

She scoffs. "You'd better be glad they followed me. What the hell would I have been able to do with Reena holding you two over the edge of a cliff?"

"It wasn't quite like that." I'd like to tell her that I practically talked Reena out of the whole thing before the cops even got there, but it doesn't seem like the time to gloat.

"You girls need to keep quiet until we've taken your statements," Malovich says. But there's a softness to his voice.

I sit there for a few minutes, letting my equilibrium return to normal. "So you were right." I whisper. "About Alis, I mean. I kissed him."

Tessa's head jerks toward me. I don't give her the satisfaction of looking back, but study my nails instead.

After a few seconds, her shock fades and she asks, "Did you get what you were looking for? About Faith, I mean?"

"Yeah. I guess. I don't have all the details, but I'm pretty sure she didn't kill herself."

"Reena's fault?"

I nod. "And Nathan's."

The cop interrupts us, and this time I can tell he means it. "Really, girls. We'll be at the station soon."

Tessa's face drifts to the far window. But I feel better. Everything's out now. Even if I haven't given my official police statement, I've talked it out with Tessa, which somehow makes me feel like everything else will be easy.

I reach into my purse and check the contents. My cell phone must still be in Reena's car, but my wallet seems intact, so I pull out my pad of paper and pen. I'm so tired of thinking, trying to process the last twenty-four hours; I feel like I'd just rather play with some poetry. Glancing beside me, I start with the word *Tessa*.

I'm just coming to the end of a stanza when our squad car pulls into the police station, where Dad and Mr. Lockbaum stand with their arms crossed, waiting for us.

I close my eyes and swallow down my nerves. There is still so much more to face.

chapter THIRTY-FIVE

ven though he's out of his bathrobe, wearing jeans and a button-down shirt, Mr. Lockbaum's hair is no better than the last time we met. His brow wrinkles as he races straight for the far side of the cop car to Tessa's door.

Detective Malovich intercepts Mr. Lockbaum and they talk for a minute. Soon the officer backs away and opens Tessa's door. She and her dad look at each other but don't say anything. I wonder how he could possibly process his six-year-old being hauled to a police station.

As much as I want to, I can't bear to watch anymore. It seems too private. I duck out behind her and walk over to

Dad. He doesn't move, and I wonder if he's mad at me. Or just scared to death.

When I'm close enough, he pulls me into a hard hug.

"I'm okay, Dad," I whisper into him. But it feels good to be held. By my dad. He doesn't let go for several minutes and I burrow into him, slowly feeling his tension subside around me.

When eventually I pull back, there doesn't seem much else to say. Things are still uncomfortable because I don't know if he wants to hear about any of this. When he backs up a step, I take that as a no, and turn back for the cop car to get my purse.

Dad just stares straight ahead as the police begin their questioning. I'm careful to keep quiet about Alis's absentee dad. I don't even tell them that Faith and Reena's meetings were held at their house. Just that the one tonight started there.

"And where were Mr. and Mrs. Monachie?"

"Mrs. Monachie died," I say softly, as if she was someone I knew. "Mr. Monachie was . . . must have been . . . out for the evening." I shrug at Malovich. "Do you know when they'll bring Alis back?" I ask.

"I'm afraid I can't say." Malovich scribbles on his notepad. "But I'm sure it'll be a long night for those two kids. Now, why don't you give me the details about the mountain."

When I reach the end of my story, Nathan running and talking a confession out of Reena, I look to Dad, but he doesn't flinch from his dull expression. It almost seems like *he's* been hypnotized.

And, in fact, our whole car ride home, he doesn't say a word. Now that it's sinking in, I wonder if he's going to start acting like Mom. Or worse, like Mr. Lockbaum.

By the time we get home, it's almost ten o'clock. Nuisance trails behind me and drops onto the floor at the edge of my bed. Lying back, trying to sleep, all I can think of is my parents. I can't stop the disappointment from rising up inside me. I figured getting some answers about Faith would somehow make things better for them. But now I wonder. Mom still spends most of her time at home locked in her bedroom. I have my doubts that she actually talks to anyone at work. Plants are probably dying due to lack of oxygen. We've had canned ravioli three nights this week.

The paper bag from my new eye shadow still sits on my dresser. It looks like a lunch sack, but a little smaller. It makes me think of the goofy puppets Faith and I used to make when we were kids.

I push myself up off my bed and go pick it up. Because I can't sleep anyway, I sit at my desk and draw two googly eyes on the bag. Then a round nose, with two large nostrils, and a long oval tongue.

When I pull it away and take it all in, the face makes me giggle. It's stupid, but I don't care. It feels good to laugh.

When we were kids, I invented something called Kid Deliveries. They weren't special-occasion gifts, just everyday things to tell Mom we loved her. Faith's were always better because she was older and much craftier with glue and crayons. I think the last one I made her was when I was about eleven. A picture of Mom and me, both the same height in the picture, even though I trailed her by at least six inches in real life. It was little better than a stick drawing, but I still remember the caption.

My Best Friend.

But that was before high school.

I stand with the puppet, ready to head for her room, but stop at my door. One more thing. I have to make it personal.

Pulling a sheet of blank paper from my drawer, I write two lines. The same two I always started with back then.

Roses are red

Violets are blue

I stop and think, but it doesn't take me long. This is like preschool bad poetry for me.

I miss my sister

But I sure miss you, too.

I fold the paper about a million times, until it's only a tiny square, and then slide it into the bag puppet. Tiptoeing to her bedroom, I push down the carpet to get it under the door without making a sound.

See, Tessa, I'm not so bad at this covert stuff after all.

I guess I thought the whole process would get something off my chest so I could go to sleep, but no. Eyes wide, forty-five minutes later, I head down to the kitchen and scour Ms. Frostbite for something to eat.

Not even leftover ravioli.

With plenty of cans in the cupboard, I can't find a single one that looks appetizing. I dig in the back and find a bag of dry linguine. After several minutes of studying it, the earth-shattering idea strikes me.

Why don't I cook something?

I search the cans for something with "tomato" in the title. Tomato sauce and tomato paste. That should do it. I stack them on the counter. At least I know how to cook pasta. Well, for the most part. I'm not actually sure how much pasta one cooks for a family of three.

The "family of three" thing still feels weird in my head. I move the bag of pasta to the middle of the counter and place a tomato can on either side. Three. It even *looks* weird.

The pot of water on the stove is starting to boil when Mom pads into the kitchen. She's dressed in yoga pants and a T-shirt—not her usual bathrobe—and her hair looks not only clean, but brushed, too.

I've gotten used to not looking her in the eye, so I naturally divert my gaze to the spices. Oregano—that sounds like a pasta spice. She intercepts me on my way across the kitchen and reaches for my arm. The first glance at her face is an awkward one and I turn away. But she doesn't let me. She pulls at my wrist, at my shoulder, and finally at my head, until I stare straight into her eyes. They're wet, but for some reason, I think that's a good thing. Without even feeling the movement of it, soon I'm wrapped up in her arms.

It takes me a long time to breathe but when I finally do, I'm not breathing air. I'm breathing saline. I nearly choke on my tears while Mom strokes my hair. It's been so long and I didn't realize until now how much I need this.

"I love you," she says. "I'm so sorry, Brie. So sorry to have left you." She backs away and looks at me again. "And I missed you, too."

"I love you, Mom." I know I need to say it as much as she needs to hear it. She cuddles me close again, and I wonder, wrapped up in the cocoon of my mother, how much Dad told her, or if they even talk at all anymore. Should I say something about Reena? Tell her the whole story? But I can't think of anything that will make it any easier for her. The only picture that keeps repeating in my mind is of her wrapping her hand over the face of the Jesus statue.

"Do you hate God?" I ask into her hair.

She doesn't answer for a long time, and her arms go limp around me. She pulls away slightly, but then renews eye contact. "No, Brie, I don't. I don't always understand things that happen, but I don't hate God for them."

I'm not sure why this makes me feel so much better, but it does. "Do you hate . . . Dad?" I venture.

She shakes her head. This question seems easier for her and that relieves me even more. "He'll come around. In his own way." She ruffles my hair. "He will, Brie."

I smile, but Mom doesn't smile back. Her eyes divert past my shoulder.

"It's boiling over," she says, and rushes past me to turn down the heat. When she faces me again, she asks, "What are we making?"

The next day I stay home from school and sleep. When I dial Alis's phone number, I get a message saying the number has been disconnected. Since I still don't have my cell phone, I wonder if Alis will take the chance to call our house, or if he'll avoid me forever now that he knows the truth about what happened to Faith.

Wednesday morning at school, I suspect someone's breaking into Tessa's locker. But then I recognize the pink turtleneck under the mop of light brown hair.

"Wow, what happened to all the black? Why the new look?" I ask.

"I guess the mourning is finally over," she says. I watch her pile several books into her arms, like she's actually planning on going to a few classes in a row.

"What's up?" I say. "Suddenly trying to get into college?"

She looks at me, but doesn't say anything for a long time. "Maybe." Now that she wears her hair loose and parted on the side, it falls in her face. She scoops it out of the way. "Dad and I had . . . an encounter or something."

"Really? What happened?"

She shakes it off. "Nothing, really. I guess." She turns to dig for something in her locker, but I can tell it's an act. A diversion. "First, at the police station, he treated me different. Then this." She holds up a folded piece of notepaper. It has a blue border, and looks like it came from the pad in my purse. "I got dressed for school today like this, I don't even know why. Anyway, Dad saw me and he put his hands on my shoulders for a long time. He just stared at me." Tessa's eyes are as clear and dry as always, but she blinks as though she's blinking away tears.

"What's that?" I ask, pointing at the folded-up piece of paper.

She opens it and places it on the top of her stack of books. When she reads the title, I know exactly what it is. The poem I wrote in the police car.

"'Terrible Tessa,'" she reads.

My face grows warm. I expect she'll leave it at that, since we both know the rest, but she reads on.

> *"A terrible thing about Tessa*
> *Is how she grew up too fast*
> *Shoes too big and too small all at once.*
> *A terrible thing about Tessa*
> *Guilt, a weighty stone around her neck*
> *Undeniably amiss for six.*
> *A terrible thing about Tessa*
> *The force she had to use, and still,*
> *It took someone so long to know her*
> *To really see her.*
> *There are many terrible things about Tessa*
> *But she*
> *Is not one of them."*

After her last words, Tessa just stares at the paper. And I'm glad, because it's better than her looking at me. I don't know what to say. The flutter in my stomach won't calm down, and suddenly I realize it's not from nerves. It's more than that. I've never heard anyone read one of my poems, out loud no less, and it actually . . . it feels good. It sounded like a real poem. It sounded like me.

"Thanks," she says, with her eyes still down.

I'm scared to ask, but I do it anyway. "And can you, um, look at yourself in the mirror?"

She opens the flap of the binder sitting on top of her pile. There's a mirror glued to the inside. We both look down.

"Yup."

She half-smiles, then shuts the book. "Heard from Alis?"

Her voice is so controlled, so even. I have to see her face. Other than the hair and clothes, the same old Tessa stares back at me. I shake my head. "No, I'm sure he's in a foster home somewhere. Probably in a different state."

"Obviously his life is getting rearranged," she says, "but no point in jumping to conclusions."

"I don't think I'm exactly jumping. He hasn't called."

"We better get to class," she says, changing the subject yet again.

I close my locker to follow Miss Responsible's lead, when I hear a familiar "Hey" from across the hall.

I turn slowly. *Celeste.*

Tessa hangs back, even though I know she's in a hurry to get to the science wing. Like she's protecting me.

"Hey," I say.

Celeste walks over and I can already tell that she's sorry, she doesn't have to say it, but she does anyway. The important thing, though, is that it's obvious she's not hiding anything anymore. She's free of her secrets.

"It's okay," I say. "I understand, or at least I think I get most of it." I smile. "Except where you disappeared to Monday night."

"I couldn't find your phone, so I ran as hard as I could down the mountain. Well, as hard as I could without being able to see two feet in front of me," she says. "Nathan caught up to me, but he was concerned only with saving himself."

"I can't believe he was actually Faith's boyfriend," I say. "I could never have seen her with someone like him."

She rolls her eyes. "He was everyone's boyfriend. Or at least he said he was. Reena's the only one who believed it."

I feel somewhat relieved. Maybe I knew my sister better than I thought.

She goes on with her Monday night play-by-play. "I finally

found the police at the base of the mountain. They already had Nathan and drove us back to the police station in a squad car. I don't know what Nathan told them, but I told the truth. About everything," she adds.

"Me too," I say. "So they must have enough information to do something about Nathan. And Reena." I can never have Faith back, but at least we may have saved anyone else from getting involved in their deadly cult.

"After *my* statement, they better," Tessa says, as if she was the one in their clutches.

There's one more thing I'm not totally convinced about, and I have to know. "Do you think . . . Could Faith have been hypnotized?"

Celeste shakes her head, without a hint of hesitation. "Faith's the one who told me you have to want to be hypnotized for it to work. Even though I believed that, I wasn't sure I was strong-minded enough. I mean, I've never been strong like her. I never seemed able to resist Reena's pressure."

"That's why you took your contacts out?" And that's why it hadn't worked on me. Maybe I do have some of Faith's strength.

Celeste nods. "Faith didn't agree with the hypnosis part of things. She insisted on knowing exactly what she was speaking about. That's why I left that night. I didn't know what to do when Reena wanted to hypnotize us and Faith was saying no way. I thought by leaving I'd be eliminating at least some of the conflict, but even as I was going Faith started talking to Reena about the orange level and their arguments got worse. Faith knew there was something off about the Higher Scriptures and wanted to set Reena straight."

"Now, that sounds like your sister," Tessa says, surprising me. Even though she'd never actually talked to Faith—I'm her only real connection—she seems to know her so well. Which probably means I do too.

"Faith really wanted me to back her up," Celeste goes on. "I thought I wasn't strong enough. I just wanted to go to a normal youth group again and forget about them, but Faith couldn't let it go." Celeste looks so sad when she says it that I know if she could have the moment back she would have stayed with Faith. Even if it had meant the end of her, too.

The way Celeste shifts, there must be something else, so I wait, even though Tessa's tapping her locker, apparently ready to go.

"I was wondering," Celeste starts, but then stops and rethinks her words. "I'm thinking about going back to Pastor Scott's youth group. I need to be hooked in somewhere, or all this is just going to eat me up."

Is she looking for my approval? Trying to find out if I think all religion is bad and scary and something everybody should run away from kicking and screaming? "I think that's a good idea, Celeste. Pastor Scott seems like an okay guy."

She stares down the hall, but still doesn't leave. Most of the students have made their way into classrooms. *Late pass, here I come.*

"I just feel weird going without Faith, and I thought maybe you, I mean both of you"—she glances at Tessa— "might want to come."

I'm trying to come up with a gentle decline, when Tessa blurts out, "Sure. When is it?"

They discuss the details, while I wonder what happened to Tessa.

After Celeste leaves, Tessa says, "Come on, we're gonna be late," and drags me along behind her. She leaves me outside my English classroom, with absolutely no explanation of what she's thinking.

Maybe she hasn't changed so much after all.

By Friday evening, Tessa still hasn't explained her motives for volunteering our attendance at youth group when Celeste swings by to pick me up. Tessa's already in the car, wearing her black clothes mixed in with the few clothing items of

DENISE JADEN

mine she has permanently borrowed. She looks brighter just
because of the makeup and hair.

When I get into the backseat behind them, they're already
in mid-conversation.

"If you listen to the *scientists*," Tessa says, emphasizing the
word, "there are plenty of other explanations."

"Like what? Some big bolt of lightning? Or, wait, better
yet, an alien." I can't believe how bold Celeste sounds. And
here I'd thought it was an act up on the mountain. "Even so,
where did the lightning or alien originate?"

Tessa isn't about to let Celeste get the last word in, and
moves on to the subject of why babies die.

I zone out on their debate. My strongest suspicions were
that Tessa was coming to youth group either for me, because
she thought I needed it, or for Celeste, because she thought
Celeste needed us. It hadn't occurred to me that maybe she's
coming for herself.

"That's bullshit," Tessa says, not quite your average Christian on her way to church. "God might be powerful, but he's
not *that* powerful. And he's not always good."

Celeste gets stronger and more confident with each sentence. "Who says He's not?"

"Believe me, I know."

They haven't asked me what I think and I'm glad. Who

370

knows what I think? One thing I'm starting to believe though, is that maybe it's not such a bad idea to talk about stuff.

Celeste leads the way into the church basement. She's obviously been here before. Many of the teens stare at us—the new kids—when we walk in. Tessa doesn't seem to notice. She sizes up Pastor Scott from across the room.

We take some seats at the back when two guys at the front start playing guitar. Words appear on an overhead projector, and soon the whole room stands and sings, kind of like at church, but with lots of extra clapping.

Celeste falls into line and sways along with the music. I look at Tessa and she's not singing, not clapping her hands, but staring intently at the words on the screen.

I hover in the middle of the two of them, trying to decide where my place is in this. Who I'm going to follow.

But I'm not going to follow either of them.

Eventually, I close my eyes. Listen to the words but don't attempt to sing any of them. Don't attempt to analyze them. I listen hard to hear if Faith's voice is among the rest. But if it is, I can't hear it. I take a deep breath and relax, just relax, for the first time maybe ever.

After the music, everyone sits and Pastor Scott introduces his new assistant. I'm glad he's got some help, and he looks way less stressed. The new guy gives a short talk, with Tessa shaking her head through the whole thing, and then dismisses us for games time.

We head into the next room and as I pass by Pastor Scott, he gives me a wave.

"Hi," I say.

He smiles. "Hey, Brie. How are you?"

Something about his tone makes me realize he's not just asking out of obligation.

"Pretty good, actually," I say.

"It looks like you're doing better," he says. "I'm glad."

I wave as I scurry into the room where they're just finishing up explaining the first game.

"It's okay," Tessa says, pulling my arm toward a small group of teens. "You're on my team."

chapter THIRTY-SIX

Plan Z: Get to all my classes on time and somehow pass the rest of this semester.

Monday morning, I pull out my cell phone, glad to finally have it back from the cops. I plan to dial it to silent before classes, but it's already on silent, and reads that I have three missed calls. I scroll through, and they're all from . . . Pastor Scott?

When I turn to talk to Tessa at her locker, my mouth drops open. Alis stands ten feet behind her, a lopsided smile on his face.

"Hi," he says, but I'm already barreling toward him. When I wrap my arms around his back, he reciprocates and whispers, "I'm the new kid," in my ear.

I laugh a little, but don't let go. He feels so good, so warm.

After a few seconds, I pull back and grab him by the shoulders. "Wait. Where are you living now? Why are you here? You're not here to say good-bye, right?"

He grins. "Pastor Scott and his wife took me in through the foster care program. I'm living with them, at least for now."

That explains the missed calls. "And you get to go to school with me?" I'm so excited, I bounce up off my heels.

"Scott suggested the nearest Christian school first. Then when you came to youth group the other night, and after he heard about all the stuff with Faith and Reena, I guess he decided this place might be a better choice. I think he figured we could both use a friend in all this."

"Really?"

He nods.

"And Reena?" I ask softly.

"She's in a psychiatric center," he says. "It's where she needs to be for a while. My Dad's pretty broken up about it all, but I know he's still not ready to be there for either of us." He looks at the floor and I snuggle back in to hug him.

Tessa clears her throat behind us. I ignore her; she can say hi to Alis later. But she continues making sounds like she's choking on peanut butter. Then she coughs out the word "PDA."

It takes me a second, between Tessa's peanut butter throat and Alis whispering how much he missed me, to understand what she's trying to tell me: *Teacher alert. Public Display of Affection.*

I pull away from Alis only seconds before Mr. Clancy gets to us.

"Miss Jenkins." He crosses his arms and taps his foot. "I should think you'd be spending more time getting caught up on schoolwork and a little less time snuggling in the hallways."

He suggests sending me to see Principal Voth, but then decides that a longer detention would probably be of greater benefit. "Bring your history book," he adds.

Before he turns to leave, Alis says, "Excuse me, sir. It was my fault too."

Clancy looks confused and I'm not sure if it's by the fact that a student's never said such a thing to him, or if it's because Alis is somehow outside of his clairvoyant radar.

"Ahem. Yes. You come for detention too," he says. "Make sure to bring some homework."

When Clancy leaves, Alis and I smile at each other.

"Do you think he recognized me, or wonders why I'm in school at 8:30 a.m.?" Alis asks.

"You know, sometimes I think he knows everything." I

watch the back of Clancy's trek down the hall. "Sometimes I think he knows nothing at all."

Tessa slaps me on the back. "See you in five." She raises her eyebrows. "Or maybe ten."

She's doing well at attending her classes and getting to them all on time. Even Art, which is first thing today.

Alis stares down at his class schedule. "I can't figure this thing out," he says. "I guess we were supposed to start biology two years ago, but Reena's not much into sciences. But then I'm way ahead in math, so I chose some extra electives." He shakes his head, looking over the paper. "And where the heck are all these classrooms?"

"Don't worry, I'll help you." I peer over the edge of the paper and scroll my hand along the line that says Block D, since that's first thing today. "Huh. Art 11. What do you know."

"What?" He must see the smile on my face.

The hallway clears, so I snap my locker shut and grab his hand. We're halfway down the hall, me pulling him along at a hundred miles an hour, before he asks, "What's the hurry?"

"Boy, you have a lot to learn." I interlock my fingers in his. "Time for a new slate. This is called Plan A." Saying it out loud makes me think about how some things *do* work out the way you want them to. And sometimes even better. "Plan A, with benefits."

He laughs, and we run down the hall together, rounding the corner into Mr. Poindexter's room just as the second bell sounds.

ACKNOWLEDGMENTS

Many writers say they couldn't do it alone, but WOW, I really could not. There are so many people who have helped me, mentored me, encouraged me, even kicked me in the butt, and this book wouldn't have been possible without them.

First, thank you to my best friend, Shelly. I'll always remember that you read the first (i.e., really bad) stuff, and kept loving me anyway. (How many times did you read Trev, again?) Without your support, I would never have found the confidence to get here. And to go along with that, thank you to my awesome home group (nothing like Reena's home group, I swear!) for giving up so many nights to talk about my writing struggles.

Thank you to my wonderful agent, Michelle Humphrey.

ACKNOWLEDGMENTS

I couldn't ask for a better advocate, advisor, cheerleader, and friend. I hope whatever's on the lunch menu today is extra-special!

Thank you to Anica Rissi and the team at Simon Pulse for putting so much thought and care into my book, and offering stellar suggestions to make it shine. Many thanks to Cara Petrus for creating the beautiful cover for this book.

To my incomparable critique partners and friends: Extra-special thanks to Sharon Knauer, who gave me the perfect mix of encouragement and brilliant suggestions in my early writing days. Enormous thanks to Shana Silver, Elle Strauss, Craig Pirrall, Jennifer Hoffine-Hoffman, Amy Brecount-White, Tara Kelly, Caroline Starr Rose, and Pendred Noyce for your boatloads of help with multiple manuscripts. Thanks to Maria, Rick, Lorrie, Pam, Liz, and Brandy, and the rest of the cool people at Critique Circle whose advice can be seen in the pages of this book.

A big thank-you to The Tenners and Class of 2k10, not only for their co-promotion efforts and support, but also for being just plain fun to be around. A great big shout-out to all my Blueboarder, LiveJournal, Twitter, and Blogger friends. And YA Book Bloggers—you ROCK!

Thanks to a few of my early readers for great advice and confidence-building: Mom, Dad, Jody, Kathryn, Kim, Harry,

ACKNOWLEDGMENTS

Norm, Duane, Natasha, Mandy, Michelle, and all others I'm probably forgetting (feel free to make me feel guilty— I deserve it!). Also thanks to Jason Goertzen, who gave me the book that sparked my love for reading, and to Paul Latta, who continues to inspire me creatively.

A few great websites I need to mention and thank the proprietors thereof: www.critiquecircle.com—this is where I met most of my amazing critique partners; www.nanowrimo.org— Losing Faith was a "Nano" novel, and I completed the first draft in twenty-one days during Nanowrimo 2007; http:// misssnarksfirstvictim.blogspot.com—wonderful educational contests where I learned about the art of hooking a reader.

This book would not have been possible without the amazing support of my friends and family. Thank you all, especially Ted and Teddy, for giving me the time and space to find my stories.

And most of all, thank you to The Great Author and Perfecter of faith, for making me who I am, surrounding me with such awesome people, and quickening my mind to so many stories to tell. I can't wait to find out what the next one will be about!

ABOUT THE AUTHOR

Denise Jaden is a former church secretary and youth group leader. When she's not writing, she can often be found homeschooling her son or dancing with her Polynesian dance troupe. She lives just outside Vancouver, Canada, with her husband, Ted, and son, Teddy. *Losing Faith* is her first novel. Find out more at denisejaden.com.

When the pressures of prep school build up, cracks can appear in the funniest places.

LEILA SALES

mostly good girls

From Simon Pulse
Published by Simon & Schuster

Love. Heartbreak.
Friendship. Trust.

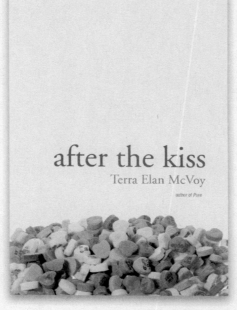

after the kiss

Terra Elan McVoy

author of *Pure*

"I love this book. Like, love it love it.
My heart expanded when I
read it—yours will too."
—Lauren Myracle,
bestselling author of *ttyl* and *ttfn*

From Simon Pulse
Published by Simon & Schuster